ANY HUMAN FACE

Charles Lambert was born in the United Kingdom in 1953. In 1976 he moved to Milan and, with brief interruptions in Ireland, Portugal and London, has lived and worked in Italy since then. Currently a university teacher, academic translator and freelance editor for international agencies, he now lives in Fondi, exactly halfway between Rome and Naples. His first novel, *Little Monsters*, is also published by Picador.

CHARLES LAMBERT

ANY HUMAN FACE

PICADOR

First published 2010 in paperback by Picador

This edition first published 2011 by Picador
an imprint of Pan Macmillan, a division of Macmillan Publishers Limited
Pan Macmillan, 20 New Wharf Road, London N1 9RR
Basingstoke and Oxford
Associated companies throughout the world
www.panmacmillan.com

ISBN 978-0-330-51245-9

1 3 5 7 9 8 6 4 2

A CIP catalogue record for this book is available
from the British Library.

Typeset by Ellipsis Digital Limited, Glasgow
Printed and bound by CPI Group (UK) Ltd, Croydon, CR0 4YY

Visit **www.picador.com** to read more about all our books
and to buy them. You will also find features, author interviews and
news of any author events, and you can sign up for e-newsletters
so that you're always first to hear about our new releases.

For Giuseppe

Any human face is a claim on you, because you can't help but understand the singularity of it, the courage and loneliness of it.

GILEAD
Marilynne Robinson

1982–2008

BRUNO AND ALEX **1983**

The bags were on the back seat of the car: three brown-paper carriers with string handles and writing on the side. Bruno had thrown his coat across the seat to hide them, but the movement of the car had shifted it and Alex could make out the letters ORE and AMO, black and bold, on the outside of the bag nearest to him. Alex liked words and fancied his skills as a linguist. He smiled to himself. *Hours*, he thought, and the Latin for *I love*; that's just what Bruno has in mind. Then, as the car drove on over cobbles and the coat slipped again to reveal VAT and RAG, it clicked. *Salvatore Ferragamo*.

'I didn't know you bought your shoes in Via Condotti,' he said, opening and snapping shut, then reopening his Zippo lighter, Bruno's most recent gift to him. He twirled the ratchet with his thumb, enjoying the sweet scent of the fuel, finally lighting a cigarette from the packet of Winston beside the gearstick.

Bruno, sweating in shirt-sleeves, was hunched over the wheel, distracted, fraught. 'Driving round Trastevere this time of night,' he said, 'is like threading strings of tripe through a fucking needle.'

'Or squeezing a Ferragamo customer through the gates of heaven,' said Alex, raising himself from the seat to slip the lighter back into his front jeans pocket, tilting his hips up at Bruno as if to remind the older man of what they'd be doing later.

'Ferragamo?' Bruno turned his head to look at Alex, puzzled. Then, with a grin of understanding, he said: 'You mean the bags? Don't be fooled by appearances. They're just what was to hand.' He stroked Alex's thigh. 'You needn't worry. I haven't been wasting my money on fancy footwear. I can't afford to.' He squeezed Alex's knee, pulled it towards him while Alex, teasing, resisted. 'I only waste money on you.'

'Quite right.' Alex wound down his window to throw the half-smoked cigarette into the gutter. 'Not that you are wasting it. I'm worth every lira.'

Bruno shifted down into second. 'Have you eaten?'

Alex shrugged. 'Have you?'

Bruno thought about this. 'I could eat again.'

'So could I.'

'Pizza?'

'Pizza?' echoed Alex. 'Why not?'

'I don't believe it,' said Bruno, swinging the car across the nose of a small green van, which swerved and stopped. 'A parking space outside the Obitorio. And they say there's no God. In Rome, of all places.' The van driver pressed his horn and shouted. Bruno strained across, his belly warm and heavy against the younger man's bare forearm, to shout back through Alex's open window. 'And you can fuck off as well, you and your whore of a sister.' The van, to Alex's relief, drove off. Wiping his mouth, with an edge of glee in his voice, Bruno said, 'That's what I like, a bit of real dialogue before dinner. A bit of genuine communication with a representative of the skiving masses.' He tweaked Alex's earlobe between his fingers. 'And then, Alessandro *mio*, a bit more after dinner.'

It took almost twenty minutes before they could sit down, at one of the tables up against the wall. Bruno told the waiter to bring some bread and a litre of local white. And four *supplì*. And four *filetti di baccalà*. Alex had his elbows on the table, waiting for Bruno to tell him to shift them, feeling in the mood for a fight, nothing too serious, a touch of friction to remind them both that Alex had a mind and body, *and not just body*, of his own. He was still smarting from being called Alessandro, his real, despised name, although it might have been worse: Bruno might have said Sandro, as Alex's mother always did. His earlobe was warm, almost sore, from the pressure of Bruno's fingers, the edge of his broken, nicotine-yellowed nail.

Alex was wearing a T-shirt he'd bought that day, white, with Greek letters round the neck, but Bruno, the only person he knew who could read what they said, didn't seem to have noticed. Alex lit the final Winston from the packet he'd found in the car, scrunching the empty carton with his free hand, while Bruno picked up one of the paper napkins from the marble tabletop and took out a pen, an expensive real-nib job with a gold clip. Mont Blanc?

Maybe not, judged Alex, but not far off. Bruno scrawled a row of dashes in red-brown ink on the paper, divided into two groups by an oblique stroke.

'Come on,' he said. 'A famous person.'

'What?'

'A famous person. Big-time famous. An international name. Give me a letter. Any letter.'

'I don't understand you,' said Alex. 'Why can't we just talk? I mean, you don't have to amuse me. I can amuse myself. I'm not just a pretty face, you know.'

Bruno looked gloomy. 'You're right,' he said. He pushed out his lower lip until Alex could see the wet red-grey part inside and tilted his head towards his shoulder, a parody of self-reproof. 'I hate myself. I'm scared you might find me boring.' This made them both laugh, to Alex's surprise. Bruno capped and put away his pen and watched while Alex grew calm and silent.

With Bruno's eyes on him, he glanced around at the other tables, at the travertine-covered walls. 'You can see why it's called the mortuary, can't you?'

'They don't actually wash the place, you know that?' Bruno shuddered. 'They hose the drying blood off the walls.'

'And the tables. It's the marble, really, isn't it? That's really why they call it the mortuary. Perfect for the odd cadaver or two.'

As soon as the waiter had left the plates of *supplì* and salt cod, and the carafe of wine and basket of bread, Alex said: 'They're all ex-boxers, in case of trouble.'

'I thought that was that other pizzeria. Down the road.'

Alex looked over Bruno's shoulder towards the street with an unexpected sense of being out of place. He wished he hadn't agreed to see Bruno that evening, wondered what other kind of life he might be living instead of this, and with whom; his equal, perhaps. He nodded. 'Right.'

Using his rejected Hangman napkin, Bruno picked up a finger of cod. He bit into it, then gasped, spitting a scrap of batter on to his plate. 'Christ, this is hot,' he said, blowing out. 'I've just burned my fucking mouth.' He held out a clean square of paper to Alex. 'Try one.'

'In a minute,' said Alex. 'When they've cooled down a bit.'

'You're such a wise young man,' said Bruno. 'I'd trust you with anything, I really would.'

'Yes, right.'

'No, seriously, I mean it,' said Bruno, and he did sound serious, Alex decided, taking another piece of *baccalà* and blowing on it. He isn't a bad man, he thought. I could do worse. He's well connected, at least.

'What do you mean, anything?'

'In fact—' said Bruno.

'Yes?'

Bruno poured them both some wine. 'This stuff always reminds me of urine samples,' he said. 'Not that I see that many. It ought to be the other way round.'

'Yes?' repeated Alex, biting. Hot oil squirted from beneath the batter onto his tongue. He would never learn, he thought, from the mistakes of others. He would never wait quite long enough. He wasn't made like that. This thought – that he might be doomed – gave him comfort. He felt like Jim Morrison, James Dean, pleased by the prospect of an early death. He swigged a mouthful of cooling, slightly apple-tasting wine, hangover guaranteed. Wise people laced it with lemonade.

Bruno sighed. 'Look, love,' he said, his voice lower now, as though they might be overheard, as though someone nearby might care what they were saying. Alex could barely catch the words. 'I need you to do me a favour. Well, I say me. It's not exactly for me. But I need a favour done.'

'Go on.'

'You wouldn't mind taking the car for a spin this evening, I don't suppose.'

It didn't sound like a question. Bruno was glancing round as though expecting to see someone he'd rather avoid. Alex wondered if he'd missed a link. 'No.'

'It's just that those bags . . .' Bruno said. 'You know, the ones on the back seat.'

'The fancy footwear.'

'That isn't.'

'So what is it?'

Bruno sighed again. He emptied his glass, grimaced, refilled it. 'It doesn't only look like piss,' he said. 'I don't know why I bother. But I do.' He drank a second time, more slowly, then took a new packet of cigarettes from his pocket and ripped it open. He flicked out a cigarette and held it with exaggerated care between his fingers, as though it might snap. 'It's something I don't want in my flat right at this moment.' He put the cigarette down beside his bread and reached across, his hand on Alex's, a brief reassuring touch, pulling away before Alex could; before anyone saw. 'It's nothing to worry about, love. It's just that, well, it's delicate. Not even that. Potentially delicate.' He smiled. 'So I thought, knowing how much you like to drive my nice fast car, you might be willing to slip the stuff round to your place for a day or two.'

'So let me get this clear. You want me to drive your nice fast car to my flat and hide those potentially delicate bags? For a day or two. And it's nothing to worry about? It's just a favour?'

Bruno leaned back. 'Not *hide*,' he said, forcing a laugh. 'Hang on to them. Give them a home. It won't be for long.'

Alex thought about this for a moment. 'All right,' he said.

Alex lived down the Casilina, but he decided he'd take the long route. He was in no rush to return to Bruno, who'd begun to wear him down. It was not that he wasn't fond of the older man, in his way, or that he didn't appreciate the long-term view of a leg-up into journalism and the short-term regime of pizzas and presents; he'd be a fool not to play willing. Besides, this wasn't the first time Bruno had lent him the car with a wink, as though he might not want it back, not at once anyway. One day, maybe not at all. So Alex felt under no obligation to rush.

Bruno would probably be asleep, in any case, and might as well be woken up in two hours' time as one.

Alex didn't give in to the temptation to look into the bags until he'd been driving through the Saturday-evening city traffic for fifteen minutes, over the river and down Via Marmorata. On an impulse, he parked by the Pyramid, outside the bar the whores warmed up in on winter nights where he'd sometimes come to be flirted with, be bought a final hot punch, accept a lift home from one of their clients. He strained back to tug the nearest carrier towards him, but couldn't quite reach it. In the end, because he was slightly drunk, he clambered over the seat and into the back, banging his funny bone on the corner of the headrest. He imagined himself jammed between the seats until he died. People would think he'd been worked over and left there by someone on the game.

When he finally did make it, winded by effort, he was annoyed to see that all the carriers contained, pushed down as far as they'd go, were smaller bags made of thick black glossy plastic, thicker than the kind used for rubbish, the kind he'd seen photographs stored in. Each carrier contained a dozen, maybe more, of these, sealed shut with two-inch duct tape. Maybe he'd open one, he thought, but later. He'd do it with the care required.

He climbed back into the front seat and drove home as fast as he dared, down beneath Via Cristoforo Colombo and past Coin – the railings outside the department store his Saturday-morning haunt until two or three years ago, when he'd still been at school and feckless – the traffic thinning as he took the curve in front of the church with the nail from the holy cross inside it. As if. That was the joke about Rome, the big sad joke, he thought, with all its talk of holy this and holy that, and all the unholy goings-on. He'd learned a thing or two already, had his own brief glimpses, and guessed the rest. And what he hadn't guessed, Bruno – old Roman lowlife hand and Vatican expert – had filled him in on.

It was after one o'clock when Alex parked the car directly beneath Bruno's flat, round the corner from Piazza in Piscinula. Tonight's our lucky night, he thought, two parking spaces found where and when they were needed. How often does that happen? Once every death of a pope, if that. He locked the car, swinging the key from his forefinger, reminding himself of someone he'd seen in a film. Bruno had given him his own key to the building so he didn't need to ring. He climbed the stairs in darkness, running his hand along the wall, until he was on the third floor. One more floor to go. But the darkness had already begun to lift before he reached Bruno's landing. Alex frowned, disconcerted, suddenly anxious. Speeding up, he saw a wedge of light from behind Bruno's door, which was half open. His heart beating fast, light-headed, he pushed the door back to the wall. 'Bruno,' he called, his voice low, as though he didn't want to be heard. He glanced into the first room on the right, the bathroom, and saw the towels on the floor, the medicines from the cabinet spilled into the bath; he smelt the Eau Sauvage

Extrême from the matt black bottle, broken beside the bidet. Someone should pick up those bits of glass, he thought – stupid to think it, he knew – before they cut themselves. He called again. 'Bruno.' He walked along the corridor until he could see into the living room.

Bruno was stripped naked and bound to a chair, legs spread, silver duct tape round his legs and chest and upper arms, across his mouth so tightly his face was deformed by it. That's the second time I've seen duct tape this evening, it struck Alex, cold with shock. Bruno's eyes were open, staring towards the door. For a second Alex thought he might still be alive. He took a step further into the room. Bruno's forearms and thighs had been burned, haphazardly, with cigarettes. His chest was covered with small neat cuts, like paper cuts, each with its fringe of drying blood. One larger cut, broad and lipped into a pout, had been made at the level of the heart. Someone had used what looked like Bruno's blood to write '*frocio*' on the wall.

Queer.

ANDREW AND MICHEL 2008

Andrew Caruso is wondering if he can shut up shop ten minutes early. His last potential customer, an American woman looking for *Foucault's Pendulum* in English translation, was sent off down the road to Feltrinelli, reluctantly on Andrew's part, more than half an hour ago. Since then a pair of Malaysian nuns has sifted through the secondhand paperbacks on the bargain table outside, clearly killing time, before crossing the square with a third nun and entering Santa Barbara. Saint B. is the patron saint of booksellers, he's been told, though it's not clear to Andrew how her patronage might work, certainly not by mere proximity. Maybe he should light a candle or two, say the odd prayer. Perhaps it would help to believe.

He starts to sort the books on the table by size, ready for their cardboard boxes, counting as he stacks to see how many have been stolen since lunchtime. They're mostly worthless, or practically worthless, although some of them, fading proof copies and large beige paperbacks with engravings on the cover, have an air of value about them, an air that occasionally attracts would-be connoisseurs. Seven down, not a bad haul in just over three hours, and he's a shrewd idea who lifted them. The boyfriend of the French girl who kept him chatting about the best, as in cheapest, places to eat while the boy slunk around outside, his rucksack open. It's so transparent sometimes that Andrew doesn't have the heart to intervene. Now and again an envoy from the group of Polish alcoholics that gathers fifty yards down the road is sent to see what he can find. Andrew watches from inside the shop, pretending to work, wondering whether the man will simply pick one up and walk off, as they often do, or pretend to drop his empty wine carton and bend over, sliding some slim volume into his pocket as he does so. Either way, Andrew continues to work, or pretends to.

He's writing a piece on a young photographer he knew some years ago, a Belgian with whom he had a brief tumultuous affair, who might have killed himself intentionally or accidentally – it wasn't clear. He'd been found in a ground-floor room behind a garage not far from Andrew's flat, a room Andrew had never seen, a mattress on bare tiles and plastic bags stuffed with, among other things, some of Andrew's more valuable stock. His art was dark stuff – objects scavenged in the streets arranged with the modish paraphernalia of broken dolls, animal parts and butchers' scraps, photographs of photographs, blurred and grainy, and sometimes, though less often, people, also found. So his death, by overdose, shouldn't have come as the surprise it did.

Andrew's been asked to produce something for a catalogue to accompany a show in Ghent, the photographer's home town, something else Andrew didn't know until he received the letter a month or so ago. The gallery owner seems to think that Andrew is a bit of a power-broker in the Roman art world, or has given this impression to flatter him into action. It's worked to the extent that Andrew has written, and rewritten, a dozen paragraphs about the photographer, whom he continues to think of as Tintin, as much for his appearance – button nose and quiff exerting their usual charm on him – as his Belgian origin. The gallery owner's assumption is even true, up to a point. There have been moments when Andrew has wielded a modicum of clout, connecting people, opening doors, standing back, arms crossed, as bigger boys did their deals. The bookshop, he still likes to think after almost thirty years, is merely a front for more exciting, creative activities, although what form these might take remains to be seen.

In the meantime, he dresses the part, his hair still strong and thick, albeit by now more grey than red, worn long and occasionally tied back with a leather thong to hide the elastic band, his taste for white shirts, tight black jeans and Converse All Stars immovable, along with a wardrobe of those coarse beige canvas waistcoats covered with pockets, favoured by fishermen and big-game hunters and Joseph Beuys. Andrew's pockets are cluttered with stubs of pencils, paper clips, supermarket receipts, business cards he hasn't got round to entering in his Rolodex. He's notoriously untidy, a fact he acknowledges, when forced to, with smug regret.

He first saw Tintin, whose real name was Michel Dela-haye, in a drinking hole in Trastevere. The Belgian – although Andrew hadn't known that then and had thought he was French – had been arguing in a drunken, belliger-ent way with two middle-aged men Andrew recognized from openings as art dealers. When the two men took the younger man's arms and appeared to be dragging him, against his will, towards the street, Andrew stepped across. Tintin pulled away and threw his arms round Andrew's neck. 'My friend,' he said fervently, in an accent that went straight to Andrew's heart. Andrew has many soft spots, so many he wonders what holds him together, what stub-born carapace of survival has roped in his wayward needs. French accents are one, and button noses another; youth, increasingly, as his own is worn down and traded up for what he likes to think of as style, as in *ageless*. If Tintin had spoken English with a German accent, or had had a Roman nose, it just wouldn't have happened.

It's easy to write about the first few days, and weeks, Andrew's found. But as Tintin became more truculent and abusive, and dependent, the words become harder to find. The final month had been one of recrimination and public rows, punctuated by dramatic shows of affection and public sex. Tintin had blown Andrew early one morning under the still vacant porticos of Piazza Esedra, no more than a dozen yards from where McDonald's now sets its tables. When they hadn't been fighting or fucking, the Bel-gian took photographs, reel after reel. Andrew, writing his piece, is tempted to play with the word 'reel', to describe not only a film, the physical object coiled in its gleaming canister, but also a state of being, aimless, unspooling, exposed. And he's suddenly moved by a memory of Tintin, of Michel, gathering up a handful of salvaged newspapers and piling them neatly to form a low stool on which he sat, naked and unadorned, to photograph himself.

This was the last photograph Andrew saw him take. After his death, most of the work was taken away by Michel's mother, who refused to talk to Andrew other than to damn his eyes and breath. Everything except the shots on the final reel, which he'd developed and given to Andrew – as though he had nowhere else to put them, it occurred to Andrew later; as though he'd already made up his mind. This photograph, of a naked, forlornly elf-like Michel, and a dozen others, dark, ill-lit shots – a man walking into Santa Barbara with the daylight behind him, the same shot adjusted so that the features of the man, a young man with a cautious smile and ruffled hair, were just visible, a close-up of Michel's own hand on a surface Andrew didn't recognize, relaxed, the fingers curled as if around an invisible ball – oddly provisional photographs that only became full of meaning when the man who had taken them was gone.

That day, in Michel's other room, the room Andrew had never previously been allowed to see, Michel's mother stood over him as he took back the bags of his stock; it had taken the threat of the police to persuade her to grant him as much as this, and even then she'd insisted on watching to make sure they contained nothing else. If she'd had her way, he'd have left with nothing. 'He killed my son,' she said, to no one, more than once, in the cold, windowless room that Michel had used to escape from him.

'You killed your son,' said Andrew, under his breath, because he had to say something and that was as likely to be true as anything else. Life killed your son.

Andrew lives in a world of dilapidated, permeable borders. The books inside the shop, on the shelves and outside the shop, on the bargain table, are fluid categories, the membrane between his home and his place of work as punched with holes as a long-distance train ticket. Half the time, he doesn't know where he's put things and it's a source of constant niggling disquiet that something important – but what? – might have gone missing. Now, as he thinks about Michel, it strikes him that not everything could have been carried off by the artist's avenging mother; that something must still be where he'd left it, in Andrew's flat. It also occurs to him, given this sudden critical interest in the work of Delahaye, photographer, Belgian but fashionably dead, that whatever he finds might have unexpected value.

Andrew makes just enough money to live, in a way he despises as modest, but feels as though this already precarious balance might tip over into penury without warning. The bookshop keeps him afloat so long as he doesn't declare three-quarters of the small amount he earns; even if he wanted to, such is the state of the shop's accounts, he'd find it impossible to trace its comings and goings. His waistcoat pockets are the nearest thing he possesses to a filing system; the obligatory till sits dusty and unused behind his desk, an *objet trouvé* from a world that has spurned, and been spurned by, its official owner. His other financial ventures – the odd review, curating an occasional show for artist friends, translating articles and, more recently, menus into his mother's tongue, English – pay for the rare treat, no more than that. Now and again, he clears out the room above the shop and uses it to put on a show of his own work or that of one of his friends, small things, objects, ready-mades, even, if they're odd enough, watercolours: avant-garde, he likes to think, though he isn't quite sure what that means any longer, other than unprofitable. He hasn't been out of Rome for years: he can't afford it. Now, as he heaves down the metal shutter and turns the key in the lock, he lets his mind wander along the walls, across the floor, of his flat, to see what it might find. Michel's stuff must be somewhere.

Thirty years ago, Andrew lived just round the corner from Campo de' Fiori, in a two-room garret above the *latteria*. The *latteria* still sells its large white bowls of *caffelatte* and rusk-like biscuits, but Andrew moved on when the intensifying effect of a picturesque tiled roof on winter cold and summer heat became too much for him. Since then, like some bobbing object impelled by a centrifugal force he can neither understand nor halt, he has lived in a series of rented flats, each one a half-mile further from the centre than the one before. By an equally mysterious process, his worldly goods have accumulated as their worth has diminished; each time he moves, the boxes and plastic sacks into which he has stuffed his life seem more forbidding, more intractable. He shuttles between the old flat and the new in whichever car he has borrowed, just one step above a bag-lady pushing an overloaded supermarket trolley, front wheel askew, his whole world teetering on a metaphorical wonky castor. He used to think corridors were wasted space. He doesn't think that now. If the last thirty years of Andrew's life have been a slow, bone-wearying history of decline and displacement, they have also brought with them an appreciation of the ever-growing need for storage space.

His current flat is near the old gasometer, a few hundred yards from the river. It has two bedrooms, one of which is used to store stock from the shop. The other is a kind of sleeping alcove-cum-study, also filled with boxes of books that might be stock, or Andrew's, spilling across the bottom of the mattress on the floor. He used to bring people home whenever the chance arose, but he stopped that after a man he'd met on the bus, from Cape Verde, had refused to take his shoes off. He found the flat through someone who worked at the Irish embassy; its owner lives in Cork, which is a comfort.

He takes off his jacket and puts it over the back of a kitchen chair, then pours himself a glass of wine from an opened carton in the fridge. He's hungry but not in the mood to cook; he should have picked up a slice of pizza on his way home but he wasn't thinking about food as he walked from the bus stop on Via Ostiense and let himself into the hall of the building. He was thinking about photographs, Tintin's photographs, trying to imagine where they might be. There's a passage from Cicero he read once, dusting the Loeb classics at the rear of the shop, about the way to remember the flow of a speech by remembering the stages of a journey or, even better, the curved and niche-riddled walls of a theatre, by placing a brightly coloured kinetic image in each of the niches so that their order represents the order in which the elements of the speech appear. A theatre of memory, Cicero called it. Mnemonic tableaux of sex and violence. What he's doing, or trying to do, now is rather like that, except that he has no idea what each imagined niche might contain. What he sees when he turns on the light is not so much Cicero's theatre of memory as an abandoned, cobwebbed honeycomb of detritus.

Finally, he takes two cheese slices from the fridge and slaps them between his standby rye bread, gummy and damp, two slices, also from the fridge. It's chewy stuff; he refills his glass, forcing some of the sandwich down. As soon as he's had enough to stave off hunger, he lays the crust on the table top and walks into the corridor.

One wall is lined with bookcases of various depths and sizes. The other is hidden to waist height by what looks like an inner buttress of cardboard boxes. Andrew opens the flaps of the first box and peers inside. Auction catalogues, yellowing copies of the *TLS*, a smaller sealed carton containing, it turns out, the packs of cards for playing *scopa* he'd bought one winter evening from a woman in Venice, toothless, old enough to be his grandmother, who'd told him she could bring a man to orgasm by beating her eyelashes against his glans; he'd been tempted, for a moment. But this won't do, he thinks, I'll be here all night at this rate. He closes the box and shifts it so that it forms the base for a new pile nearer the kitchen door. He continues like this for an hour, an hour and a half, discovering folders, letters, objects he thought he'd lost, or forgotten the existence of, or imagined sold or stolen, gradually dismantling and reassembling the stacks until he is a third of the way down the wall and is beginning to give up hope. If there were a sense of chronology it might be more encouraging, but the effect is less of strata laid down by time than of atemporal disarray, as though Schliemann had excavated Troy with a gigantic digger and heaped what he'd found beside the hole to poke through later, when later was too late. He opens another carton of generic white wine, finishes his crust, fills and empties a glass, then starts again.

He's at the last but one stack, two layers from the bottom, when he finds a box with a drawing of Tintin's face on the outer flap. He recognizes his own hand and almost weeps because all at once he recalls exactly when he did this: the day Michel had been found and he had carried this box away from the shop where Michel had left it, perhaps on purpose, perhaps not. He recalls taking a black felt marker from the pile on the desk and drawing this rapidly, the oval of the head, the button nose, the quiff of hair, the eyes undifferentiated blobs of ink; this hasty, infantile icon of love. Slumped on the floor, with the almost empty carton of wine beside him, he remembers, with unexpectedly painful clarity, reaching for the packing tape on his desk and sealing it down because he didn't want anyone to look inside, not yet; he didn't want to look inside himself. He hadn't forgiven Michel for leaving him as he did, without a note to prove that it was wanted at least, that Michel had made an actual decision to die and not simply cocked up and taken the wrong pills, the wrong number of pills, at the wrong time.

Tears prick the corners of Andrew's eyes as he slides a forefinger under the tape and feels it lift without resistance, the glue dried out.

The girl's been handing out flyers to make some extra money, leaflets advertising a new shop selling cosmetics near the Corso. It isn't hard, but it's boring, and she's been tempted to throw the second pack in her rucksack into a bin and just pretend she's given them to passers-by. She'd do it if she didn't feel she was being watched. It's madness, she knows, madness to pay her and then pay someone else to watch her, but she can't help it, she feels she's being followed. She's felt it since she left the shop and headed off towards the river, popping the flyers under the windscreen wipers of cars until someone told her to stop it, it was illegal. Which isn't true, but she'd also been told not to do it by the shop. Look out for girls your age, the man had said, late teens or older, smile at them, make them feel they're being treated personally. It's hardly worth answering rubbish like this, but she nodded and said she'd do her best. She still can't quite believe how much she's getting paid for this. It's more than her parents give her in a month. She'd thought there was something odd about it at first, but then he pushed the money into her hand and she couldn't say no. She'll keep quiet about how much she's making, though, she knows what her parents would think if they knew. They'd make her stop right away or, even worse, carry on and give some of what she makes to the poor. She's planning to get to the Vatican for when her father finishes work, and surprise him. She's still got a couple of hundred to get rid of before that. She crosses the river and heads off towards Via Cola di Rienzo. At this time of day, the shops have already been open for more than an hour and there'll be thousands of people walking around. She'll stand outside the cinema and grin like a total idiot until all the flyers are handed out, then nip down the road. It's a good thing he's regular as clockwork – it must be working alongside all those Swiss Guards that does it. But even outside the cinema, with people going in and out, the sensation's still there, the sensation of being watched. She shakes her head as if it were going on inside and all she has to do is dislodge it somehow. A school friend of hers was followed into Villa Borghese a few weeks ago, near the racetrack, and nearly raped, but that was evening, it was dark, there was no one around. Her friend had told her afterwards she'd known something would happen, she'd felt it in her bones, but the girl didn't believe her: she'd thought it was hindsight. Now she's not so sure.

ANDREW 1960–82

Andrew's mother expected him to return to Scotland, where he'd been born and passed the first months of his life; his childhood was a preparation for this. Against his father's will, which was mean and egalitarian in equal measure, she sent him to over-priced international schools in the suburbs of Rome, which left him with an Anglo-American accent she abhorred, but accepted as better than nothing, better than not speaking English, her native tongue, at all. When he finished school and told her he wanted to become an artist and travel, by which he meant live in New York and have constant sex with rough young men who'd been filmed by Andy Warhol, she hurried him off to study languages at St Andrews. She said he had a gift for languages.

At first he'd thought it was a joke. 'Andrew's at St Andrews,' she liked to tell her English-speaking friends. It felt pointed, and cruel, the sort of thing the local Roman boys, who had never quite become his friends, might say to hurt him. At school the other children had teased him about his surname, Caruso, hooting fake arias behind him as he walked away. In the streets and scraps of park around his house, they'd imitated his mother's sibilant, unutterably snobbish take on 'Andrew'. *Anderrroowe*. Either way, he was doomed to solitude.

At St Andrews he acquired a substantial book debt, a dope habit and genital warts, the last from a Spanish man who worked in the kitchens. He came back to Rome after three years, with an ordinary degree, and found work in a second-hand bookshop, run by a middle-aged Dutchman called Joost, who also dealt in home-grown grass and forged Byzantine icons. When Andrew's father died unexpectedly of heart failure and his mother returned to Edinburgh, he stayed in Rome, in his single room above the *latteria*. When his mother died, equally unexpectedly, and left him more money than he'd hoped for but not enough to buy a place to live, he bought the shop from Joost, who retired to Thailand. For the first time in his life Andrew had no one. He could hear his own breath slow down, feel his own blood in his own veins, uncontested. He didn't experience this as happiness; it was more like calm, as though the dogs had been called off.

He wasn't an artist, he knew that; his mother had been right. He still made odd collages from shredded magazines and arranged found bits and pieces in wooden boxes, Joseph Cornell style. He wandered around the city centre taking photographs of graffiti and doors with a camera he barely knew how to use, a second-hand Nikon Joost had bestowed on him as a parting gift. He recorded, late at night on a small portable tape-recorder, tuneless, repetitive spoken songs that reminded him of Laurie Anderson at the time, but only then, that subsequently made him cringe with shame and a sense of his utter uselessness. In the pockets of his canvas waistcoats, he carried notebooks of ideas, even lines, for poems he would never write, torn where he'd ripped strips off to pencil his phone number for men.

But this didn't mean he couldn't be part of what people called the art world. He knew all kinds of artists. His mother had been right about his gift for languages as well. He found himself called on when writers and painters and film companies dropped into Rome and needed help. His French was excellent, his German good, his Spanish, thanks to the kitchen hand at St Andrews, acceptable though basic. He'd even picked up a smattering of Dutch from Joost, though he was cautious about using it; it struck him as dated drug argot and he was afraid of appearing ridiculous. He had a way with people that people liked. He worked for a while as assistant to a playwright, feeding the feral cats and the colony of ants the man kept in his kitchen in a slice of red earth sandwiched between plates of glass, answering his mail with promises of future work or repayment of debts. When the playwright was arrested and sentenced to eight months' jail for corrupting minors, Andrew continued to feed the cats and ants until a cat fight knocked the colony to the kitchen floor, and the glass smashed, and the ants, in their structured unsentimental way, escaped in single file behind the sink. Later, after meeting a woman in a bar who worked for Channel 4, he was paid a monthly retainer to scout papers and local television stations for news items about Italy that would make the English laugh and feel superior: a Mafioso with a stutter, who sang his demands for protection money; an unmarried mother who hadn't left her room for fifteen years, out of shame, and thought Pope John XXIII was still alive. But he stopped doing this, also out of shame. Shame for Italy, which can bear such things with equanimity, and for England, which can find them droll.

The thing about Andrew is that in his heart he's neither Italian nor British. His colouring, red-haired, freckled, is foreign, an Anglo-Celtic mix that marks him out. But his intimate language, the tongue in which he thinks about his life and dreams, is the Roman of the streets and markets, the Roman his mother once slapped him, in front of Scottish cousins, for using. She'd accused him of showing off, but what he was trying to do was to win them over, to charm them in his shy, small way. He falls in love with foreigners, invariably. A man he knew once said, with a grin, that he batted for the other team and Andrew recognized himself immediately in that; he recognized himself as one who would always bat for the other team, who would always, in a sense, betray those around him, if only to win them over, and, in doing so, betray himself. It had nothing to do with sex, although that was what the man had meant. It had to do with him.

His first big love, after the Spanish kitchen hand, was English, which made him a rare exception among Andrew's boyfriends, with a keen, old-fashioned air that reminded him of one of Enid Blyton's young heroes, the kind that wear sandals without socks and khaki shorts and attract all manner of animals to their side. He came into the shop one day, saw Andrew alone and almost left, backing towards the door as though he'd entered the wrong place, as, in one sense, he had. This still happened: people would wander in and look for Joost, hoping to score some grass. Andrew was dusting shelves at the back, stopping every now and then to read a phrase or two. He shook his head and said, in Italian, that if it was Joost he was looking for he'd have to wait; adding, in customarily wry fashion, that Joost had gone out just under two years ago and was now in Thailand. It was clear from the young man's hesitation that he hadn't understood. Andrew tried again, in English. This had more effect. Looking like an overgrown boy, twenty at most, which made him almost ten years younger than Andrew, the young man shrugged and came back into the shop.

'I see,' he said. He glanced around the shelves. 'Lots to read.'

'Well,' said Andrew, 'it is a bookshop.'

The young man nodded, glancing round the room.

'As long as you aren't looking for anything specific,' continued Andrew. He studied the young man in silence for a moment. What was the one called in the Famous Five? Dick? Surely not Dick. 'On holiday?' he said.

The young man shrugged. 'Not really. I've been living here almost a month now, in a hostel run by nuns. Or they say they are. Half of them have got moustaches. I'm supposed to be improving my Italian.'

'For fun?'

'Not really. Not at all, to be honest. For work. I'm a journalist – well, I plan to be. I've got an interview for an internship at a news agency here, at the English desk. If it works out, I'll stay for a while. I'm just a bit worried about my Italian. I actually did it at university, as a subsidiary. I can read it, I just don't seem to get it when people talk to me. I wish they wouldn't, sometimes.' He paused. 'I didn't understand a word you said. But you aren't Italian, are you?'

'Half,' said Andrew.

'Which half?' The young man looked him up and down.

Good God, thought Andrew, heart leaping, mouth suddenly dry. He's flirting with me. 'It's not that simple,' he said. 'It's not like being divided down the middle. It's more like being a solution, like salt in water. You'd have to shake me up and then let me settle to see.'

This was met by another grin. 'That sounds like fun. Do you know, I've hardly spoken to anyone since I got here. Everyone goes on about how friendly the Italians are, but I don't get it. They're pretty cool with me. Even the nuns. Well, especially the nuns. Which makes sense, I suppose. I don't expect you'd have time to give me a little language practice, would you? Or would that shake you up too much?'

'Not at all,' said Andrew, nodding, hand held out, not

believing his luck. 'I'd be happy to. My name's Andrew. Andrew Caruso.'

The young man shook Andrew's hand. 'James,' he said. 'James Bond.'

Andrew laughed. 'Yes, right.'

'No, seriously.'

'You're not joking?'

'I wish I was. My parents didn't think he'd catch on, you see, and James is an old family name, so—'

'So I have to call you James?'

'Well, I'd prefer Jamie. It's marginally less embarrassing.' He grimaced.

Andrew nodded. 'Jamie it is, Mr Bond.'

That evening, after a pizza, they smoked some grass, walking along the empty banks beside the river, then went back to Andrew's room. Andrew, nervous, excited, had done most of the talking during dinner but once they were alone, inside, his words dried up and Jamie took over. He made them both coffee while Andrew shifted dirty clothes and piles of paper from the bed to the floor. There was nowhere to sit apart from a tin trunk, painted by Andrew in green and white stripes, that he had taken to university, now filled with home-made music cassettes – Echo and the Bunnymen, Joy Division, Nick Cave, the Cure – and Italian gay porn magazines, folded to Andrew's favourite pages. Jamie talked as he waited for the coffee to bubble up, but Andrew was only half listening: he'd had an erection for much of the meal and now his balls were aching, not to speak of his head after sharing two

litres of local white wine. Throughout the meal, Jamie had
not once referred to sex, nor to the possibility of it,
although his tone had been uninterruptedly flirtatious.
Neither had Andrew. Andrew had babbled on about art
and cheap places to eat in Rome. Now he'd begun to
wonder if he'd somehow misread the signals, a prospect
so humiliating he felt physically sick at the thought of it.
He wondered what would happen if he pounced the
minute the coffee was safely dispatched, and rolled Jamie
onto the floor and towards the bed, like a carpet. He wondered if Jamie would stay, or run.

But pouncing wasn't necessary. Jamie didn't even pour
the coffee. As soon as it had risen and begun to gurgle in
the *caffettiera* he turned off the gas. 'I don't actually want
any coffee,' he said. 'Do you?'

Andrew shook his head.

Jamie pulled off his T-shirt and sat on the edge of the
bed, patting the sheet beside him. 'Come on, then,' he said.

Jamie left the nuns' hostel the next day and moved in.
Andrew closed the shop for a week, most of which they
passed on the mattress, going downstairs for bowls of
caffelatte and cakes when they needed sugar. The sex was
good in its way, but that way was also odd, unsatisfying
even. Jamie was child-like, affectionate, kissing Andrew's
face and hands and neck, playing with his earlobes and
nipples, snuggling his sweet little snub nose into Andrew's
armpits, until Andrew wanted to scream out loud. There's
just too much foreplay, he'd decide, and then Jamie would

start to whisper hot breathy sex-talk into his ear, and he'd be lost. It was good, but it wasn't enough; it wasn't *genital* enough. At one point, he decided to show Jamie some of his porn magazines from the trunk, not to excite him – that wasn't necessary – just to remind him of one or two of the more basic positions. But Jamie made it clear at once that he didn't need pornography, announcing that he considered it exploitative, and sexist. Andrew, thwarted, dropped the lid shut.

When they weren't making love, as Jamie called it – despite Andrew's misgivings that what he was making was less love than a trial run for it with someone whose instinct was elsewhere, in some more infantile, polymorphous place that Andrew had long abandoned – Jamie talked about how they should be living, about what life was for. Not just for the two of them. For everyone. Despite his improbably school-boyish manner, Jamie had palled up with a gang of punks and their rake-thin dogs who gathered beneath the statue of Giordano Bruno in Campo de' Fiori. They ranted about heresy and revolution in broken English, broken Italian, their dogs sniffing out refuse left from the morning market. Jamie adored them; he said they were real. Andrew, who'd picketed with the best of them at university, recognized the rhetoric and was touched by it, but felt too old to be taken in. 'Somebody's got to work,' he said, when Jamie went on, half drunk, about freedom from bourgeois restraints. What he wanted to say, in his bourgeois way, was who paid for all their wine?

When Jamie, to their surprise, was offered a three-month stint of barely paid work experience at the news agency, he had to be persuaded to accept. Ironically, the dreadful salary was what clinched it. On Andrew's first morning back at work, he watched Jamie set off in a pair of new linen trousers, slightly too big for him, cinched with a canvas belt, and a clean white button-down shirt he'd borrowed from Andrew, the sleeves rolled up to his elbows. Andrew's heart ached with anxious affection. He'll never stick it out, he thought. But it wasn't the job he was thinking about.

Andrew had never had a relationship before this. He'd had sex, with friends and strangers, sometimes more than once with the same person, but he'd never imagined himself living a shared life with someone. Except that, he knew, wasn't true. For the last fifteen years he'd done nothing *but* imagine himself living such a life, piecing together an image of coupledom from whatever lay closest to hand. Barely aware of what he was doing, he slipped his own needs into the faces and clothes of the happily married in films and books, the people who'd made it, somehow, against all odds. Who'd persuaded someone else that they were worth it. Even Andrew's wank mags provided him with sequences, often stretching over several pages, suggesting a rough-and-ready continuity of intent.

So the morning Jamie went off for his first shift, sauntering in his boy-hero way, and Andrew went back to the bookshop, it was hard not to feel that something had finally been achieved. Already he missed what he thought of as the honeymoon of the past few days.

ALEX **1983**

Using his shirt to wipe the handle clean, Alex closed the door of the flat behind him. He crept down the stairs, pressed to the wall, placing his feet on each step as lightly as possible, until he was on the ground floor, had crossed the entrance hall and was outside the building. The road was empty. In the square to his left, maybe fifty yards away, a man and a woman were walking slowly towards their car, the woman gripping the man's arm, their heads together as if wrapped in argument; they hadn't noticed him. He moved a few yards from the door and stood there, trying to control his breathing. Closing his eyes, he saw Bruno before him, dead, his chest covered in cuts, his mouth taped shut, his own eyes blank and staring. He shook himself, moved towards the car. For a moment, with a sense of panic, he thought he had put the keys down on the hall table, as he usually did, in the ashtray Bruno also used for small change. But no, he had them in his pocket.

He pulled them out, then stood with his hand on the car door handle, trying to decide what to do. It would be madness to take the car, he knew that, but it was all he had. If he'd had the courage, or been stupid enough, he would have gone back to the flat to see what he could find. He almost did, but realized he wasn't thinking straight. He was furious that Bruno was dead, furious that he would never see the man again, spend time with him, furious that there would be nothing more to be had, no presents, no help, from someone who had promised so much. Alex found these thoughts, more sensations than thoughts, welling up, one behind the other, and was appalled at himself. How could he have such feelings? For a moment he was on the point of crying. Someone had taken Bruno away from him and he didn't know why, except that hatred was involved.

He opened the car door, then took off his shirt and used it to clean the wheel, the inner handle, the gearstick. He tried to remember exactly what he might have touched, what people touch when they drive, his brain racing. He sat in the driver's seat and then wriggled over and wiped the door on the passenger side as well. Where else had he been? For a moment he wondered if his bare skin against the seat back might have left a trace of sweat, some smear that might be used to pick him out. Calm down, he told himself. Then: Why did I close the door? he thought. He should have left everything exactly the way it was. Perhaps there was someone still inside. Perhaps he'd been seen. When footsteps came towards the car, he crouched as low as he could until they'd passed. 'Please, God,' he whispered to himself. 'Please, God, don't let them kill me too.' He started to shake. Wriggling into his shirt, he put the key in the ignition, got out of the car, swore, wiped the handles clean a second time, then walked down the road towards the river.

There was nothing in the newspaper the next morning. Alex woke up late; he'd walked much of the way home, only catching a night bus for the last mile or so, when exhaustion had overcome his need to be on the move, to distance himself from what he had seen. As he hurried along the empty pavement, his shirt unbuttoned, sweating and shivering all at once, ticking the streetlights off, the image of Bruno returned, and was fought off, and returned. At one point, he stopped and threw up, both hands against the wall as he freed himself of his final meal with the man who had vowed to care for him. Who might even have meant it, Alex thought now, his throat burning with the bile of what he had eaten.

The first thing he saw when he woke were the carrier bags Bruno had entrusted to him. He'd dumped them in the corner of his room the evening before, eager to be behind the wheel, to return the car to Bruno. Now he glanced across at them with a sense of unease, and unwilling curiosity, as though they might tell him something he didn't want to know. What was it Bruno had said? That what they contained was delicate? Potentially delicate? He'd have opened them last night if it hadn't been for the duct tape, the same sort of duct tape he'd later seen cutting into Bruno's thighs and calves and wrists, strapped tight across his mouth.

He lay in bed for a few minutes, then looked at his watch. Half past eleven. There would be no one else at home at this time: his parents were both at work, his sister at school. He had three hours to himself before anyone came back, three hours in which the flat belonged to him. Crossing his bedroom, he picked up a pair of scissors from his desk and set to work.

There were twenty of the smaller sealed envelopes, identical in size, shape and, he judged, weight. They had been sealed with care: strips of duct tape had been cut and wrapped round the folded-down part, each strip over-lapping with the one before, as though their purpose was to protect the contents as much from the atmosphere as from prying eyes. He picked up the first of the bags and inserted the tip of a scissor blade into a small gap left between the tape and the fold, then cut down, careful not to cut the bag itself, until one side of the flap was free. The second side was easier: he started at the bottom and worked the blade up until the flap could be lifted and the bag flipped open. He peered in, irrationally afraid that something might leap out, then started to empty the con-tents onto the floor between his bare knees. It took some time, and a little manoeuvring, before he could see that his guess the previous evening had been right. They *were* photographs. Wrapped, they had seemed the same size but now, spread out on the floor, he could see that they varied not only in their dimensions but also in what they portrayed.

Most of them were police photographs, full face and

profile side by side; some had a full-length image of the man – or, less often, woman – on the same sheet. Serial numbers or other forms of identification could be seen along the edges of some; others appeared to have been trimmed. The photos looked old, but not that old, slightly torn at the corners, some slightly bent, as though they'd been forced into the bag by someone who wanted them hidden as rapidly as possible. In several, the full-length figures were standing against a chart that measured their height. In others, they'd been taken against a bare grey wall, with a socket and plug and dangling flex leading out of the frame. The women were mostly prostitutes, or looked like prostitutes, wearing stuff he'd seen women wear when he was younger, maybe five years earlier: miniskirts, backcombed hair, halter tops; half-smoked cigarettes in their hands. A few, though, showed scenes of crimes – broken windows and doors, forced locks, a Fiat 127 crumpled against a tree, the body of a woman hurled across the bonnet. Unsettled, he gathered the photos together and slipped them back into their bag.

He opened the next, found more of the same. Mug shots, men and women, scowling, indifferent, defiant, scared, drunk. In the third, alongside more faces, there were objects: weapons or goods that must have been seized by the police, again with serial numbers on the negatives or scratched onto the surface of the photograph itself. An axe, with what might have been blood along the edge of the blade, lying beside a pair of electrician's pliers and a car jack. Hundreds of house keys arranged on a table, all turned one way, half stacked like fallen dominoes, splayed out like a pack of cards. Paintings of the Madonna, saints, the crucified Christ, a vase of flowers, a dog. A bare tabletop covered with Roman pottery, in pieces or whole. Cigarettes – Marlboro, Kent, other brands he'd never seen before – still in their cartons, piled into a rough wall ten cartons high. A room full of television sets.

Another bag had photos of groups of handcuffed men, hostile, resigned, staring into the lens, surrounded by police, and photographs of a bank heist, with running figures turned towards the camera, their faces concealed behind balaclavas. One man, in one of the groups, had a sickle dangling from his grasp.

Altogether, when all the bags had been emptied out and their contents sorted, roughly, into categories, Alex counted almost three hundred photos. What had Bruno wanted with all this, he wondered. And where had they come from? He gathered them up and repacked them, as they came, into the bags. He didn't want them in his bedroom, in his parents' flat, he knew that. But they were all he had, of Bruno and of Bruno's promise. They must have value to someone, he thought, or Bruno would have thrown them away, instead of packing them into carriers and giving them to Alex to hide. They must be worth something to someone. But how much, and to whom? He didn't know. Could Bruno have been killed for these? And if he had been, what did that mean? That Alex was also in danger?

*

The next day, in the Rome pages of *Il Messaggero*, there were two pictures of Bruno. One must have been taken years before Alex met him, a thinner Bruno with thick short hair, staring at the camera, expressionless. It looked like one of the mug shots from the bags, but had probably been taken for an identity card or driving licence, some kind of official document. In the other, more recent, photograph Bruno was laughing and clearly had his arm round the shoulder of someone who'd been cropped from the image as irrelevant, or worthy of protection. This was the Bruno Alex had thought he knew and, for a moment, he was hurt to see the man so cheerful, his image already smudged by the fingers of other bar customers who'd read the paper before Alex had got to it. He was jealous to think Bruno had enjoyed the company of someone else, someone he would never know. The story, two columns long, was entitled 'Brutal Murder of Rome Journalist'. Alex read it rapidly, his coffee going cold beside him on the bar.

There was nothing about the word on the wall, '*frocio*', the word for 'queer' that Bruno had often used as a wry joke directed at himself; nothing to suggest the murder might have been sexually motivated. The police had no idea where to look, the article said, but had begun to investigate possible links with Bruno's recent work on organized crime for *Il Messaggero* itself. Alex knew nothing about this. Bruno had never wanted to discuss his work. 'There'll be time for all that when you're my cub reporter,' he'd say, one arm behind his head, a cigarette between his lips. 'Like Jimmy Olsen.'

'Who's Jimmy Olsen?' Alex had asked.

'You don't know Jimmy Olsen? He's Superman's pal,' laughed Bruno. Bruno loved American superheroes – he had a bookcase in his bedroom full of vintage DC and Marvel comics, *Superman*, *Spider-Man*, *Thor*, *The Fantastic Four*, *Captain America*, most of them wrapped in transparent plastic, too valuable to read or even touch. I should have taken some of those, thought Alex, for a second, but half-heartedly; that anger had passed. He was too relieved to be free, so far at least, to care that much about what he might have lost. Besides, he had the photographs. He'd taken some out that morning and looked at them again, at the faces of people he had begun to feel he knew as they stared back out at him, as if to stare him down, as curious in their way, it seemed, as he was in his.

La Repubblica had more information, Alex discovered when he stopped in another bar for a second coffee. Someone must have laid their hands on photographs taken by the police, as Bruno himself had, or even entered the murdered man's flat. There was a shot of the bathroom, as Alex had seen it, and another of the damage that had been done to the kitchen, which Alex hadn't seen. But the largest photograph was of the wall where '*frocio*' had been written. They would have had a photograph of Bruno as well, it occurred to Alex, but they wouldn't have been able to use it, not with Bruno in that state.

The article itself had no more information than the one in *Il Messaggero*, repeating the organized-crime theory without naming the rival newspaper. But this time the journalist had interviewed some of Bruno's neighbours, who were more than willing to talk but preferred not to be identified. One woman said the flat was always full of young foreign men, at all hours of the day and night. Alex, who knew, or thought he knew, this wasn't true, had a good idea which neighbour she was. The one on the third floor who'd tried to make Bruno pay for the installation of a lift. 'Gay parties,' she'd said, *festini gay*, and he could see her lip curl as the journalist wrote the words down in his pad. Assuming these words were hers, of course: Bruno had told him how rarely the quotes in an article corresponded to the truth. A man said he'd heard raised voices coming through the door, and slaps and moans, as though someone were being slapped around. Not that night, he added, of course: no one had heard a thing that night, when it might have mattered; besides, it wasn't his business. Someone else said that Bruno had always been discreet, whatever that meant. That he'd had something to hide? Isn't being called discreet a sort of veiled accusation? All the old grudges and jealousies would be coming out into the open, thought Alex, who wondered now how often he'd been seen by these people, these neighbours, on the stairs, on Bruno's landing, letting himself in with a key he wished he'd never had. Still, as long as they were talking about foreigners he was safe.

That must have been what had happened then, that other men Alex had never even met had entered the flat and killed him. But it still didn't make sense. Bruno had known that Alex was coming back: he'd never have let anyone else into the flat, certainly not for sex, for *festini gay*. He knew that wasn't Alex's thing. Besides, he'd always said Alex was all the love he needed, or had the energy for. None of it squared up. He tried to remember if the front door had been forced, but couldn't; all he could recall was the fact that it was open and that the light from inside shone onto the landing, and he had walked in and found his lover, because he knew now that this was what Bruno had been, strapped dead to a chair in his own house. But it was odd that neither of the newspapers had said anything about how the murderer – murderers? – might have got into the flat, as though that didn't matter to them, as though they knew but didn't want to say. Surely it mattered more than anything. Had he, or they, been friends of Bruno's, or not? And if not, who were they, and what did they want? Bruno had been tortured, that much was obvious. There was no mention of that. And what if he had told them about Alex before he died?

He thought about the photographs in their black plastic bags, like sleeves, hidden beneath his bed where his mother had sworn she would never look. He didn't trust her; he would have to move them as soon as he could. What were they all about? What should he do with them?

That was when he remembered the Birdman.

The girl's crossing the road when the car stops right beside her and both doors open so that she's trapped in the space between. She starts to cry out but the man in the front seat pulls her into the car, onto his lap, while whoever's opened the other door, the door behind, gets out and bundles her legs in, then returns to the car and slams his own door shut. There's a hand over her face. She tries to bite it but can't open her mouth far enough, he's gripping her jaw so tightly. She's being held by more hands than one, she can't work out how many, as someone pulls something soft over her head and everything goes black. Then the front seat is moved somehow, flattened, and she's being dragged through into the back. She's kicking but there's no purchase – she can't get any force behind the kicks. Once, she makes contact and there's a cry and a swear word before she's slapped hard on the thigh like a naughty little girl. Her skirt's ridden up – they can see her legs, her knickers. They're going to rape me, she thinks, and she tries to calm down, breathe more slowly, remember what she's been told to do if anyone tries to rape her. What did her friend do, the one in Villa Borghese? She can't remember. Run? She must have run. But that was different – they were in the open, in a park. The girl's in this massive car, and it's driving quite fast now, she can feel it; she doesn't know how many men there are with her, but it can't be more than two and the driver. They're in the centre of Rome, in broad daylight. She thinks, This can't be happening. What do they want with me? A man's voice tells her to behave and they'll take the bag off, but she has to promise she'll behave. She tries to speak but the fabric muffles her voice. She nods, hard, so they'll see. She says, as loudly and clearly as she can, I promise, and they take the bag off. They're stationary, waiting for lights to change, and she seems to know where she is, though she isn't sure. There are people only feet away from the car. One of them sees her and lifts something to his face. She scuttles across the seat towards the door and tries to open it, her fingers reaching for the handle, staring out, about to scream for help, but already the man beside her has grabbed her shoulder and is pulling her back. I'll teach you how to keep a promise, he says.

ANDREW **2008**

Andrew lifts out the neatly folded pullover from the top of the cardboard box. It's one he remembers Michel wearing, a loose-knit green V-neck pullover he'd bought, second-hand, from one of the shops in Via del Governo Vecchio. Andrew had offered to buy him a new one, but Michel had refused. He said he loved the colour, a musky greyish-green, not quite military, almost feminine. I wonder why he loves it, thought Andrew at the time, and finds himself thinking now, after years have passed and the pullover has ceased to exist for Michel, and only Andrew knows what it once meant. Holding it to his face, breathing in, Andrew smells dust, cigarette smoke and the faintest, probably imagined, trace of sweat. He puts it down, still folded, on his knees, sits back on his heels before continuing to search, unexpectedly shaken by what he has found, his eyes half closed. Michel used to wear it over a T-shirt, he remembers, a yellow T-shirt gone ragged at the neck, with baggy corduroy trousers and desert boots, a sort of uniform, an artist's uniform. If not this pullover, then another, equally shabby, the colour of rust or the dried and powdered blood people use to feed their plants.

Clothes were the last thing he'd expected, the last thing Andrew had wanted to find for a host of reasons. Disturbed, dissatisfied, he looks back into the box, and his heart lifts. Photographs.

He takes out the first stiff plastic envelope and examines it. There are traces of duct tape around the upper section where it's been folded shut, but the tape has been scissored through at each side and the envelope is no longer sealed. He reaches inside, extracts the bundle of photographs, flicks through them, initially perplexed and then with mounting disappointment. These aren't what he expected either. They're black and white, but he can see at once they weren't taken by Michel. He lifts the box and carries it into the kitchen, pushing dirty plates to one side to make room, then, with a sigh, sick of himself, he gathers the plates and transfers them to the sink. When he has made enough space, he opens another envelope to find more of the same. And another, until all the envelopes are open and the table is covered. Faces, mostly of middle-aged men from the front and side, a rogues' gallery, sometimes full-length, followed by their booty, the whole sad assortment of what they have stolen. Then scenes of the crime and images of the victims. A bunch of photographs, blurred, askew, of people running across streets and out of buildings with guns in their hands and masks over their faces, a corpse in the gutter outside a bar, which must have been taken by witnesses. He picks them up and puts them down, blankly, not understanding what he has found, not understanding what it has to do with Michel, or with him. There's no art to them. Yet these photographs are also the kind of sad, dark thing Michel would have liked, and Andrew's aware of that. He'd have pronounced them *genuine* in a way guaranteed to irritate Andrew, who, deep down, is a sentimentalist, or someone who thinks the idea that suffering is more genuine than, say, pleasure is essentially a sentimental idea: he's not sure which. But what Michel would also have liked is their serial feel, as though they were variants on a single theme, their individuality both sapped and accentuated through quasi-repetition.

All of which is beside the point, thinks Andrew, as the irony sinks in. That of all Michel's possessions, he should be left with a cardboard box of photographs that someone else had taken and preserved for bureaucratic reasons, of no apparent worth, of no sentimental value. Because Andrew *is* a sentimentalist, when it comes to it. He wants to have something of Tintin, his Tintin, something that will last and have meaning. He wants to have something that will bring his Tintin back.

He is returning the pictures to their bags when one image catches his eye. A large dark car, a Mercedes, possibly, or a BMW – Andrew isn't much good on cars – is pulling away from the pavement. Whoever took the picture is standing close enough to frame the body of the car, its driver, a middle-aged man in a black jacket and sunglasses staring straight ahead, his face invisible, and the person sitting behind him in the back, a teenage girl who is twisting round and staring through the closed window at someone or something outside the photograph, apparently unaware she's been spotted, her eyes wide open, her expression distraught, lips parted in what might be a cry. Behind her, a man is holding her shoulder, as if to prevent her leaping from the car. The girl's face looks familiar to Andrew, the face but not the person, as though he has seen her in someone's house or on television. He can't quite place her, and doesn't really want to.

He is alone, as usual, in the flat, but tonight he feels it both as something new and as something that will go on, perhaps for the rest of his life.

He slides the photograph back into its bag.

The next day is Sunday. He'll open the shop for an hour or two in the afternoon, in the hope of some post-lunch tourist trade drifting between Largo Argentina and Campo de' Fiori, but plans to spend the morning working on his piece about Michel. He's slept badly, waking from dreams that aren't exactly about Michel, but that might have been dreamt by him, if that makes sense, although the details escape him now. Dreams of a city he doesn't know but identifies as Ghent. Dreams in which Michel is the protagonist and Andrew a reluctant, often panic-stricken observer. He makes himself a large pot of coffee, takes it through to the bedroom with a packet of biscuits and sits at his desk, his laptop on. The final photograph of Michel, perched naked on his pile of newspapers, is propped against an empty wine bottle, to remind him of what he has lost. This must be how he saw himself, Andrew thinks, picking up the photograph, one of the bunch Michel had taken and given to Andrew on the last but one day of his life.

Andrew reads through what he has written so far. He's been trying to capture some day-to-day sense of Michel, of what the fabric of their lives was like, but this isn't working; it isn't lifting above itself as he'd hoped. It's thoughtful, polite stuff, he thinks, generous towards the dead; even Michel's mother, assuming the bitch is still alive and in control, will be happy to see her dead son treated with such respect. But it doesn't ring true, not a word of it. He doesn't delete it, he's too frugal for that, but he decides to take a different tack. He starts to write.

There was something angry about Michel, especially in bed. I don't think he ever had, or wanted to have, a sense of intimacy. He saw sex as a challenge, a deadly serious game he had to win, or possibly as a performance, except that no one was there to witness it except the other, who didn't quite count, who didn't quite constitute an audience, who imagined himself, against all odds, to be involved. I'm talking about me, obviously. His favourite type of sex was public, risk-running, but I don't see him as an exhibitionist so much as someone who just didn't work in private spaces, bedrooms, bathrooms, kitchens, who didn't like what they meant. His photography is part of that, part of that fuck-off attitude towards everything normal. He hated the way people defined themselves by their possessions; ironically, for someone so vain, he hated the importance Italians gave to their appearance, their clothes, the objects they used to define them in the world. He always used cheap biros, exercise books from UPIM. He was angry about the way people wasted so much money on things, but he was also the first to say that people deprived of their things didn't really exist at all. And it wasn't a criticism for Michel: he saw not existing as a blessed relief. That was why his work gradually excluded people, images of people, and what he called 'the lie of personality', in favour of the crap we surround ourselves with, which told 'the truth'. And that was his big idea, his big paradox. It isn't particularly original, but neither was Michel. That was his problem, or part of it. He might have been happier as a criminal – he flirted with the idea of crime. He was like another man I loved, who also imagined himself to be a rebel in some way, who'd read his Artaud and harmed himself, gingerly, a couple of times. Except that Michel may have killed himself, in a room he kept hidden from me. So maybe he did like privacy as much as the next man. What he didn't like was sharing it. What he didn't like was sharing it with someone. By which I mean with me.

Well, this won't do, Andrew thinks. This self-pity won't do at all. And how odd that he should think of Jamie, out of the blue, like this. He eats a biscuit and pours himself some lukewarm coffee from the pot, wondering how long it will be before he has to close the shop and find a regular, paid job, 'give in', as both Jamie and Michel might have said; wondering why he should find such defeated, self-satisfied, self-serving men so attractive when all they have ever done is make him suffer. He picks up the photograph of Michel and touches it lightly to his lips. He will resist for as long as is humanly possible, he decides, and is unexpectedly cheered by this decision. He stands up, and his chair flips over with the weightof the accumulated jackets on its back. 'And now,' he says, in a loud voice to no one, 'I shall tidy up this fucking bedroom.'

Jamie left the news agency after a month and a half, before his stint was finished. All he seemed to do there, in any case, was arrange his drinking circle for the evening. He'd adopted the wine bar just round the corner from Andrew's flat, which had a sprinkling of ex-pat foreigners among the locals but – at that time – few tourists. He persuaded Andrew, initially with some difficulty, to go with him. Andrew generally avoided bars like that but found that he enjoyed himself, to his surprise. He enjoyed the company of English-speaking people, whose experience of Rome was equal to, but different from, his. More than anything, he enjoyed being seen with Jamie, bright, keen, extreme little Jamie, his other half.

Jamie introduced him to some of the people he worked with – Matilda, a wire-haired woman from Newcastle, who'd recently been arrested, and released without charge after protesting against cruise missiles in Sicily; a large-boned, red-faced man called Martin Frame, who was supposed to be or once have been a spy; a Spanish amateur playwright with a harelip, whose name Andrew constantly forgot. They were all, including Andrew, heavy drinkers, but Jamie would always drink the most, emptying his glass with a child-like relish, the tips of his pixie-like ears glowing pink, his fine blond hair increasingly ruffled and standing on end; it was impossible not to see his antics as innocent, thought Andrew. Sometimes he'd bounce on his stool in a state of nervous excitement; other times, his face would take on the beatified expression it wore when his back was being scratched by Andrew's willing hands. Andrew adored him constantly, and was constantly terrified of what he might do. Sober, Jamie was impulsive, in a harmless, endearing, puppyish way. Drunk, he was capable of any madness that entered his head. He liked to hold hands with Andrew across the table and didn't care this wasn't done in public, not in this bar; sometimes he'd lean across and kiss him on the mouth, then sit back, grinning and smacking his lips. One evening he launched at the top of his voice into an IRA song he'd learned from someone, about Bobby Sands, martyr, and ended up in a sloppy theatrical tussle with three English tourists. Once, when it was clear Jamie could barely stand, Andrew had hinted they should go home, finally attempting to lift him from the stool and into the square outside. But Jamie had not only brushed this suggestion – and Andrew – aside, he'd regarded it as a challenge to take his naughtiness up an extra notch, extravagantly throwing his arms round Andrew's neck and dragging him to the floor for a snogging session. On this occasion, Martin Frame had manhandled Jamie out of the bar, while Andrew got up, too mortified to meet the other customers' eyes.

Jamie left his internship soon after that evening. They continued to go to the wine bar, but Jamie had begun to fall asleep without warning, often tumbling from his stool to the ground. Before long they were asked to leave. Matilda and the Spanish man disappeared from the scene at that point. Martin would meet them now and again in other bars, but it was clear that Jamie had ceased to amuse him and, not long after, he was also gone. Andrew missed Martin, missed his conversation. Jamie wrote the man off as a fascist, but that meant nothing; even Jamie couldn't be bothered to explain.

Walking home across Piazza Navona one night, after sharing a pizza and too much wine with Andrew, Jamie kicked off his shoes, tugged off his socks, then threw himself into the fountain in front of Sant'Agnese and tried to mount one of the sea monsters, struggling onto its slippery back, sliding off, struggling up again. Andrew hissed at him to get out, but Jamie, in a state of exaltation, ignored him. He flung himself like a saddle-bag across the creature's curved haunches, his hands and bare feet dangling in the water at each side. Eventually Andrew clambered in and waded across to the monster himself, to haul him off. Wriggling, dripping wet, Jamie resisted until he was pulled over the fountain edge.

Andrew was furious. 'You could have broken something off it.'

Jamie shrugged. 'It's only stone,' he sneered, because everything Andrew thought and said and believed in was hopelessly off the point. 'It isn't alive.'

'It's fucking Bernini,' said Andrew.

'Dead white males,' said Jamie, in a slurred, sing-song way.

Andrew hadn't heard this phrase before and didn't immediately understand. It seemed important. He stared down as Jamie slumped to the ground, his clothes clinging, his hair plastered to his head. You've never looked lovelier, he thought. I don't know what I'll do when you go. The idea that this might happen overwhelmed him. I won't be able to bear it. 'You could have been arrested,' he said.

Jamie grinned. 'I know.'

ALEX AND THE BIRDMAN **1983**

The Birdman lived in Piazza Vittorio, above the daily market, in a large flat with three windows overlooking the square. These were festooned with strips of fatty rind, string bags filled with various kinds of seed, peanuts threaded, still in their shells, on a fringe of dangling wire. The sills were lined with water containers of one sort or another, cut-down plastic bottles, handleless cups, recycled tomato cans. The shutters had been permanently fastened back to increase the amount of feeding space available. The Birdman was fat, with a loosely jowled face and plucked eyebrows; he favoured kaftans at home and extra-large T-shirts with pyjama trousers for when he left the flat. Around his head, tucked into a strip of tartan ribbon, he often wore feathers, pigeon feathers. Most of the birds he fed were pigeons from the square below, already overweight, squawking and jostling for space, squeezing out smaller birds. At times, the Birdman would drive them off and click his fingers or emit a low keening noise designed to attract other species, to no effect.

The main room of the flat had a low stage to one side

where the Birdman would put on shows, or plan to. He'd been an actor, had appeared in a couple of films made by Fellini as one of the director's grotesques, but his speaking lines had been removed, or dubbed by others. More often his part was simply excised as superfluous. When his parents died within months of each other and left him this flat, the flat in which he had spent his childhood, he had taken to letting rooms and living off the rent. Later sources of income involved dealing in small quantities of grass and helping young men with documents they otherwise wouldn't have been able to obtain, only to give the money back to them later for services rendered. His flat was generally full of young men.

Alex had met him one evening at the station. The Birdman had offered him a coffee and Alex, wary but intrigued, had accepted. This was before he'd met Bruno, before he'd met anyone to speak of. After their coffee, the Birdman asked him if he'd like to come back and meet some friends of his. Alex, after thinking about this for a moment, shook his head. 'You're a wise boy,' the Birdman said, and patted his hand. 'Trust no one. That's my considered advice, and I make no charge for it.' The next time they saw each other, some weeks later, Alex went back to the Birdman's flat.

The Birdman cooked him a meal, poured him a glass of wine, rolled a joint for them both from a foil-lined bag of grass. Apart from the joint, it reminded Alex of going to have Sunday lunch with his grandmother. The Birdman chatted about his time in the film world, and people he knew, journalists, artists, poets, so that Alex felt privileged to know him. By the time they'd finished the joint, he was ready to be approached for sex and to rebuff it, gently, because he didn't feel like hurting the older man. But the Birdman didn't seem to be bothered about sex, which put Alex in the odd, and offended, position of waiting – even wanting – to be propositioned so that he could refuse with grace. Instead, the Birdman asked if he would like to have his photograph taken, and when Alex said yes, he led him through to the living room and told him to stand on a bare stage in the corner. 'You can take off your T-shirt if you want,' he said, and, with a knowing grin, because this was how it would start, Alex did.

The Birdman set up a camera on a tripod, then stood back, using a button attached to the camera by a wire to take the photographs. Alex posed, then stopped posing, then posed once more as the Birdman clicked on the button. He wanted to look at the camera, but the Birdman's presence to one side of it distracted him.

'You're a very striking young man,' the Birdman said, pressing the button, and Alex was flattered, though slightly tense with anticipation. Surely, sooner or later, the man would pounce. But the Birdman simply unhitched the button from the camera and thanked him with a stiff, ironic bow before leaving him alone to dress. Alex, snubbed, pulled his T-shirt back on, then walked to the window, peering out through the hanging bags of bird seed, the ribbons of fat, scaring away a clutch of pigeons, unsettled, wanting both to leave and to stay. The next time he visited, some days later, the Birdman said that all his most special birds came home to roost.

Alex was never shown the photographs the Birdman had taken and wondered sometimes what had become of them. He suspected they might have been sold and wasn't pleased, although what he most wanted was less to protect himself than to see how he looked. He was worried they might not have done him justice. When he asked if he could take a glance at them, the Birdman shrugged and pouted, then changed the subject, which confirmed Alex's suspicions. He stopped visiting for a while, affronted, angry that he'd been used. But he soon drifted back. There were always new people to talk to, and sometimes – if he wanted – to have sex with, though never the Birdman. Nobody, as far as he could tell, had sex with the Birdman.

It was through a Sardinian soldier on national service, who was spending his few days' leave in the Birdman's flat, that Alex first met Bruno. After their meeting he stayed away for months, but Bruno had wanted grass one evening and Alex said he knew where to get it. The Birdman raised an eyebrow when he opened the door to Alex but, apart from that, behaved as if nothing had happened. Perhaps, thought Alex, nothing had. He must be used to people coming and going like this.

So he didn't feel bad about turning up at the Birdman's four days after Bruno's murder. The Birdman took Alex's head between his hands to study his face for a moment, then kissed him on both cheeks in what struck Alex as commiseration. It hadn't occurred to him that his relationship with Bruno might not have been private; knowing this might not be the case unnerved him. But the moment passed; maybe he'd misunderstood. He followed the Birdman's swishing kaftan into the living room. Sitting on floor cushions against the wall were two men he'd seen there before, waiters in a nearby restaurant. They nodded, but didn't move. Alex was about to sit down beside them, to share whatever they were doing, when someone came into the room behind him. He turned round to see who it was.

He was a few years older than Alex, twenty-three, twenty-four at the most. He had dirty blond hair, the fringe almost covering his eyes, and needed a shave. He grinned at Alex, revealing a missing canine, as though the two of them were old friends. Alex was about to smile back, offer his hand, when the other man shook his head. '*Scusami*,' he said, in a strong, almost comic English accent. He sounded very drunk. Standing closer to Alex, swaying a little, he introduced himself as Jamie. He gestured with his head towards the other two. '*Non sono molto simpatici*,' he said, in passable, slurred Italian. Alex thrust out his bottom lip, as if to say: What do you expect? then asked him where he came from to show that he, on the other hand, was *molto simpatico*. Jamie shrugged. Before he could answer, assuming he would have done, the Birdman came up and put an arm around their shoulders, drawing the three of them together into a loose, ungainly hug.

'Be nice to him,' he said.

Alex, whose face was pressed up against Jamie's hair, couldn't see who the Birdman had said this to, but assumed it must be him. He pulled away. 'Of course,' he said. The Birdman led them across to a corner of the room with two chairs and a small table. 'I'll get you something to drink,' he said. He looked at Alex, warningly it seemed. He mouthed, 'He's a good boy,' once again as if to remonstrate with Alex's failure to realize this.

'I'm sure he is,' said Alex.

Jamie glanced at the Birdman's back as he walked off, then shook his head slowly as though he'd remembered something unpleasant and wanted to dislodge the memory. The two men across the room laughed, Alex didn't know at what. At nothing to do with them. It was likely enough.

When they were both sitting down in their corner, as they had been told, and the Birdman had brought them bottles of beer, Alex wondered what he was doing there. He should have spoken directly to the Birdman. He should have come clean, if only to see whether the Birdman knew about him and Bruno because if he did he wouldn't be the only one. The police would also know, sooner or later. And so would the people who had killed him, if Alex was right and it hadn't been what the papers had begun to refer to as an '*omicidio gay*', but something more sinister.

Jamie was talking to him with great earnestness. His Italian was hard to follow but Alex grasped enough to understand he was being told about the end of an affair. Fractured, confused, repetitive, Jamie had evidently been hurt. He'd been kicked out by his lover, or had walked out: it wasn't clear which, perhaps not even to Jamie. There'd been a row and the police had been called. Jamie was leaning forward, one hand on Alex's knee, holding him there the way drunks do, his face too close to Alex's. It hadn't been Jamie's fault, but the other man, whose name Alex couldn't catch although it sounded foreign, had blamed him. Jamie had said he was sorry, but it was too late. He repeated this several times, as though he had lost the thread of his story, which wasn't so much a story as a lament, thought Alex, like one of the Portuguese folk songs Bruno had loved so much.

'I didn't mean to hit him,' Jamie said. 'I made him cry,' he said. He told me to go, but he didn't want me to go, I know he didn't. He was scared.'

'When did this happen?' Alex asked, out of politeness. 'What?'

'When did you leave each other?'

'Oh, ages ago,' Jamie said, distracted, as if he'd been talking about something else. Slumping back, he looked down at his grubby, nail-bitten hand, which was still on Alex's leg, then lifted it off and used it to fish a cigarette out of a packet on the table. 'I haven't seen him for ages,' he said. 'He's got someone else now anyway. Some French photographer.'

Alex, fidgety with boredom, was about to seek out the Birdman, presumably busy preparing food for them all in the kitchen, cheese and bread, chopped-up fruit and nuts that would otherwise be given to the birds. But the word 'photographer' fixed him to his chair. 'What was his name again?'

'Who?'

'Your friend?'

Jamie thought about this for a moment. 'Andrew,' he said.

'And his new friend? He's a photographer?' Alex asked. Jamie didn't seem to know, or to have understood, or possibly to care. He drew in a lungful of smoke with surprising energy, his head tilted back, his mouth in a sort of rictus. Alex took this chance to look at him more closely. It was impossible to place his age, he thought. His skin looked older than the rest of him, crêpe round the eyes, cheeks reddened by a maze of tiny broken veins. Maybe he was older than Alex had first thought – mid- to late twenties, even. He wondered how old the other man had been. Older than Jamie, he guessed. He could see that he and Jamie had that in common, like most of the youths who drifted through the Birdman's flat: their attractiveness to older men. Still, at least he had never hit Bruno or made him suffer, as Jamie obviously had his older man. He'd made him cry, but maybe the man was happy now with his French photographer. Alex thought of the photographs that must have been taken of Bruno, taped to the chair, his chest covered with blood, his dick messed up. What was that Chinese torture called? Death by a thousand cuts?

'What does he do?' he asked Jamie, who breathed out to examine him.

'Sells books. He buys and sells used books. They used

to sell dope there. And anything else that can be bought and sold. He's got a shop.'

'Where is it?'

'Near Campo de' Fiori,' said Jamie, in a bored voice, lowered to make sure no one heard. 'Do you want to go somewhere and have another drink?' He glanced round. 'I've had enough of this place.'

'I haven't got any money,' Alex said.

Jamie smiled. 'No problem.'

It *was* a problem, as things turned out, because Jamie didn't have any money either. Alex discovered this when they'd both had a couple more beers in a place near San Giovanni and the man behind the bar wanted them to settle up before he drew them a third and, in Jamie's case, a whisky chaser. Alex had a sense that he'd been in this particular bar before, with friends, but didn't feel it would be useful to remind the man of this, so he let Jamie do the talking, in his loud, rambling Italian, his forefinger prodding at the man's chest until the man lost his temper and dragged Jamie to the door by the shoulder of his shirt. Before he could do the same to Alex, Alex stood up and joined Jamie on the pavement, spreading his arms and bowing slightly from the waist in an effort to appease the man, who marched back into the bar, sweeping a damp cloth across the table they'd used, to cancel their presence.

It was dark by now. 'Let's find someone to fuck,' slurred Jamie, slumped against the wall. 'The night is young.'

Alex shook his head. He was hungry and Jamie was clearly in no position to feed him, even if he'd wanted to eat, which didn't seem to be the case. 'I'm going home,' he said, taking a step away from Jamie, as if he thought Jamie might try to prevent him physically from leaving. After all, Alex had no reason to stay. He knew all he needed to know about Andrew and his second-hand bookshop. He knew that Andrew was interested in buying stuff, including photographs, and enjoyed meeting boys like him. If Andrew couldn't help him, no one could.

Jamie shrugged. 'See you around,' he said, and headed off towards the metro.

The girl is led from the car down a passage between two buildings. She doesn't know where she is but thinks it might be Monteverde. She's trying not to panic, trying to notice everything that might be needed later, when she's been freed, to identify these men, this place. She notices the colour of the walls, the roughness of the plaster, the weathered slabs, moss-covered at the sides, beneath her feet. It's getting dark now, it must be half-past seven, eight o'clock, but it's still not too dark to see. The two men, one in front of her and one behind, are making sure she walks at their pace, which is faster than she'd like. It doesn't give her the time she needs to think, to look for ways to escape. Both the men are much taller than she is, though she's tall for her age, and broadly built, thugs really, she thinks, and she's scared again, despite herself. She's decided not to be scared – she decided in the car as it drove along what looked like Viale Trastevere. The man beside her had his hand on her head, holding it down, but she saw the top of something she's sure was the Ministry of Education. Whatever they want to do with her, she's decided, she'll survive. At the end of the passage they go down some steps and there's a gate. She's frightened again as the man in front of her slips a key into a lock and the gate opens, and he turns to take her arm above the elbow, squeezing until it hurts. He leads her down some more steps into what ought to be a garage but looks as if it's been converted into somewhere to live. The man behind her pulls the door closed and there's a moment's darkness – she thinks, I'll make a break for it! – before a light comes on and she sees where she is. She's standing in the middle of a small room that's been rigged out as a kitchen, with a stove and sink against one wall and a small fridge in the corner. There's a table, with two chairs, and a dresser, one of those sixties ones – notice everything, she tells herself, remember everything – with the sliding glass doors. Beside the dresser, an open door reveals another room – a corridor? She can't make it out. There aren't any windows, but there's a sort of slit along the top of the wall behind her that must let in some light during the day. She looks from one man to the other, as if to say, Now what? What happens now?

'But these are simply fascinating,' Daniela says.

'I thought you'd like them.' Andrew opens another folder and takes out a dozen more photographs. 'Look at these,' he says. 'Crime scenes.'

Daniela glances at them briefly, but her eyes soon return to the mug shots, spread over the bookshop counter like playing cards. 'These are the genuine article, though, aren't they?' she says. 'They're utterly extraordinary. So material, somehow. They almost convince you Lombroso was right about criminal physiognomy. Just look at them. Their destiny's marked. Beetle-browed, weak-chinned. Dreadful skin.'

'That's probably more to do with their diet than any criminal inclination in their genes,' says Andrew. He picks up one of the photos, a triple shot: full face, profile, full figure of a young man. 'This one certainly isn't weak-chinned. He's actually rather good-looking.'

Daniela takes the photo, gives it a judicious glance, shakes her head. 'Well, he won't be good-looking now, darling. Look at the clothes they're all wearing. These must have been taken at least twenty years ago. Probably more like thirty. It won't be that difficult to establish a date, I shouldn't think. The cars in the crime scenes are bound to have number plates we can track down, that sort of thing, if we have to. At the same time, they're just so fantastically atemporal.'

'Why should we have to establish a date?' says Andrew.

'Well, you're surely going to do something with all of this, aren't you? You'd be mad not to. They'd make a wonderful little show, maybe a book. I'll give you a hand, you know that. I'd like to have a project on right now.' She pulls a face. 'Regime change has left me with time on my hands. I've been pushed to one side. I'm on the shelf, professionally speaking.'

This is exactly what Andrew wants.

'Here, you mean?' He's all innocence. 'Do the show here?'

'Why not? Your space upstairs is perfect, above a second-hand bookshop. I mean, what could be more appropriate? These images are pure *text*, Andrew, used, abused, discarded text, crying out to be reinterpreted.'

Delighted and relieved though he is, because without her support he'd be fucked, he doesn't quite know whether to take her seriously. He met Daniela dell'Orto years ago, when he translated a piece she'd written for a catalogue. She was famous within the art world for having thrown together a group of young artists and invented a school, *I nuovipittorici*, upping the asking – and selling – prices of its exponents by a factor of several thousand. Beyond the art world, she'd later become notorious for having posed naked with a porn actor, more or less *in flagrante*, for the cover of a weekly magazine for which she wrote a column. Her journalism was more or less comprehensible, tossed off in a bar outside the magazine's offices. Her more serious writing, critical reviews for specialist magazines, presentations, catalogues, was appalling, subject-less sentences that went nowhere and ended without resolution, grammatical or otherwise, logorrhoeic accumulation, neologisms, modish transliterations from English and French. Andrew tried to make sense of the essay she'd given him and then decided, What the fuck, I'll do it word for word. He spent a day and night at his typewriter with a bottle of grappa and a dictionary, then realized the dictionary served no useful purpose because all he had to do was take the word, any word, and make it look English. Half the words didn't exist in their own language: what harm could it do? He could defend his choice as a sign of respect towards the original. He was particularly proud of this piece: *The event puts itself forward as a pure differential of plane; a sensitive alteration produced by the expansion of a flowing of materiality but without the burden of materiality, through a pure qualification of space according to anidea of completely pictoric concretion that conserves, without mimicry, the complex sense of expressive tension.* Fantastic stuff, he thought, emptying what was left of the bottle into a glass.

Hung-over, fraudulent, he handed in the finished translation the following day, wondering what his chances were of being paid, rating them slight. A few mornings later he had a phone call from Daniela dell'Orto herself. He almost put the receiver down, but what was the point? He was ruined. She knew everyone in Rome and beyond. She'd find him wherever he went. Everyone owed her a favour.

He needn't have worried. She'd called because she wanted to thank him from the heart. Finally, she said, she'd found someone who could actually *feel* what she was creating and rebirth it into English. She loved him, would love him for ever, and wanted to meet him that very day. He would work for no one else, she said, which turned out not to be the case. But she bought him an excellent meal, and then another that was almost as good, and he was seen with her at various events, which helped. He even had the chance to acquire a couple of small works by one of her protégés, which he sold on at a very decent profit some years later. In Roman terms, they're friends. And now she's taken with the idea of the exhibition.

'Where did you find them?'

'I bought them.'

'Really?' She looks doubtful, maybe because she knows how little money Andrew has.

'Well, sort of. Someone I know gave them to me with some other stuff. Ages ago.' He doesn't know what makes him lie, some instinct for secrecy, perhaps a desire to keep Michel's name out of it. On the other hand, his involvement in the history of the photographs might add to their value. Andrew decides he'll tell her the truth later, when she's forgotten his first story. Even better, he'll tell her when she's done some coke and deny the first story altogether.

'Other stuff?'

'They're mine, Daniela,' he says firmly. 'I can do what I like with them.'

'I don't doubt that,' she says, although she clearly does. She's letting her hair colour grow out, he notices, the way intellectual women tend to do when they hit fifty, though she must have hit that wall some years ago now. Grey is the new red, as he knows to his own cost. But surely she's older than he is. She's pencil thin – from the back, with her hair dyed, she could be fifteen, sixteen. He's reminded of that old, ungenerous crack: *liceo* from behind, *museo* from the front. Despite this, she's had several lovers he's envied, students and would-be artists, and doesn't seem to care that their interest in her might be self-interest. Andrew's been thinking about love too much these past few days, in a way that brings him no comfort. He blames Michel for it.

'Who's Alex?' she says. 'Is he your secret contact?'

'Alex?'

She's holding a scrap of paper in her hand.

'Where did that come from?'

She looks mysterious. 'Alex?'

'I don't know anyone called Alex.' Edgy, he grabs the paper from her. It's been torn from an exercise book. There's an address written in red pen and, as Daniela has noticed, the name Alex, maybe the name of the person who wrote it, maybe not. The address is in Rome, Piazza

Vittorio, and there's another name scribbled above it, a surname that might be Morelli or Moretti, or neither of these, and a pencil drawing of a fat, legless bird. Judging from the colour and texture of the paper, it dates from the same period as the photographs; it certainly isn't much more recent.

'Relax, darling,' Daniela says. 'I'd rather not be told. I don't need to know any more than what these wonderful faces tell me. I'm inspired by them, honestly. I don't care a fig where you got them from.' She smiles. 'Though I do rather like that little drawing of the bird. Perhaps we could find a use for it.'

But Andrew isn't listening. He's trying to work out which bell is being rung so distantly and with such insistence by this scrappy little note. He's trying to remember if he's ever known an Alex, or someone called Moretti – Morelli, Marelli? – who lives in Piazza Vittorio. He's trying to identify the icon of the tubby bird.

'Where did you say you found this?' he says.

'It was stuck to the back of one of these.' Daniela waves her hand at the pile on the counter. 'I don't remember which.' She picks up a photo of a young woman. 'This one, perhaps.'

'Stuck?'

'Well, not deliberately, I don't think. It had been there for a long time.' She pauses. 'I imagine.'

'Yes.'

'Are you all right, Andrew?'

'Yes,' he says again. 'Why do you ask?'

'Because you look as though you've seen a ghost.'

What Andrew has seen isn't a ghost but a memory. A memory of Michel walking beside a fat man with bird feathers sticking from his hair.

That lunchtime Andrew turns down Daniela's offer to take him somewhere to eat and catches a 64 towards the station, getting off near the top end of Via Nazionale. He walks past the opera house and round the side of Santa Maria Maggiore, along a street filled with Chinese wholesalers and supermarkets, until he gets to Piazza Vittorio.

He hasn't been here for years. He's surprised to find that the daily market, with its scent of spices and fish, and hubbub of voices, has been moved somewhere else, to be replaced by unattractive public gardens. He stands beneath the building that corresponds to the number on the scrap of paper in his pocket, then crosses the road and looks up at the facade. The windows on the second floor, above the portico, have their shutters fastened back and are covered with wired-on cups and containers of various kinds and sizes. The windows themselves are wide open. He can hear music, Puccini, coming from within.

As he watches, a fat man approaches the central window and claps his hands. Within seconds a host of pigeons has gathered to eat from the sill, and the man can no longer be seen. Andrew continues to stare up until the birds have gone, but the man has also moved back into the room behind and all Andrew has is the barely glimpsed vision of a round bald head and something flowing. Is this the man he saw with Michel, he wonders. He's lost his hair; the man he remembers had hair down to his shoulders. But years have passed since then.

Stepping back beneath the portico, he's tempted to ring the bell, to make sure that the man he has seen and Morelli, because that is the name engraved beside the button on the brass plate of the entry-phone, are the same. But if they are, then what will he do? What will he say? The more he tries to find out where the photographs might have come from, the greater the risk that he, in his turn, will be discovered. And for what? Because he feels that by understanding where Michel got them from he will somehow, retrospectively, incompletely, irremediably, understand him.

This morning he mentioned Michel to Daniela, told her about the show in Ghent. She'd met him once or twice and remembers a little of his work, but it didn't impress her that much. If she'd shown more interest he might have told her then about the link between Michel and the mug shots, but it occurred to him that if she knew about the connection she might just as easily lose what interest she had. Also, obscurely, she tends, or tended, to be jealous of his boyfriends although she has never shown the slightest sexual curiosity in him herself and is often irritatingly girlish with him, as though expecting girlishness in return. She might have dropped the project for that reason, or some other reason of her own, which is the last thing he wants. Without Daniela, there's no show.

Finally, he supposes, he didn't want her involved in his

own project, which isn't even clear to him but which involves Michel and his death, and the death of love, and which has brought him here, his finger on the bell. Despite his better instincts, he's about to press it when the main door to the building opens and the fat man walks out.

He's wearing what look like pyjamas, but made from the kind of material Andrew associates with curtains in English cottages, flowery and crimson. His head is swathed in a similar fabric. He glances up and down the portico, paying no attention to Andrew, perhaps not even noticing him, while Andrew takes in every detail: the shaven eyebrows, the makeup, the swollen look to the skin, as though the face has been inflated, the bleary eyes. The man looks ill. He's like a tribal queen, or brothel-keeper in some distant Asiatic port, thinks Andrew, watching him as he turns away and waddles off.

He knows now that he's seen this man before, and more than once. He's a figure that's hovered round the edge of Andrew's vision for years, peripheral but constant, in the corner of the eye, apparently as unaware of Andrew as Andrew has been of him. He's sure now that he saw him with Michel, this large soft man beside his red-headed little Tintin, angrily recording the world with his camera. Perhaps there is even a photograph of the man among Michel's own work, most of which he hasn't seen for so long that it's no more than a blur to him, a mood. And, yes, he saw the man years ago with Joost, in the bookshop, one of his other customers, as Andrew used to consider them, the ones who traded odd, fake artworks for home-grown grass. And after that, when Joost had gone, he's not sure where. He knows this man in the way people say they know a recurring figure in a dream.

The Birdman heads off in a determined shuffling way towards the station, his feet in trodden-down tartan slippers, Andrew sees now. After a moment's hesitation, he doesn't follow him but walks away in the opposite direction, heading home.

ALEX AND MICHEL **1983**

Alex was expecting someone English, but the person behind the counter, who raised his head briefly to greet him with an abrupt, unwelcoming '*Buon giorno*', had an accent that sounded French. It must be the photographer Jamie talked about, he thought, and smiled to himself. Things are looking up. He glanced round the shop, dark, stuffy, a single unwashed window high up on the back wall with stairs rising across it, a door half open to the left. He walked to the nearest shelf and pulled out a small brown book no bigger than a packet of cigarettes. It was old, leather-bound; it creaked along the spine as he forced it open. Inside was crumbling yellow paper, words in a language he couldn't speak, a language that looked like German. He put it back, picked out another, opening it more gently. This one had poetry in it, in Italian. He read a few lines, but didn't recognize them, although he'd read a lot of poetry in his time and not just Leopardi at school. Not sure what else to do now that he was in the shop, after days of hesitation, he read on. Five minutes passed before the man behind the counter spoke.

'He'll be back soon. He's gone to the bank.'

Alex said, 'Who?'

The man gave him a wry, unexpected grin. 'I'm sorry, I thought you were one of Caruso's friends.'

'Caruso's the owner?' said Alex, replacing the book. He'd expected an English name. Jamie had called him Andrew, and laughed when Alex tried to repeat it. 'No,' he'd said, 'without the big fat *r* in the middle. You sound like a rattlesnake.'

The man behind the counter nodded. He had a tuft of red-blond hair at the front and a roundish, small-featured face, but was otherwise thin, unhealthily so, and pale, as though he'd never seen the sun. His pullover sleeves pulled up over scrawny elbows, he was fiddling with the parts of a dismantled camera, spread out before him.

'Are you cleaning it?' Alex said.

'It's broken. I'm trying to see why.'

'You're a photographer?'

'Sometimes. It depends.'

'I'm interested in photographs,' said Alex.

'Really?' The man seemed amused. 'What sort of photographs?'

Alex shrugged and looked around the small, airless shop. 'Does Caruso buy all this stuff himself?' he said.

'It's the only way.'

'To do what?' said Alex. He's taking the piss, he thought.

'To fill a shop with stuff that no one else wants. It's not so much a shop as a symptom of Andrew's generosity to others.'

Encouraged by this, Alex nodded towards some framed

photographs on the far wall behind the counter. 'Did you do those?' he said.

The man laughed. 'No.' He picked up the long black lens and held it to his eye, pointing it at Alex like a truncated telescope, moving it backwards and forwards as if to focus. 'They're by Cartier-Bresson. He's fairly famous.'

Alex knew perfectly well who Cartier-Bresson was and wished he'd had the sense to hold his tongue – he had, in fact, recognized one of the photographs the moment he'd spoken, the one of a man's fist sticking out through the bars of a cell. 'Are you French too?' he said, to prove it.

'Belgian. I have that fortune.'

'Does he buy photographs as well as books?'

'What kind of photographs?'

It was obvious the Belgian thought Alex was there to shift pornography. Alex could see the likeness between him and Jamie, the same neat features and tuft of hair. They might have been brothers. If Alex cut his own hair the way they had, something he'd be loath to do, he might look similar, except that he was dark and fit while this guy looked ill, and so did Jamie. He wondered if Caruso would find him attractive, or if you had to be fair and foreign and half dead. It came to him, acid as heartburn, how much he missed Bruno. 'Old photographs,' he said.

For the first time, the Belgian seemed interested. He held out his hand. 'My name's Michel,' he said. 'I'm Caruso's assistant. Among other things.'

Alex took his hand and grinned, holding his head to one side in a questioning way.

'I like old photographs,' Michel said.

'Because I've got some I'd like to sell,' Alex said.

'I thought you had.' And Michel grinned back, as if to say, We understand each other. Slowly, he let go of Alex's hand.

Alex glanced back at the door. 'You said he'd gone out to the bank?'

Michel shrugged. 'He isn't necessary. I'm the photography expert, not him. You can talk to me.'

Alex brought the rest of the photographs round later that day, not to the shop but to the small church beside it. Michel had told him to wait if he wasn't there. He'd need to get hold of the money, he'd said, although he didn't say from where or whom, and Alex didn't care, so long as he had it. It wasn't as much as he'd hoped, but what he really wanted was to be rid of them. The papers had stopped talking about Bruno's murder, which shocked Alex: it was as though he'd simply been wiped off the board. But it was also a relief. If the papers had lost interest, maybe the police had as well. Maybe, though he doubted it, the murderers themselves, whoever they were. As soon as he was freed of the photos, Alex tried to convince himself, he'd be free of it all.

Walking past the bookshop he glanced in to see if Michel was there, but the only person he could make out in the gloom was a tall man with long reddish hair pulled back into a ponytail, standing behind the counter where Michel had stood that morning. He was wearing one of those fishermen's waistcoats with pockets, over a Rolling Stones T-shirt. He looked up as Alex paused beside the door, then smiled. Alex felt as if he had been caught stealing. He stepped back, stumbling into the wooden tray of used books balanced on trestles outside the shop. It tilted, rocked, and he swivelled to catch it before the first row of books slid to the ground. Immediately the man was next to him, his hands held out. Before he could say anything, Alex hurried off into the church, the plastic bag with the photographs inside banging against his leg.

Michel was sitting beside the altar, one ankle resting on the other knee, his hand folded loosely around it. His eyes were closed, his face turned up as if to receive the sun. His arm was thin, lightly etched with fine parallel scars, white against the pallid, hairless skin, as though a cat had scratched him time and time again. He must have sensed Alex had come in because he turned his head towards the door before opening his eyes. 'You made it,' he said. 'I was starting to think you'd chickened out.' He pulled his camera, now assembled, from a leather bag beside his chair. 'Wait there,' he said. 'Don't move.'

Alex froze as Michel uncapped his lens and lifted the camera. He knew enough about photography to realize he'd not be much more than a silhouette surrounded by a halo of light and, enclosing that, the darkness of the doorframe. 'I won't come out,' he told Michel. 'You won't be able to see me.' He wasn't sure why he said this, other than to show that he knew something about backlight, that he wasn't a fool: the Cartier-Bresson thing of the morning still smarted. In one sense, he was relieved he would be nothing more than a crisp black hole at the centre, the anonymous form of a young man holding an anonymous plastic bag.

But Michel shook his head, unexpectedly playful. 'That all depends,' he said, 'on what I do. You'd be surprised what a camera can see in the right hands.'

Alex stared around the church. It was small, too small, he thought, to be a proper church, wider than it was deep, its walls painted to resemble a hundred different types of marble. It reminded him of a sample card.

'Some people think she's the patron saint of booksellers,' Michel said.

'Who?'

'Saint Barbara. This is her church. There used to be a lot of booksellers here, but now there's just Andrew. That's why it's called Saint Barbara of the Booksellers, unless it's the other way round and they named the church after the square. She's actually the patron saint of artillerymen and the fire brigade, even though she probably never existed. Most saints didn't exist when you actually look into it. They're about as real as elves.'

'That's quite a difference,' said Alex, interested despite his better, or more urgent, intentions, which were to sell the photographs for whatever Michel would give him and get out of there. 'Booksellers and artillerymen. And the fire brigade.'

'Well, books can be weapons too, and they can burn

like brands,' said Michel, drawing out the last three words in a ghoulish fashion. 'And so can photographs, if you know what to do with them.' He stood up, no longer amused, beckoning Alex into the far corner of the church beneath the organ. 'So, let's see what weapons you've brought to sell me.'

Alex followed him, gave him the bag. He'd pushed all the photographs in together, feeling that a single bag would look less conspicuous. Now, as Michel tried to wrestle one of the slim black envelopes out, he wasn't so sure. It made them seem less valuable. He turned to glance behind him, towards the door, while Michel reached into the envelope and pulled out a handful of photos. Careful not to touch their surfaces, he thumbed through slowly, expressionless at first, gradually smiling and shaking his head, so that Alex wasn't sure what he was thinking. 'Very nice,' he said finally, as if to himself. 'Very nice indeed.'

Ten minutes later, he had looked through everything Alex had to offer. 'I can't give you much for them,' he said. 'Not today anyway. But I can give you something now and something later.'

'I thought we'd agreed,' said Alex, but he couldn't put much anger into his voice. Michel must have realized this. He pushed the photographs back into the bag, and handed it over. Alex stepped away hurriedly, raising his hands. 'I don't mean you can't buy them. I just thought—'

'I can let you have half what I said today and the other half this time next week,' Michel said, holding the bag to his chest. 'Right here, beneath the organ, a week today.'

Alex nodded. He gave Michel a piece of paper. 'If you need to get in touch with me,' he said.

A week later Alex waited in the church for more than half an hour, but Michel didn't show. He wasn't surprised. He knew he'd been stupid, but all week long he'd felt the relief of knowing that no one could link him to Bruno any longer. The money Michel had given him, which he'd spent on albums and a pair of shoes, was beside the point. He sat where Michel had been sitting, watching the door, in the same position as the Belgian, his right ankle resting on his left knee. The weather had turned for the worse and he was wearing a jacket that Bruno had bought him earlier that year, at the start of it all. He hadn't much liked it then, but hadn't known how to get what he really wanted without looking spoilt and greedy. He'd worked that out later, or Bruno had let him think he had.

This afternoon, though, he'd picked out the jacket, a dark blue linen one that was too old for him, too serious, and slipped it on over his T-shirt. He hadn't meant it as a gesture of love towards Bruno but that, he supposed now, was what it was. A sort of apology. He wondered what Bruno had known about the photographs for the hundredth, thousandth, time, and was sorry for a moment that he'd let him down, although what else could he have done? At times he felt as though Bruno were waiting somewhere and might want them back.

Leaving the church ten minutes later, he glanced towards the bookshop. The door was closed, the lights turned off.

The trestle table he'd stumbled against the week before had been emptied of its books and folded away; he wasn't sure if it had been there when he'd arrived. On purpose, he hadn't looked; he hadn't wanted to be seen by anyone inside. Now, though, he walked across and peered in, his nose to the glass. The counter was stacked with books, there were more piled on the floor, and the photograph of the convict's hand was just visible on the far wall. He tried the handle, but the door was locked.

He was walking off when a man putting out tables at the *baccalà* place opposite called, 'He closed early. He had to go somewhere.'

Alex nodded. The man walked across, wiping his hands on his apron, obviously keen to talk. He lowered his voice. 'The police came for him,' he said. 'There's been a death.'

'A death?' said Alex, against his will, afraid to hear what the man might say.

'A friend of his. Well, let's say a friend. Some young guy, foreign,' the man said, the corners of his mouth turned down. He looked at Alex more closely. 'Wait a minute. Didn't I see you here last week?' Alex shook his head. 'I did,' the man said. 'I know your face. You were here with him, weren't you? You were in the church with him.'

'I don't know what you mean,' said Alex, turning his face away from the eyes of the man. 'I've never been here before.'

The girl's been alone for half an hour, maybe more, when a woman comes in with a tray. She's been sitting at the table, trying to keep calm and not let herself get frightened, wondering what her parents will be thinking. Her father will be home by now; her mother will have told him about their daughter's part-time job, because the girl has told him nothing. She'd wanted it to be a surprise for him – she'd planned to turn up outside the Vatican and tell him what she'd been doing, and see his surprise. He's always saying she should be more independent. Besides, she wasn't quite sure if he'd be pleased or not. Her mother hadn't been sure about it when she'd phoned to tell her. She'd said, 'Be careful.' Her father's funny about her being out alone: he thinks fifteen is too young for practically everything except staying in her bedroom with the radio off, doing her homework. He says it's because he loves her. But that doesn't mean he has the right to keep her prisoner. She said that to him once, when they were shouting at each other through her bedroom door because she'd locked him out. She was old enough to decide for herself, she'd screamed. Now she wonders what he's thinking as the woman walks across to her, not speaking, and puts the tray down on the table in front of her, then steps back. Where am I? the girl says, trying not to sound afraid, but her voice trembles anyway. The woman's face doesn't change. She just shakes her head, and the girl wonders for a moment if maybe she's foreign or mute. But then the woman says, Don't worry, eat something, and the girl can tell she's from Rome. She's old enough to be the girl's mother, thin and tired-looking, in the sort of overall-dress country women wear and flat black shoes. The girl looks at the tray: there's a bowl of pasta in broth and a slice of meat with some salad beside it, and a glass of water. I'm not hungry, she says. I want to go home. She looks at the tray again. How can I cut the meat, she says, without a knife? The woman tut-tuts. I knew there was something, she says. Hang on. She hurries out of the room and leaves the door ajar, the door the men closed behind them when they left. The girl stands up and walks across. She can see the corridor and the other room, and it strikes her that the woman must have come from somewhere, not from outside but from somewhere in the building. Which means there must be another way out apart from the door they used when they brought her in, some other way to get out of here. Holding her breath, she tiptoes into the corridor.

ANDREW AND MARTIN **2008**

A few days after their meeting, Daniela dell'Orto calls Andrew in the shop. It's early evening, the place that sells *filetti di baccalà* opposite is putting out its slatted wooden tables and folding chairs to catch those tourists who can't wait for the restaurants to open at eight. Andrew has sold no more than a dozen books all day and is wondering how much longer he can go on. For the last two hours, he's been playing Spider on his computer and has won only once; the percentage of successful games is now down to single figures. His mobile phone is concealed beneath a set of prints of classical Rome, removed from a book he bought last week, ripped out against his better judgement. He is thinking of putting them in the window in the hope that someone might imagine they have value when the phone rings. Scrabbling to answer it, he tips the prints onto the floor, temples and fora and circuses, the spine side jagged where they've been torn from their binding. Look on my works, he thinks.

'There you are.' Daniela sighs, already exasperated because she has so much more to accomplish than Andrew and it's essential that he knows this, knows that the interest she is showing in his footling little project is already more trouble than it's worth. It constitutes a favour in her currency, and should be recognized as such. 'I've been thinking that what we absolutely need for this show is a short piece by a working journalist, a crime journalist ideally. Something, I don't know, gritty, authentic, sincere. Unmediated.'

'Sounds good,' he says. Unmediated by what? he wonders. Intelligence, critical expertise? He waits for her to suggest a name, because surely she has some friend in mind, some protégé who needs to branch out into artier circles. When she doesn't, when all he can hear is silence, apart from what might be breathing, he says: 'Do you have anyone special in mind?'

'Well, I was hoping you'd have some ideas.'

She sounds irritated. She's either regretting the whole business and is hoping to shift the responsibility onto him, where it belongs, or she's genuinely too busy to think about dishing out a favour, or calling one in, hard though that is to credit in Daniela's world. Either way, it looks as though it's in Andrew's hands. And, he has to admit, it's a good idea. It will bulk out the catalogue nicely and involve a new set of people – the journalist and his friends – with some kind of investment in the show. At the very least, a dozen or so extra copies of the damn thing will be sold. So long as he doesn't have to pay for the privilege. It's already a miracle Daniela hasn't mentioned money: normally she'd charge at least a thousand euros for a job like this.

'There's someone at *Repubblica*,' he says.

'No, no, I'll deal with them,' says Daniela. 'I want the arts page to preview the show so it wouldn't do to have one of the staff writers in the catalogue as well.' She laughs. 'We don't want anyone accusing us of collusion, now, do we? No, I was thinking of some foreign interest. Come on, Andrew dear, you must know someone who'd do us this little favour, with your mixed origins. Some kilted barbarian Scot? Even better, what about an American? They're used to crime, aren't they? *CSI*? *Bones*? I'm thinking we could maybe trace a diachronic virtual blood-line from the wanted posters of the Wild West through, I don't know, Dillinger, Capone, Bonnie and Clyde, because what isn't fiction, finally?'

'Yes, well, I'll have to think about it.' He's playing for time, but already he's remembered Martin Frame. Andrew's never lost touch with Martin, although he can't say they're friends, despite an intimacy Andrew has never fully under-stood; if they're not quite friends, they're something both rawer and more formal. One afternoon, some weeks after Jamie had disappeared from his life into whatever his own became, the details of which remain mercifully unknown to Andrew, Martin came into the shop and waited there until Andrew was free to nip out for a quick espresso. He asked after Jamie but seemed to want to talk about himself. That afternoon, and for some time after, Andrew wondered if Martin was gay and about to confess, a situ-ation Andrew would have preferred to avoid. The last thing he needed in the smarting of Jamie's absence was to take someone else's sexual issues on to his shoulders. But

Martin's conversation soon made it clear that he wasn't gay and Andrew, thrown, had never understood what was wanted from him, other than a skewed, oddly tender friendship. The two of them chatted – and continue to chat – about books in the shop on Martin's frequent visits, or over coffee in the neighbouring bar, or during one of the half-dozen evenings each year they've spent getting drunk together in the neutral ground of medium-priced restaurants and drinking holes. This has been happening less often these past three years, since Martin, to Andrew's surprise, has married a much younger woman from somewhere in Eastern Europe and has seemed to pull himself together.

'Well, think about it as quickly as you can,' says Daniela.

Andrew calls Martin just before closing up, suggesting they meet for a drink. At first Martin hesitates. Andrew can hear him speaking to someone else, but not what is said nor the voice of the other person, presumably his wife. Martin comes back. 'Yes, that would be lovely. Usual place? Give me half an hour.'

It takes him longer than that. Andrew has already finished a second glass of red wine and a bowl of peanuts by the time Martin comes in. He's using a steel-tipped wooden stick, limping slightly from an accident three years ago, when a motorbike ran him down in the street. Andrew's asked him about it, without much result. He's a big, bullish man, with an odd, resilient softness. 'It's age,' he tends to say, shrugging it off. 'Even a scratch takes weeks to heal after you're sixty.' All Andrew knows is that the accident coincided almost to the day with Martin's meeting his wife. He wants to ask how she is, but can't remember her name.

'How's . . . ?' he says, and Martin obliges him.

'Alina?' He sits down slowly, sliding the stick beneath his chair. 'She's up to her armpits in anatomy books at the moment. God knows what possessed her to want an Italian degree. About as useful as a dose of the clap, I'd have thought, and a lot less fun involved in the getting of it.' He stares at the table. 'You're not going by the glass, I hope?'

'I wasn't sure what you'd want.'

Martin picks up Andrew's glass and sniffs. 'No, no, don't tell me, let me guess. Shiraz?'

'Primitivo, actually.' Andrew grins. He's feeling drunk already. He rarely feels drunk, these days, which may simply mean he drinks too much and doesn't notice.

'How very appropriate,' says Martin, 'in these primitive times. We'll have a bottle, then, shall we? To be going on with.' He waves across to the bar. 'And some of those tasty little sandwiches?'

Andrew agrees to everything. One of the best things about Martin is that he makes decisions. Whether they're the right ones – because Andrew has already eaten and isn't hungry – feels irrelevant.

'So, how's retirement suiting you?' he says, when Martin has ordered.

Martin grimaces. 'Semi-retirement, if you don't mind.

I'm trying to keep my hand in. Besides, the English desk would collapse without me, under the weight of general agency indifference. They'd like to close the whole show down, or hive us off somewhere. No one actually cares about news any longer, that's the trouble. It's all about knicker sizes and who's fucking whom. And that's just the politics section. I hark back to the glory days, which makes me about as popular as a priest in a brothel. Rather less popular, actually. Still, the money's useful. And it gets me out of Alina's hair for a few hours. Which must be nice for her.'

Andrew's often wondered what Martin must have been like when he was young, when he first arrived in Rome. Even now, despite the paunch and the webs of veins in the cheeks and nose, there's a charm about him that might be called boyish if that didn't sound absurd for a man in his sixties, and coming from Andrew, who's always had a thing for boyish looks. But it's still there, like some earlier version of the man that hasn't quite been erased. He's still capable of surprise, thinks Andrew, with a trace of envy, still capable of curiosity. Still capable, it would seem, of love.

'I don't suppose there'd be a job for me at the agency,' says Andrew, as the bottle and second glass arrive with a plate of sandwiches. Martin pours the wine and Andrew wonders if what he has just said is more than a joke. Could he really change career at this point in his life? Perhaps if he had a career to change from, he thinks, and not the dead weight of a bookshop nobody uses.

'You wouldn't want it, believe me.' Martin looks at Andrew more closely. 'The edge gone off the bookselling business, has it?'

'The bookselling business hasn't had an edge for years. I'm wondering whether to open one of those boy bordellos Proust used to go to.'

'That sounds very enterprising,' says Martin. 'Over the shop?'

'Well, actually, yes,' says Andrew, 'in a way. I'm thinking of using my upstairs room again for a little exhibition.'

'And the link with your rather excellent bordello idea?'

Andrew smiles. 'Well, apart from the fact that it may be slightly illegal, none at all.'

'Illegal, you say. Reminds me of the times when your shop was run by that Dutch chappie as a front for his other more lucrative activities.'

Andrew laughs. 'Not exactly a front. I mean, Joost did care about books as well as grass. Besides, books weren't so much a sideline then as they are now. We actually made a little money out of them every now and again. I sometimes wonder if reading's even being taught in schools, these days.'

'Judging from the agency interns we've been getting recently, I'd say probably not. Our old friend Jamie was a literary genius by comparison.' Martin fills his glass. 'Just catching up, old chap.' He looks again at Andrew, more searchingly. 'You're not in the best of moods, are you? I hope my mentioning Jamie—'

'No, no, of course not. To be honest, I wanted to ask

you a favour,' Andrew says, deflecting Martin's question, he isn't sure why. It's not that he doesn't trust Martin, but he feels as though what's troubling him is both so nebulous and so vast that any attempt to grasp it and offer it to someone else, even Martin, a man who is both a friend and detached enough to play the role of confessor, is doomed to failure. He feels less like a man with a problem than a problem in human form.

'Ask away.'

'I'd like you to write something for the catalogue,' he says.

'Of this illegal exhibition?'

'I did say *slightly*.' Andrew frowns. 'I hope to God it *isn't* illegal.'

'I'm intrigued,' says Martin, pushing his chair away from the table a little to give himself room to relax, picking up a sandwich, immediately tiny in his large hand. 'Tell me more.'

And Andrew does. He tells him about the photographs, but doesn't mention where they came from; doesn't mention Michel. He knows he's being secretive, but that's all right. Michel is no one else's business. When Martin presses him, gently but firmly, he mumbles something about contacts through Porta Portese, the second-hand book world, he can't reveal people's names. This is perfectly true: he has a bulging notebook full of the names and numbers of small-time dealers in slightly shady goods, but, in this case, it's quite irrelevant. Martin thinks about this for a moment, clearly unsatisfied, then seems to brush the thought aside. He wants to know how many photographs there are, when they were taken, if any of the faces look familiar. The more he asks, the greater is Andrew's anxiety, as though his casual remark about illegality has turned out to have more weight than he intended.

When the bottle is empty, Martin stands up. 'I'll just have a quick slash and then you can take me to see these illicit snaps of yours,' he says, reaching down for his stick and stumbling off before Andrew has a chance to protest. He calls over his shoulder: 'And get them to give you another bottle of this excellent Primitivo to take with us. We may need it.'

Andrew hasn't planned to show Martin anything, not just yet. His plan was to sort the pictures out and have them framed so that their impact would be greater and, also, to make them look more like art and less like what they really are. He's worried Martin will simply flip through a dozen or so and tell him the whole idea's madness. He's worried, essentially, that Martin will confirm his own doubts, so recently sidelined by Daniela's enthusiasm and his own sadly pressing need for a little attention and the money such attention might bring. If that's the case, he doesn't know what he will do: he doesn't feel robust enough to brush off Martin's objections and find someone else. He senses he'll simply give up – although, carrying the empty glasses back to the bar, it occurs to him Martin might just as easily share Daniela's enthusiasm and be only too happy to become involved; this might be just the sort of diversion he needs. Cheered by the thought, Andrew asks for a bottle to take away and is about to pay for it when Martin's hand on his sleeve stops him.

'I'll get these,' he says.

ALEX AND THE BIRDMAN **1983**

Alex told the Birdman he thought Michel had died. He hadn't planned to, but the Birdman had taken him into the kitchen and made him coffee and he'd thought, Why not? Why not tell the truth for once? And then the Birdman said: 'You can trust me, you know that, don't you?' and Alex glanced over from his own upturned and empty hands towards the older man, overweight, ungainly in his ridiculous kaftan, with the slowly untwining bandanna, as he spooned fresh coffee into the bottom half of the pot and tamped it down. 'People do. Well, most people do.' He screwed the two halves together, shaking back his sleeves from white, surprisingly scrawny forearms. 'It's what I'm here for,' he said, pursing his lips as he placed the pot on the flame. 'To help you with your secrets.'

'It's nothing, really.' Alex listened as the coffee bubbled, took the cup when the Birdman had sugared it, and stirred. 'You know I told you I had something I wanted to sell?'

The Birdman nodded.

'They were photographs. Of people. Not of people I knew. I didn't want them. I mean, I wanted to get rid of them.' Alex wrapped his hands round the cup for as long as he could stand the heat, then put it down. 'They weren't mine in the first place.'

'Go on.' After a moment, because Alex was silent, the Birdman continued: 'You've found someone who'll take them off your hands?'

Alex nodded. 'He was someone Jamie knew. He introduced me – well, not really introduced me. He told me where to find him. In this bookshop in the centre. Some man he'd had a thing with. So I went there to talk to him, but the one Jamie told me about wasn't there. There was this foreign man, French, I think, and, I don't know why, but I told him what I was doing there instead of just going back later. And he said he wanted them. He gave me half the money and I let him have the whole lot. He said I'd get the other half the next week. I trusted him, I don't know why. I suppose I didn't really care about the money. That was yesterday. I went to get the rest of it yesterday.' Alex stared up. 'The only thing is, he's dead.'

'Dead?'

'He wasn't much older than me. I don't know what happened to him. That's the problem. Because he's dead and I don't know who to ask about it. I don't want anyone finding me and thinking he got the stuff from me.'

'The stuff? You said they were photographs?'

'Yes, yes. Photographs.' Alex paused. 'It's just that, well, he's the second one, you see. He's the second one to die. It doesn't make any sense to me. I mean, there can't be any connection, but – I don't know – it's as if they're cursed or something.' Now that these words, which he'd been thinking for the past few weeks and had felt confirmed by Michel's death, were said, they felt less real; he almost laughed. But that didn't last long.

'Photographs of what?' asked the Birdman. 'What do you mean – of people?'

He sounded cautious, thought Alex, but not because he was scared of what he might hear. He sounded scared because he knew.

'Police stuff – people they'd arrested, crime scenes, nothing, really,' he said. 'I can't see what all the fuss is about. I mean, I could if I was one of the people and they were going to stick my face on television or somewhere, but otherwise, who cares? They're only photographs.'

'Who was the other one?'

'The other one?'

'The other one who died? You told me there was someone else.'

Alex hadn't meant to say so much but felt such relief, such ease, now that he had spoken, as though his blood had been freed to flow, as though the hit had arrived where it was intended to arrive, that he went on: 'He was my friend,' he said, and this was the first time he had used the word friend to describe Bruno, which was also a source of release, and of recognition. He felt hot tears well up and sighed; he slumped as the Birdman came round to comfort him, pressing his head into the older man's soft, warm chest. 'I'm sorry,' he said, but the Birdman shook his head and started to sing in a low, humming way, the way a mother would, which made Alex smile, his mouth crushed up against the embroidered cotton of the Birdman's kaftan, tobacco-scented, sweat-scented, the edge of a tiny mirror cutting into his cheek.

'How did he die?' the Birdman said, when Alex finally pulled away.

'He was murdered.'

'Did you see it happen? Were you there?'

Alex shook his head.

'Do you know who did it?'

'Nobody does.'

The Birdman smiled wryly. 'In the case of murder, there is always someone who knows.'

'I mean I don't know, the police don't know.'

The Birdman shrugged and pulled a face. 'The police,' he said dismissively. 'The police know what they're allowed to know.'

'They'd tied him to a chair and gagged him,' said Alex, his voice raised, furious suddenly, as though the full weight of Bruno's death had never struck him before this moment. 'He'd got tape across his mouth. They'd stabbed him all over.'

'You saw this?' said the Birdman.

Alex nodded. 'I didn't want to.'

'I'm sure you didn't,' the Birdman consoled him.

'He'd given me the photographs that night. He wanted me to look after them for him.'

'And you were scared,' said the Birdman. 'That's understandable.'

'The papers said he'd been killed by rent-boys.'

'Is that what you think?'

'No, he was waiting for me. He'd never have let anyone else in for – well, that. For sex. I think they were looking for the photographs. And he wouldn't tell them where they were. And they killed him and made it look like they'd done it because he was gay. They wrote *"frocio"* on the wall. In blood.'

The older man threw back his head and whistled, the long, low whistle he used when he summoned his birds to feed. 'What a delicate touch. Like signing a canvas. Murder as a fine art.' He took the empty coffee cup away. 'And now this other man is dead as well.'

Alex nodded.

'You say he was someone Jamie knew.'

'Jamie knew the man he worked for. I don't know if he knew him too.'

'And this man he worked for. Who is he?'

'He's got a bookshop. Not new books. Second-hand stuff, prints. Near Campo de' Fiori.'

'And you say Jamie knew this man?'

Alex looked up and nodded a third time. He supposed that Jamie had been the bookseller's – what? Boyfriend? Lover? Rent-boy? Perhaps 'friend' was enough. *Il mio amico.* How odd, though, that he didn't have the words to talk about this. Not even with the Birdman. That he didn't have the words he needed to talk about his friend-ship – or whatever it was – with Bruno; about Jamie's, and maybe Michel's, friendship with the bookseller. He thought of the boys who passed through the flat in which he was sitting with the Birdman, boys and young men from every corner of the world, and of the older men they knew, and had sex with, and maybe liked or even loved. All these nameless friendships that entangled the city in a taut invisible web. A secretive web, because no one knew anything about it, or everyone pretended to know nothing about it. A web that stretched across hotels and galleries and studio flats in the richest parts of the city, from the Vatican to the senate to the station, of favours and small, sweet acts of generosity and asked-for, insisted-on violence. And then it went wrong and someone died, and the web closed to hide the rift so quickly no one would know it had ever been torn. Webs heal themselves. The boy runs off; all evidence is destroyed or brushed to one side. But Alex hadn't run off like that, and Bruno's death had been different. And now Michel was dead.

'Your friend was a journalist?'

'Yes.' Alex was startled. 'How did you know?'

'Rome's a small world. I heard about his murder and then you showed up again, you remember, and I could see you were shaken. Besides, you know how these things are, my dear, these deaths. You notice. It's as if they happen to you.' The Birdman sat down beside Alex, hitching his kaftan up the way Alex's grandmother used to lift her dress, his hairless knees against Alex's. Is it that simple to connect me to Bruno's death? Alex was thinking. If the Birdman can do it, anyone can. 'I could find out more about it if that's what you want,' the Birdman continued. Then, after a pause: 'If you're sure that's what you want.'

Alex wasn't sure of anything, but that didn't stop him saying, yes, he wanted to know. He wanted to know what had happened to Bruno, because knowing the truth, he felt, might free him. As long as no one else had been blamed, he would never be safe.

'And this other man, what did he do?'

Alex frowned. 'I don't know. He looked as if he was working in the shop, but he said he was a photographer. That's what Jamie told me too.' He shook his head as he remembered. 'He took a picture of me as I was walking into the church. I told him it wouldn't come out because I had the light behind me, but he said it depended. I didn't like him very much. I thought he was showing off.'

'Well, let's hope it didn't,' said the Birdman, under his breath. Alex was about to ask what he meant but a second's thought gave him the answer.

'You don't think—?'

The Birdman squeezed his arm. Alex could feel the inside of the man's rings hard and cold and smooth on his skin. 'Come and help me,' he said. 'I need to look after my birds.'

A few days later the Birdman and Alex left Rome together in a clapped-out 2CV the Birdman had borrowed from someone. He didn't have a car himself, or a licence. He'd told Alex once that everything he needed he could find within a square mile of his flat, with the market beneath his window and the station, by which he meant the world, only two blocks away. But Alex didn't bring this up when the Birdman tossed him a bunch of keys and said they'd be taking a little trip together.

A trip was fine with Alex. He'd more or less left his parents' home by this time, more or less abandoned his first year at university. He slept at the Birdman's most nights, in a small room next to the kitchen that looked as if it might have been designed for a maid. In a sense, that was what Alex had become – part of the day-to-day background in the Birdman's flat. A working part, he supposed, although the work was minimal: gathering glasses, emptying ashtrays, suggesting when people should leave with a hint more force than the Birdman was prepared to muster. He felt safe there, which was why he stayed. At home, he was always waiting for someone to come and ask him questions he couldn't answer: the police or worse. At the Birdman's, he felt like the man of the house. The Birdman had never tried it on with him, or with anyone else as far as Alex could see, though he was happy enough to watch if the men about the place messed around with one another, which sometimes happened. And some days he'd take photographs of them, as he had done with Alex, and sometimes he'd ask Alex to pose with whoever it was, and Alex did, the two of them standing together. But he never asked for any more than that.

'Where are we going?' he asked, when they were sitting together in the car.

The Birdman gathered his coat about him like a shawl. 'I'll tell you what to do as we drive,' he said. He waved a plump white hand. 'Go that way,' he said, 'to start with.'

The car handled well, and the Birdman's directions were clear. They skirted Termini, passing through the tunnel beneath the railway lines, down through San Lorenzo, past the flower stalls and the high wall of the cemetery, the coach park to Alex's left, beyond that the bus terminus and Tiburtina station. Alex began to enjoy himself, pushing the car as hard as it would go whenever he had a chance, which wasn't often; he could barely get out of third. Still, it was good to be driving again. The last time he'd been behind the wheel was the night of Bruno's death. As soon as they were on Via Tiburtina, in the steady flow of east-bound traffic, the Birdman slumped back in his seat. 'Just go straight on for a while, my dear. I'll tell you when to turn.'

'Where are we going?'

'You'll see soon enough.'

They were half a mile further on when the Birdman said: 'You haven't been going to the university?'

'No.'

'Why not?'

Alex shrugged.

'So what do you plan to do with your life?'

'Why do you want to know?' Alex said, not hostile, genuinely curious.

The Birdman told him to slow down: they'd soon be turning left. They drove between blocks of flats, six, seven storeys high, like the block in which Alex had grown up. Each flat had its balcony, each balcony its gas heater and broom cupboard and line of smog-choked plants. Beneath them there were shops selling clothes and shoes and food, bars and laundries, the whole business of living strung out behind a clutter of double-parked cars.

'Because you needn't throw your life away. It isn't required of you, you know.' The Birdman's tone was casual, as though what he said was barely worth the breath he used to say it. 'Would you like to act? To model? I don't mean the kind of thing I do, you understand that, I'm sure. My little sideline. You're a striking-looking young man, but I'm sure you know that. I have friends in the film world who could help you.'

'No,' said Alex. 'I wouldn't like to act.'

'I don't think you understand how bright you are. That's a pity. Most people are less bright than they imagine themselves to be. You mustn't let yourself go to waste.'

'I want to be a journalist.' Alex was crawling along, slowing the traffic, waiting to be told to turn.

'Like your dead friend.'

'Yes. He promised he'd help me. Now he's dead—'

'Well, yes,' said the Birdman, 'I can see that might be a problem.' He jerked up. 'Here,' he said, waving his arm. 'Down here.'

'This is the prison,' said Alex. 'We're at Rebibbia.'

The Birdman nodded. 'You'll need to be patient,' he said. 'Patience is a virtue. You do know how to be patient, don't you?'

The girl's gone no more than two or three yards when a loud voice tells her to stop, and she turns to see one of the men who brought her there. He's reaching towards her, as if she's fallen into water and needs to be rescued. She thinks for a moment that if she runs down the corridor, away from him, she might find a way out before he understands what's going on, but she realizes that won't happen. He already understands. In any case, there's no sense in running into darkness in a building she doesn't know. She's tempted to scream, to call for help, but that, too, will only make things worse. Suddenly she's scared, really scared, because it has only now occurred to her that whoever these people are, and whatever they want, they might decide to kill her. It's as if she has just woken up, been woken by a slap across her face. She's never thought about dying before and she doesn't know what to do with the idea. She isn't even sure if what she feels is scared. She's seen their faces, she thinks, these men and the woman too: she'd recognize them at once if the police showed her photographs. There are bound to be photographs of people like them. She's heard them speak as well: she'd know their voices immediately. She stops and turns, slowly, not to tease him, although that's what he's thinking – she can see that from the way he taps his feet and gestures with his hand to speed her up. She's worried she might wet herself if she moves too fast – she's concentrating all her muscles to stop herself losing control. This is what being scared means. As soon as she's within reach, he grabs her and pulls her back into the room, flinging her towards the table. She stumbles against it, bangs her hip. I'll have a bruise, she thinks, she's already sore from a tumble in volleyball the day before. I'll never play volleyball again, it comes to her, a second slap, never – but she doesn't believe this. She can't. He pushes her down into the chair, with the food in front of her, and she stares at the plate, the sight of which makes her sick, to avoid his eyes. She doesn't want him to see how defiant she feels suddenly: she wants them all to think she's given up or she'll never be given another chance to get away. She'll have to play along and see what kind of opportunity that might bring. She can hear someone shouting some distance off, one bad word after another, and the woman who brought her the food shouting back. She slumps into her chair. The man is standing beside her. Waiting for her to eat.

ANDREW AND MARTIN **2008**

Alina is making bread when Martin gets home. She makes it according to a recipe she has found in a new book of Eastern European food, but it amuses them both to pretend that she learnt it twenty-five years ago at her mother's knee in the Ukraine. The fact that her mother could barely boil an egg, and worked in hospital administration, is something they keep to themselves. Alina doesn't know that Martin also keeps secrets from her, although she suspects it: she knows he's a secretive man, whose life has obliged him to keep much silent, only partly through choice. They'd already been married for more than a year when he let slip one evening, as they watched the news, that he'd visited the small town in which she was born. It was soon after the Second World War, when the hospital in which her mother worked had yet to be built and Alina had yet to be conceived. Alina would spend five long years of her life as a nurse in wards that hadn't existed then, that were nothing but empty fields when Martin passed through the barren war-torn streets in which both her parents had lived and died, with passion and then resignation. She still isn't sure which side he was on, nor why

113

he was there. And she doesn't really care, although she might have done in the past, pestering him until he told her the truth and ruined everything, as though truth were the only thing that counted. A man, thinks Alina, is entitled to a few secrets. It's enough to know he's here beside her now, taking off his coat, swaying a little, which is only natural after an evening with Andrew or any of Martin's English-speaking friends, but entirely cogent, because wine is one thing and vodka another. Wine mellows, she feels – at least, it mellows Martin. Wine humanizes in a way that vodka doesn't. She doesn't care what business took him to a country she barely considers hers any more. She's no longer even sure where she last saw her Russian–Italian dictionary, the one she always used to carry in her handbag, just in case. These days her second, if not first, language is English.

'Andrew is well?' she says, wiping the flour from her hands.

'No,' says Martin, pulling from the pocket of his coat a single chocolate, with a rum-soaked cherry inside it, a variety of which Alina is particularly fond. 'I'm rather worried about him, to tell you the truth.'

Alina unwraps the chocolate, rolling the paper into a wand. She has a vase beside the fridge filled with coloured wands like this, of varying lengths, silver, gold, steel-blue. She wonders at times if there might be money to be made from what she does with her chocolate wrappers, some low-level craft-cum-recycling activity, as though she is still living hand-to-mouth, or worse. But Martin's saved her from that, and her vase full of wands, her useless, glittering wands, is there to prove it.

'What's wrong?'

'He's got this idea for an exhibition in the room over the shop. You remember, where he did that dreadful watercolour show a couple of years ago? Couldn't swing a cat in it, but there you go. The space is on a par with the rest of the idea as far as I can see. Crackpot, utterly crackpot.'

'What sort of exhibition?'

He thinks for a moment. 'Photographs, I suppose you'd call them.'

'People like photographs,' says Alina.

Martin shakes his head. 'That's not the point, dear. Well, it is, in the sense that he hopes he's going to make some money out of it, though there's not much chance of that. No chance at all, to be honest. An act of sheer desperation. He's got that mad dell'Orto woman involved as well.'

'Dell'Orto?'

'Art critic, so-called. Skin-and-bones windbag with too much makeup, if you ask me. Not that Andrew did.' He glances round the kitchen. 'I don't suppose there's any of that *polpettone* left from lunch? I've eaten absolutely nothing. Apart from a sandwich. One of those tiny things they do. Size of a thumbnail.'

'So what is the point?'

Martin shakes his head.

'Well, I'm not sure he should even have the things. They're police material, you know, scenes of the crime, mug shots.' He sees she doesn't understand. 'Identification photographs. They're all from a good twenty, maybe thirty years back, but even so. Most of the people will still be alive, and might not be very thrilled to see their faces plastered over the walls of an art gallery as criminal exhibits. Dell'Orto says Andrew should cover the eyes with a strip of black ribbon or some such half-baked nonsense, as though that will make everything all right. And this is quite apart from the fact that he doesn't seem to know where he got them from, or doesn't want to tell anyone – not even me – which is more likely. He beat around the bush, then told me the source can't be revealed, with this mysterious look on his face, which might sound all right in an article but, quite frankly, won't wash. It's perfectly obvious that whoever he got the damned things from must have obtained them in some illegal fashion. They should never have left the police archive in the first place.'

'Did you say all this to him?'

Martin sighs. 'Not really. I wish I had. He seems to think he's on to a winner, Alina. I know I should have said something to warn him off, but there's a good chance nothing will come of it and he seems so keen on the idea. He's not a happy man, Alina. I don't want to dampen his spirits any more than I have to. The problem is that he wants me to write something for the catalogue.'

'What sort of thing?'

'I wish I knew. Dell'Orto's put him up to it, I'm sure of that. He'd never have thought of it himself.'

Alina puts a plate on the table with a slice of meatloaf on it and some bread. 'Eat this,' she says, her tone more abrupt than she intends.

'And there's something else.' He breaks off a corner of the meatloaf with his fingers, but immediately puts it down. 'You weren't here when it happened, Alina, but there was a nasty case of kidnapping round about when these photographs were taken. A girl, the daughter of someone who worked at the Vatican.'

'A girl? How old was she?'

'Fifteen, sixteen. They never found her.'

'Who kidnapped her?'

Martin lifts his shoulders, hopeless. 'It was one of those cans of worms they do so well here. You know, everybody guilty, nobody guilty. The government, the Church, the Mafia. Utter chaos. It wasn't long after that shaven-headed Turkish lunatic tried to assassinate the Pope, so that was thrown into the stew-pot with all the rest.'

'But what does this have to do with Andrew?'

Martin looks up. 'I'm positive he's got a photograph of her after she'd been kidnapped. And I'm sure, I'm absolutely sure, I've never seen it before. No one has. I had to cover the story – I did a piece for the bloody *Sunday Telegraph*. You know how the English papers love that sort of thing. I know I'd remember something like that. You can see her face.' He pauses. 'And that's not all. You can see who she's with.'

'She isn't alone?'

Martin shakes his head. 'It isn't particularly clear, but

it's clear enough. I mean, if I saw him on the street I'd recognize him.'

'You don't already?'

'I'm not sure,' Martin says, but Alina isn't convinced. 'I don't think so, but I can't be sure. There is something familiar about him. But you know what it's like – I've lived in Rome for almost forty years. I sometimes think I've seen every human face the city has to offer.'

'And you didn't mention this either? To Andrew?'

'Good heavens, no. But I think he may have noticed something himself. He looked rather shifty when he showed me the one I'm talking about, then whipped it out of my hands. As though he wished he hadn't shown me.'

'That's good,' says Alina, firmly. 'If he understands the photograph is dangerous, he will listen to you. You must tell him to make sure it is not exhibited. There is no point in taking risks.'

'Risks,' repeats Martin.

'If this photograph has never been seen before, there will be a reason, surely? Someone must know it exists. Maybe the person who provided Andrew with the photographs in the first place.' She thinks for a moment. 'Or maybe not. Maybe someone before that person. I wonder how many people know about this photograph.'

Martin puts his arms around her waist and pulls her down on to his lap. She laughs. 'You'll cover yourself in flour.'

'I don't care if I do,' he says, blowing into her ear.

'You're a wonderful woman, you know that, don't you? A wonderful woman.'

'You're changing the subject,' she murmurs. 'You naughty man.'

Andrew is sitting in the shop, with the shutters pulled down almost to street level. He has put the box of photographs away again, now that Martin has seen them, and finished the wine, less out of thirst than a need to see the bottle empty, done with. He is feeling sick, but doesn't know whether to blame it on what he has drunk, which is far too much even by Andrew's standards, or on the sensation he has had since Martin left him; the sensation of being alone, more alone than he remembers ever having felt before. Alone in the world.

The shop is poorly illuminated at the best of times and now the only light, apart from that filtering under the shutters from the street, is provided by the blue-white screen of his laptop. He is surrounded by semi-darkness, the book-filled room in which he passes most of his waking hours, on which he depends for his livelihood, no more than a dusty, airless gloom without form or substance. He feels as though he is standing, wavering, on the edge of something too deep, too vast, for him to fully comprehend or measure, encircled by a silently lapping moat. Except that moats are designed to protect, are built around castles, and what Andrew senses is threat, the threat of engulfment and of dissolution, as though his castle is made of sand.

He watches the man on the screen take off his U2 T-shirt, step forward to adjust the webcam, grin to himself – to Andrew? – with satisfaction at what he sees, slide down his sweatpants, with a slow teasing motion, below his hips and then off, ungainly as he balances on one foot, and then his boxer shorts, the stretch kind, so that he's naked apart from his socks. Andrew watches him execute a perfunctory, semi-ironic dance around an imagined pole until his dick is fully hard, watches the man spit into his hand to lubricate it, then jack himself off, performing to an audience dispersed over time and place. The video has been seen more than seventeen thousand times, Andrew notes, and he wonders how many men have seen it more than once or over and over again, have included it among their favourites, as he has, because the man on the screen reminds them of someone else, someone who has gone and won't, or can't, come back. What he's watching is nostalgia. Nostalgia porn. Maybe that's all porn is, he thinks now, his hand pushing down the front of his jeans to adjust his hard-on: a search for something lost. Lost innocence, lost complicity, lost guilt, except that, of these three, only innocence can truly be lost; the others, as permanent as a sense of one's own foolishness, refuse to leave.

Behind the masturbating man on the screen is a room that could be anywhere: a curtain, the corner of a desk, a shelf with a dozen books dumped on it as if from above, paperbacks, airport novels, a couple of larger volumes that might be college texts, a magazine or two. Once again, Andrew finds himself tilting his head in a frustrated attempt to read the titles, to see what this man, who looks so like Michel it hurts, might be reading. He wants to get to know this man whose grimace as he comes – his head thrown back but still with one eye on the screen, where he sees himself exactly as Andrew sees him – is identical to Michel's. Except, of course, that it isn't; it's nothing like. Michel is dead.

Still, he'd have liked the anonymity of it, thinks Andrew, withdrawing his hand from his trousers, lifting his fingers to his nose to sniff them, breathing in his own mushroomy scent with a sort of hunger he can't explain, as though it belonged to someone else. Michel would sometimes take photographs of himself as he wanked. Andrew saw them once, by accident, a series of monochrome prints of Michel sprawled on a bed, the sheet rucked up beneath his thin white limbs, his eyes fixed on the lens as if daring it to look away. He must have set the self-timer and thrown himself down on the mattress, his hand on his dick as the camera ticked its way towards the shot, no going back, no second thoughts. He'd have appreciated the possibilities offered by all this new technology, unimaginable then. He'd have been on XTube with the best of them. He hated privacy, the vanity of it, as though people thought they were special and worthy of special treatment when all they were, stripped down, exposed, was bare forked animals.

That was what Michel had in common with Jamie, it occurs to Andrew now, more even than the Tintin tuft or the freckles or the startled look they shared, when it suited them, which he loved. They both had that anger-filled affair with privacy, as though it were a privilege denied them, that anger with closed mouths, closed eyes, closed books. *I want my life to be an open book*. They'd both said that, and he'd wondered what they meant, when his own life seemed both sealed and empty, one of those jewellery boxes fatuously, blasphemously, designed as Bibles, barely worth the effort needed to force them open. How odd that Michel, though, the most private person he's ever known, should have raged with such fury against the lies, the deceit, the veils. All of it to be stripped away was what he wanted, because it is better to be nothing, to be revealed as nothing, than to be rendered valuable by a lie.

And Andrew suddenly understands what attracted Michel to the photographs – their nakedness. The people in them have nothing left to hide; everything that gave them currency in the world has been stripped away from them, every subterfuge, every social lie. I shall call the show *Exposure*, he decides.

He's straightening up to turn off the computer when, from the corner of his right eye, he sees something move. He thinks it's a rat at first, scurrying into the shop beneath the shutter, and jumps; he has an irrational fear of rats. But a second look and he realizes that what's slipped into the shop is a cat, a thin black and white cat he's seen hovering outside the salt-cod place opposite all day. He leans down and rubs his fingers together. '*Micio*,' he says, and then – because who knows what language the cat might speak? – translates: 'Pussy. Pussy, *vieni qua*. Come over here.' The cat freezes, stares at him, eyes like balls, hunkered down as though it has never been spoken to before. The last thing I need is a cat, thinks Andrew, coaxing the half-starved creature towards him as though his life depends on it.

ALEX AND THE BIRDMAN **1983**

The Birdman didn't mention his visit to the prison until more than a month had passed and Alex had almost forgotten about that afternoon, waiting outside Rebibbia in the rusting 2CV. They were shopping together, late one morning, in the market beneath the Birdman's flat. The Birdman had his favourite meat and vegetable stalls, usually run by foreigners – Sri Lankans, Chinese, North Africans. 'I've had my fill of *la bella Italia*,' he liked to say, 'its mindless conformism. Forget all that Fascist guff about heroes and poets and navigators. It's a country of liars and priests and their bleating hypocritical flocks. You're a fool to stay,' he'd said more than once to Alex, and Alex had suggested, half playfully, that the Birdman finance a holiday for them both in some other, less suffocating, country. The Birdman had sniffed.

That morning they stood and watched the stallholder, a Malaysian adolescent in a bright yellow singlet and jeans, shovelling Basmati rice from a jute sack into a paper bag. 'Here, in this meeting of the ways, one breathes a different air,' the Birdman said, his eyes on the smooth brown forearm as it worked. 'Purer. Less corrupt.' He glanced at

Alex, then turned away, as though he'd compromised himself on purpose and wanted it to be known.

'Corrupt?' Alex said.

'You have no idea.'

Alex didn't need to answer. Ten minutes later they were in the back room of a bar, the Birdman spooning hot chocolate from his cup to his mouth. When he'd finished, he put down the cup and took one of Alex's hands in both of his, the way he'd pick up a bird that entered the flat and finally, exhausted, allowed itself to be caught. Alex resisted the urge to pull away.

'I've found out a little bit more about your friend.'

Alex knew at once which friend he meant. 'Bruno,' he said, wanting the name spoken, wanting Bruno to be there with them in that small way at least. 'Go on.'

'He was nosing into some dark places,' the Birdman said. 'Very dark. He was inquisitive, which is bad enough. He was careless, which is worse.'

'It wasn't because he was – you know – with me?'

The Birdman shook his head. 'They don't care about that. Well, they do care about it, of course. They care about it profoundly because they have minds like gutters. But what your friend did with you, and others, my darling, because you weren't the only one – well, that wasn't the problem. That isn't why he's dead.'

Alex, smarting, wanted to ask about the others, but the Birdman stood up before he had a chance. 'You're not involved, Alessandro *mio*. That's all you need to know.'

*

Back at the flat, Alex watched the Birdman put away the vegetables and rice, his left hand spinning his lighter from one finger to the next and back, a trick he'd perfected at school. He still had his jacket on, the jacket Bruno had bought for him. The kitchen was cool, almost cold: the Birdman kept the windows open during the day, and most nights, so that he could hear the noise of the birds as they fluttered around the food. Some birds, he claimed, he recognized from the sound their wings made against the dangling bags of peanuts and ribbons of fat as their claws fought for purchase.

As soon as the Birdman had finished and was sitting at the table opposite him, Alex said: 'So what was he looking for?'

'He never spoke about his work to you?'

'Not properly. He'd say things now and again. He wasn't being secretive. I don't think he realized I was interested. Or maybe it didn't matter to him that I was.' Alex smiled to himself. 'He didn't think of me as work.'

'He didn't take you seriously, though? That was foolish of him. I think your friend Bruno was foolish in more ways than one.'

'Yes,' said Alex. 'How else was he foolish?' Apart from not respecting me, he thought. Apart from dying too soon and leaving me alone.

'It looks as though he'd found out something about a bunch of rather powerful men who were trafficking in girls,' the Birdman said, pursing his lips. 'Or he thought he had.'

'Girls? You mean prostitutes?'

'No, my dear.' The Birdman shook his head. 'These girls weren't – how shall I put it? – on the game. Which doesn't make it any worse – or better, of course – just more dangerous. As your friend found out.'

'So who were they?'

The Birdman spread his hands. 'They were *good* girls.' As though he thought he might not be understood, he continued, '*Good* girls from *good* homes.'

Alex didn't know how to take this. 'Homes like mine, you mean?' He'd never thought before of his own home, of his parents' home, as being good or not good. He wasn't sure why he'd suggested it; perhaps it was because an image of his mother's kitchen had all at once appeared to him and made him feel sad, displaced, as though he was neither where he was nor there, where he once had been and might never be again. He felt ashamed and even a little angry, as though he'd set himself up to be mocked.

Confirming this, the Birdman laughed. 'Oh, no, my dear. I don't mean decent, respectable working-class homes like yours. I'm talking about our ruling classes. Bureaucrats, pimps, upholders of the faith. The worst kind of scum, but they don't know that because nobody has the nerve to tell them, and if they do they're branded as mad, or bad. As I have been, to my cost. I'm talking about people with money and power. The kind who prefer their girls to have a bit of class.'

They were interrupted by someone ringing the bell. Alex, at the Birdman's nod, walked over to the entry-phone and pressed the button that opened the main door to the building downstairs. The Birdman turned no one away. Alex knew that and was glad of it, because otherwise he might not have been allowed to stay. But that morning he'd have preferred it to be the two of them, alone; he'd have preferred to talk. He knew that the Birdman had been on the point of telling him more of what he'd found out, and that might not happen now. He would have to wait, which wasn't easy. Besides, the Birdman might change his mind and refuse to tell him at all, or tease him, or make something up to close his mouth. The Birdman, Alex knew, was unpredictable. But there was something he'd remembered, something he wanted to tell the Birdman. Bruno had said that he was looking after the photographs for someone else; he'd wanted Alex to keep them safe for some person he hadn't named. Alex was sure of this now. He'd said something about a favour being done, but not for Bruno. And if not for Bruno, for whom? Why would Bruno have wanted the favour done?

Opening the main door to the flat, Alex stepped out onto the landing to wait for the lift, one hand on the ornate metal grille that enclosed the lift shaft, shivering slightly in the cold damp air of the stairwell. He might never know the truth about Bruno, he thought, with a mixture of despair and relief as the lift appeared behind the grille and he saw a figure he didn't recognize reach out towards him through the frosted glass.

*

The Birdman closed the curtains at each of the windows overlooking the square below. Throughout the session, the three of them could hear the scratching of claws, wings beating on wood and air, swift bouts of squawking as pigeons and smaller birds fought for room. The young man wasn't Italian, but Alex couldn't place his accent; he might have been Turkish, Lebanese, a Kurd. Alex had never seen him before, but he seemed to know what to do. As soon as he was inside the flat he had gone into the room and stripped, throwing his clothes untidily into a corner. The Birdman had glanced with disapproval at the pile and, for a moment, Alex wondered if he was expected to pick them up and fold them, and was ready to refuse. He wouldn't pick up another man's clothes. But the Birdman walked across to the young man, now naked in the middle of the room, and led him across to the raised platform, almost a stage, at the far end, that he used for photographs. He spoke to him, in a voice too low for Alex to catch the words, although he recognized the language: French. The young man pulled a face, shrugged, then, to Alex's surprise, gave a brilliant smile and threw his head back to laugh. His penis, darker than the rest of him, had begun to stiffen. The Birdman reached down and gave it a brisk shake, making a coaxing noise with his lips, as though it were some recalcitrant dog. The young man laughed again, raising his thin shoulders in a shrug.

'Fetch me a chair,' the Birdman said, over his shoulder.

'Which one?' said Alex.

'From the kitchen.' He sounded impatient. 'One of the kitchen chairs.'

Alex carried a chair through and stood at the door with it until the Birdman pointed to the stage. 'Put it down over there, next to him.' Alex did as he was told, placing the chair close to the young man's thigh, then straightening up, his arm almost touching the other's. The young man didn't move away but turned his head so that Alex couldn't see his face, as though he was all at once ashamed to be there. He smelt of sweat, Alex noticed, and something else he couldn't place, some spice. 'No,' said the Birdman, 'in the middle.' He snapped some phrase, again in French, and the young man stepped to one side, making room for the chair. And then the Birdman told Alex to turn on the lights. 'Not all of them,' he said. He pointed. 'Just the ones over there.'

It was odd to see what a difference this made. Alex adjusted the lights until one side of the young man's body was brightly lit, the other in deep shadow. One half like polished stone, but warm, so not like stone, and less polished than burnished, more like buffed bronze. The Birdman barked orders in French from behind his camera, massive on its tripod. The young man opened his legs, stroking his penis into erection, staring ahead, then stood up to show himself from the side, now three-quarters on, his buttocks gleaming like aubergines on a market stall, thought Alex, as he bent a little from the waist to accentuate their curve. Alex wondered how often he had done this in the past, how much of what he did now was being dictated to him by the Birdman, in this language Alex couldn't quite follow. Even with the man in front of him, only feet away, with the smell of his skin lingering in Alex's nostrils, he was beyond Alex's understanding.

Alex had seen pornography before, a thousand times, and used it, alone and with others, with Bruno, even. But he'd never thought to wonder how little of the men before the lens was on display. How closed this young man seemed, sealed off from what was happening, indifferent to it, despite his nakedness, his erection. The way a life model would be, he imagined, as though what the Birdman was doing had the dignity and detachment of art. Perhaps it is art, thought Alex, with the lights and everything, perhaps this isn't pornography at all, but I still couldn't do it, not like this. Not knowing where you'd end up, in which magazine, in whose hands. It's not like fucking someone who's bought you dinner or something to wear. That way at least there's a person doing it, someone you can see and touch. You know where you are. This way there's nothing. I'd feel I'd betrayed myself. At least I kept my jeans on, he thought.

Jamie had told him about a session one afternoon, with an Algerian man of about his age. The Birdman had paid them both to have sex while he took photographs. Alex had listened to the story in Jamie's broken Italian, not quite believing it, not because he was innocent enough to suppose these things didn't happen – he knew full well what purpose the Birdman's camera served. He simply couldn't understand how amused, and untouched, by it

Jamie was, as though he'd helped out in a restaurant for tips or parked someone's car. Maybe the young man flexing his muscles on the stage right now was the one who'd had sex with Jamie. Not that it mattered. He hadn't thought to ask Jamie how much he'd been paid, but Jamie had told him in any case. And Alex had wondered for a moment if he might be tempted after all.

The girl's been alone for what feels like hours when the central light – the only light – is turned on from outside the room, where the switch must be, and the door opens. She blinks, startled, and wipes her face – she's been crying but she doesn't want them to know that. She sees the two men who brought her here in the car, followed by a third man. He's much older than the first two, and taller as well. He's wearing a long black coat and shiny black shoes that look as if they've been painted. He's old enough to be her grandfather, she thinks, and the thought of her grandfather carries her back to the brink of crying. He walks across to where she's lying, on a mattress against the wall. She tries to stand up, she wants to move away but it's too late, he's leaning over her so close she can smell his breath, an aniseed smell that makes her feel sick, and she's trapped between his body and the wall. When he puts out his hand to touch her face, she turns away quickly, hiding her cheek from his fingers. But he takes her chin and forces her head round until she can either close her eyes or look at him. She stares into his eyes and, for a moment, she thinks she knows him, and she's pleased, as if this will make her safe.

She's seen him somewhere before this, not to speak to, on television perhaps. His hand is strong, stronger than she expected, and he's hurting her a little. He stares back, without expression, then smiles and lets her go. It isn't a smile for her, she can see that, it's the smile a man gives when he gets what he wants. And now she's more afraid than ever as he nods and steps away. The two men come forward and pull her to her feet as the big man walks around the room, looking at the bare walls as if he's thinking of buying the place. He's bald except for a fringe of soft white hair at the back. There's a ring around his head as though he's been wearing a hat that's too tight for him. From behind, he looks like a prize fighter. When he swivels on his heels to face her again, she flinches. Now they're both standing up she sees how tall he is, and she wonders what he's going to do with her, and why her. Why her? He gestures towards the table with his head and the two men half lead, half drag her across to where she was seated before. They pull the chair out from under the table and push her into it.

ANDREW AND MARTIN **2008**

Daniela dell'Orto's changed her mind. She's decided someone should come from one of the Rome newspapers, to
get the buzz rolling. She's just learned the word 'buzz',
and drops it into her Italian as often as she can, though
she isn't quite sure how it's used, nor how it's pronounced.
Does it rhyme with 'loose' or 'fez'? Andrew, who refuses
to help her out, is less than thrilled about reporters coming
to look at the photographs, which are still unframed, still
stacked in the original box, just as they were when he
showed them to Martin. He's started to have cold feet
about the whole business, mostly because of Martin's reaction, which was less wholehearted than Andrew had hoped
it would be.

Martin's called since, a couple of times, and given
Andrew the impression there's something he wants to say,
if only because he's said nothing of any purpose, which
isn't Martin's style: Martin doesn't do small-talk without
a reason. The fact that he won't come out with it, whatever *it* might be, only makes Andrew more concerned. He
trusts Martin. More to the point, he knows that Martin
isn't the type to hide what's on his mind unless he has to.

At the same time, Andrew's more convinced than ever that these photographs had meaning for Michel and that, by showing them, he is making up for what he understands as his own failure, because suicide is always a sort of accusation, and he's starting to realize how much he's taken his sense of guilt for granted these past twenty-five years.

He's decided that the show will be dedicated to Michel. He's toyed with the idea of including his name as joint curator, next to his own, and might yet do this. He still has a month to decide what form the catalogue will take. Daniela will throw her piece down at the last moment, as usual, faxing it through so that he'll have to key it in himself, because one of her many affectations is that she can't, or won't, use a computer. He isn't sure what Martin will do, and doesn't want to take it into account until it's required of him. Daniela wrinkled her nose at *Exposure*, but accepted it as a working title until she could think of something better, more *ambivalent*, as though the word enacted itself in a way she didn't like, exposing her. Andrew hopes she won't be able to because *Exposure* is what he wants; he's made his mind up now and doesn't need to have to argue with her. What he does need to do is select the photographs he wants to use. And this is where Martin could help him, if only he would. Andrew decides he'll call tomorrow and ask Martin what his problem is. Better, he'll suggest they meet for a drink. He'll make him talk.

He picks up the photograph of Michel that's propped in front of him and stares into the soft creased cardboard

eyes of the dead man squatting naked on his improvised
pile of decades-old newspapers, long since thrown away,
long since discarded and trashed, as though he expects
some response. He expects it so much, so deeply, he dares
Michel's eyes to react, to recognize him, both thrilled and
frightened by that possibility. He's drunk, but not lost. He
knows what he's doing. If he had three magic words to
use he'd use them. It occurs to him now that he would
like to use this photograph as the cover of the catalogue,
to make explicit the sense he has of owing something to
Michel, and because there is finally no difference between
this face, which he has loved, and the faces of all the
others, of people he has never known, who were made
to stand against a soiled white wall all those years ago,
full face and profile, their shoulders taut, their eyes as
unsmiling and wary, mistrustful even, as Michel's are in
this final self-portrait, as though he was both accused and
accuser, the impotent victim and the man with the camera
who won't take no for an answer and yet doesn't know
what he's asking, despite his power. He would like to make
this plain to everyone, this *ambivalence*, as Daniela would
say. He's drunk, but not incapable of thought, of feeling,
never that. 'Is this what you'd want?' he says to the photograph, and pauses for a moment to allow it to speak,
his head slightly cocked. 'This exposure? Is this why you
somehow obtained these photographs and then hid them
away beneath your favourite soft green pullover for me
to find?'

Leaning forward, he studies the black and white contours

of Michel's face in the picture more closely and with greater urgency than he was ever allowed to do in life, because Michel would always turn away, or grimace, or pull Andrew's own face in to be stroked and kissed. Kissing is always a way to not speak, not see, thinks Andrew now, the way we close our eyes and open our mouths, one tongue silencing the other. It is some months since he has been kissed – he can't quite remember when it was nor by whom – and even more since he has been kissed with love. Three magic words. He'd used them with Michel, and with Jamie too, but they hadn't worked, or hadn't worked long enough or well enough, as well as they were meant to do, as charms against loneliness, against death. 'I love you,' he whispers to the photograph, taking it and lifting it to his face until the skin of it, cold and slightly clammy, touches his lips and seems to wake him to what he's doing.

Exasperated with himself, he pushes his chair back and goes into the kitchen for something else to drink. The cat is asleep on the table.

The next morning, hung-over, he calls Martin first on his mobile, to find the number no longer exists, and then at home. Martin, sounding distracted, agrees to see him later that day. Andrew suggests a bar, but Martin insists they meet at the shop. Andrew reminds him that it's Sunday and says he hasn't planned to go into the shop, but Martin repeats that, no, he prefers the shop, or wherever Andrew keeps the photographs, and Andrew understands. Martin has a problem with the photographs. He puts down the phone and looks around himself, at his personal chaos, then spends the first hour of the day sorting out the boxes he piled up outside the kitchen door when he was looking for Michel's things. He tries to decide what to throw away and what to keep, but gives up the minute he finds himself shifting things from pile to pile, forgetting which is which. He takes two soluble aspirin and lies on the sofa. When he wakes up, the cat arranged neatly on his chest as if in reproof, he realizes he just has time to shave and shower and get to the shop.

Martin is waiting for him at the bar in the square in front of the church.

'Sunday,' says Andrew. 'The bus didn't come. I walked here in the end.'

'No problem,' says Martin. 'Isn't that a dreadful expression? Euro-friendly, I suppose you'd call it. People never mean it either – though, oddly enough, I do. This time anyway. I've been enjoying the sight of people young enough to be my granddaughter, quite unashamedly. One of the joys of old age is that people see you as harmless. You can ogle all you want.'

'I'm sure Alina doesn't see you as harmless. Or ogling as harmless.'

Martin sighs. 'Alina has far too high an opinion of me, if the truth be told.' He lifts his stick from the other chair at the table. 'Sit down, old chap. What will you have?'

Andrew slumps into the chair. 'Coffee,' he says. 'Water.'

'In a bit of a bad way?'

Andrew rubs his face with both hands. 'Oh, God,

Martin, I don't know. I had a bit of a miserable evening, to be honest. I know sorrows won't be drowned but it doesn't stop me trying every now and again.'

Martin is silent for a moment, staring at the waiter by the door to the bar, whose eyes are closed, his empty tray dangling from his fingers. 'If there's anything I can do,' he says finally. 'Is it money?'

Andrew smiles. 'No. Well, yes, it's that as well, of course, but no. Thank you for thinking of it, Martin, but it isn't money.' The waiter, suddenly brisk, hurries across. 'It's what you do when you're bored, I suppose, and by yourself. I mean I don't *know* what you do. I just know what I do.' He looks at Martin. 'What *did* you do, Martin? Before Alina?'

Martin orders a coffee, a glass of water and two brandies. 'I managed,' he says, as soon as the waiter has left them. 'Which reminds me. Alina has made me change the thingamajig in my phone. Apparently this one's cheaper. Madness, really, I hardly ever use the damn thing.' He fumbles in his pocket, produces a card. 'And now I've had to have these printed with my new number.'

Andrew pulls a face at the idea of brandy, and of managing. 'I feel as though I've spent my whole life rehearsing for something.' He sighs, slipping the card, unread, into the pocket of his leather jacket. 'And then suddenly it's too late. I think the actual performance is the dress rehearsal and I'll get another chance the minute I get it right, but it's the next act and I'm still not ready. I'll never be ready for anything. I haven't grown up, I think that's what it is.' He studies Martin. 'All these years and I've never asked you if you have any children. Isn't that odd? Because I'm starting to think the only way you can stop being a child is by having one.'

'No.' Martin waits until the waiter has left their drinks. 'No children. I've wanted them or I've been married to women who wanted them, which comes to the same thing very often. I don't know how much men really *do* want children, whatever we say. But, no, no children. I'm not sure if I prove your point or not. I don't feel particularly grown-up, certainly. I haven't done for decades.'

Andrew drinks his water. Then, with a groan, he tips the brandy into his coffee. 'Jamie adored you, you know. He told me once you were the only man he respected. He never respected me, I'm sure of that. I was jealous of you for a while. I even thought there might be something going on. I must have been mad.'

'Yes, you needn't have worried about that.' Martin laughs. 'In any case,' he adds, to the surprise of them both, 'respect's a poor substitute for love.'

'I'm not sure he did that either,' says Andrew. 'Love me, I mean. I don't know, I've been thinking a lot about Jamie recently.' Despite his confessional mood, which has startled and disturbed him as much as it may be startling Martin, he doesn't want to talk about Michel, not yet. In one sense, he's talking about himself, and Jamie, to put off talking about what Martin might want from him, from the photographs, something he already knows he won't be willing to provide.

'I saw him, you know, years ago now,' says Martin. 'I didn't mention it at the time. I wasn't sure whether you'd want to have news of him or not. I imagined probably not. And then it completely slipped my mind, as these things do. Unlike you, I haven't thought about Jamie for ages. I used to associate the two of you, which was only natural, of course, but then he fell away, so to speak, and I was left with you.' Martin smiles. 'I think I got the better bargain.'

'Where did you see him? Here in Rome?' Andrew hasn't really heard the last, generous, thing Martin said, or doesn't care. His voice sounds urgent, almost shrill, even to himself.

'No,' says Martin. 'In London. He was walking along Tottenham Court Road with a tall black woman, quite striking. I noticed her first.'

'Did he look happy?'

'He looked healthy, which I remember surprised me at the time, given the way he behaved here in Rome.' Martin thinks for a moment, his eyes half closed as if he is trying to recall the scene. 'Yes . . . I think, on the whole, he did.'

'I'm glad.' Andrew drinks his brandy-laced coffee in one gulp, then watches Martin empty his own stubby glass, tilting it to the sky. 'You want to see the photographs again.'

'One of them,' says Martin. 'I want to see one of them again.'

'You're worried about something?'

Martin shakes his head with a sort of weariness,

reluctant to speak. 'I think you're being a fool,' he says finally.

Andrew feels himself stiffen, as he always does when a choice of his is questioned. He's lived alone too long. 'Really? Why?'

'It's too soon, Andrew. For God's sake, half the people in those photographs are probably still alive. They won't want to see themselves exhibited as art.'

'They're hardly the sort of people who'd come to a piddling little show above a second-hand bookshop.'

Martin looks disappointed, then irritated. 'But how do we know that, Andrew? We're in no position to say what sort of people they are now, or were then for that matter. People do have lives. Just because they got into a spot of bother twenty-odd years ago doesn't mean they want to see themselves hanging on a gallery wall as criminals.'

'I'm sorry, that sounded snobbish. I didn't mean that. I just think they'll never even know about it, like most people. It's not exactly the biggest event in the social calendar. It'll be tricky enough to attract the attention of the handful of people who might actually be interested, never mind anyone else. To be honest, I'm beginning to think it's hardly worth doing.'

Martin spreads his hands. 'So why do it?'

'Well,' says Andrew, too quickly, 'Daniela would kill me if I pulled out at this point.'

'Daniela dell'Orto?' Martin laughs. 'With what? Her poison-filled pen?'

Andrew has no answer to this. 'Which photograph do you want to see?'

'The one with the girl in the car.' Martin looks at him more closely. 'You realized that, didn't you? You understood there was something odd about it when you showed it to me.'

Andrew sighs deeply, as though he has been found doing something shameful, then shrugs, as if to say it wasn't his idea; he's innocent. 'I wasn't certain. I thought it might be that one. You recognized her. I'm right, aren't I? You know who she is?'

'I'm not one hundred per cent sure,' says Martin, although it's clear from his tone he's lying. 'That's why I'd like to look at it again.'

'I thought she seemed familiar but I couldn't put my finger on it. And then I decided I didn't want to know. Until I saw the way you stared at it and my heart sank.' Andrew stands up. 'I suppose we'd better go and check.' He's thinking, This will make no difference. I won't let him stop me.

Martin waits beside him, resting lopsidedly on his stick, as Andrew crouches to unlock the shutters protecting the shop. Martin has always thought of Andrew as much younger than he is but, seeing him bent over, his fine hair pulled back and stuffed into an orange elastic band, his bared neck oddly frail and sinewy, bird-like in a way Martin can't pin down, not even clean, as though it has been wiped rather than washed, he no longer seems any younger than himself. Two childless men growing old, he thinks. In the end, after a certain age, we are all the same. '"Life is like playing a violin solo in public and learning the instrument as one goes along,"' he says. Thank God I have Alina, he thinks. My constantly forgiving public.

'What?' Andrew straightens up, then bends again to heave the shutter free of the shop front.

'What you were saying earlier, about the rehearsal being the only chance you get. Samuel Butler said it first. In his own way.'

'That doesn't make me feel any better, Martin.'

Ten minutes later, they are side by side behind the cluttered shop counter, Andrew's desk light shining onto the photograph. Tilting it slightly to reduce the reflection, Martin nods. 'Yes, it's her,' he says, in a tone Andrew can't decipher, between relief and disappointment. 'I was sure it was. It's Silvia Castellani.' He puts it down. 'I'll need a copy of this, Andrew.'

ALEX **1983–1985**

Alex changed degree course later that year, from eco-
nomics, his parents' idea, to Italian literature. If you want
to be a journalist, the Birdman said, you'll need to know
how to write, and the best way to know how to write
is to know how to read. He didn't tell his parents.
They didn't matter to him by now; he saw them once or
twice a month, if that, slamming the door as he left after
some futile argument, his father shouting behind him as
he ran down the stairs because the lift took too long, and
was too small, too airless. Besides, the Birdman had offered
to pay his fees, and, without having said a word, was
paying for everything else. Alex ate what he was given,
accepted small presents of money and clothes, helped in
his own way around the flat as a sort of recompense in
kind. Not only money and clothes: the Birdman began to
lend, and then buy, him books, encourage him to talk
about them.

Alex was shy at first. Bruno, who'd worked with words,
had never regarded him as worth this effort, although the
Birdman didn't seem to see it as effort. On the contrary.
More than once, he said how rewarding it was to find a

boy who wasn't just a pretty face, *a very pretty face indeed*, and Alex was flattered on both counts: to be considered a pretty face and to be seen as more than that. This helped him as he worked his way through anthologies the faculty obliged him to use, anthologies his professors had edited and assigned as required reading. One morning, the Birdman picked up one such anthology, weighing it in his hands, and sighed. 'Dear God, what do they think they're doing? As though you can expect a growing mind to learn to love Dante from extracts and exegesis.' Alex looked across. Exegesis? The Birdman explained, as always, and Alex listened.

He soon stopped going to lectures and studied at home, the Birdman's home. He had his own room by now, not much larger than a broom cupboard, a window the size of a letterbox, but with space for a single bed and a brand-new bookcase, gradually filling up with the Birdman's gifts and the few books he had brought from his parents' home as and when he thought of it. He kept his clothes in a wardrobe in the hall, and studied on the kitchen table. He was used to reading in the midst of chaos, and found it harder to concentrate in silence than otherwise. The Birdman had taken to introducing him as his assistant, which meant that, nominally at least, he was seen to be earning his keep. He had never been happier.

Sometimes, when he felt like it, he'd have sex with one of the men passing through the flat, but he didn't want ties. Afterwards he was rough, off-hand, with them, which seemed to please the Birdman. Alex wondered if this meant he was jealous and, finally, asked him. But the Birdman laughed and shook his head. 'I don't care what you do in bed,' he said, and Alex decided to believe him. When they worked together on the photo sets the Birdman made, and sold, Alex now knew, to private collectors – because one of his jobs was to pack the photographs into padded envelopes and take them across Rome to the main post office in Piazza San Silvestro, to be sent all over the world – he found himself excited by them, but also repelled, as if he knew too much.

He thought sometimes about what a journalist might do with the information he had, the names he wrote on the labels, some of them known to him from newspapers, the specialist requests the Birdman tried to meet. He thought about what he might do, if he chose. But he pushed these thoughts away; he would never knowingly betray the Birdman.

Certain days, occasional days, he was sent out for an hour or so, fresh money in his hand, told to buy something new to wear or to watch a film. One afternoon, in a cinema he'd never been to before, he saw a film called *The Elephant Man*, and cried to himself in the darkness, wiping his tears, in rapid shame, with the palm of his hand. He didn't know what happened when he was sent away from the Birdman's flat. He didn't want to know. The Birdman had never treated him with anything but respect. It struck him, these hours in exile, as he queued alone for his ticket or wandered from window to window, that he had no one he could call, no friends from school or the area he'd grown up in – as though he had wiped his whole life clean of his past. He was pleased to find this didn't matter. It was better like this, to have no one drag you back.

Perhaps that was why they hadn't talked any more about Bruno, or about the photographs, not until months had passed. The Birdman brought the subject up; Alex had practically forgotten, unless he was reminded.

'I went to see that bookseller you told me about,' the Birdman said.

'What bookseller?'

'Wake up, light of my life. The bookseller you wanted to sell those embarrassing photographs to.'

'Why did you do that?'

The Birdman hummed along with the radio for a moment. Culture Club. 'Do You Really Want to Hurt Me'. Alex refused to become impatient. He couldn't understand why the Birdman was being so arch. The last time the affair had been mentioned, when he'd talked about powerful men, and girls, he'd seemed almost scared.

'I wanted to see what he was like,' the Birdman said eventually, when Alex's eyes had returned to his book.

'And now you have.'

'I knew him already.'

Alex hadn't expected this.

'Not well,' the Birdman said. 'Not even to speak to. But now that I've seen him, I know who bought your photographs.' The Birdman's tone changed, as if he had decided to be serious. 'He was Belgian, not French. His name was

Michel. I don't remember his surname.' He paused, his voice unexpectedly choked. 'He helped me out for a while, the way you do now. Then he left, without explaining why. I thought, Well, he's found something better. I didn't mind. Well, perhaps I minded a little. Yes, I minded. The last time I saw him was just before he died, I realize that now. I'm surprised you didn't bump into each other here. He told me he was happy, but I didn't believe him, not entirely. Happiness didn't come into it. Michel wasn't made for happiness. He was too curious, too probing.' Another pause. 'I didn't realize who he was when you told me about him. I had no idea. I thought he'd gone back to Belgium when he disappeared like that. You said he was French. That threw me off. I know it sounds stupid, but it simply didn't occur to me that it might be Michel. Belgium and France are different places, you see. People confuse them, but that's out of ignorance. They're quite different places.'

Alex nodded, anxious. He'd never seen the Birdman lose control, but now he seemed to be rambling, as though Alex weren't there. He'd turned away and was staring at the birds gathered in the window nearest him.

'And then when I saw the bookseller everything fell into place. I could see why he'd gone then. He wanted something he could strike against, the way a match does against the box.' The Birdman looked sharply at Alex. 'Have you seen him, this bookseller?'

Alex nodded. 'Not properly. Through the window.'

'Of course,' said the Birdman. 'He wasn't there, was he,

when you went? Just think what might have happened, if he had been.'

'What?'

'Well, for one thing, Michel might still be alive.' The Birdman came over and gripped Alex by his shoulders, his fat thighs pushed heavily against Alex's knees so that he seemed to be half resting on him, using him for support but also pinning him to his chair, as if afraid he might run off, the way Michel had done. 'Because I think you're right about the photographs. I wasn't sure at first. I'd asked around a little, as you know, but there didn't seem to be any link between that nasty business your journalist friend was poking his nose into and a bunch of police photos. At least, I couldn't see the link. But now, with Michel dead, and knowing Michel, the way he worked, the way he was, I'm less convinced. I think his death has something to do with it as well. I don't think he killed himself.'

'He was your assistant?' said Alex. 'Before me?'

The Birdman's fingers loosened their grip. 'Yes.'

'What did he do? What I do?'

'No. He was difficult.'

'And I'm easy?'

The Birdman shook his head. 'Not in the sense you mean. You're easy in the good sense. Michel made life hard for himself, and for everyone else. I don't envy his bookseller friend one bit. He must have been a patient man to have stood Michel all that time, if they were together after he left me. But I don't know that they were. There's no reason to think that. Michel wasn't reliable in that way. He didn't need to be with someone else. I think he was happier alone – his anger had more room to move. I also think he may have enjoyed making the other person suffer. That's why he wasn't anything like you, why he was difficult to live with, though not to love, and you're easy to live with and to love. Although easy's not the word – you're right to be offended. You like to see people happy. You know what happiness means, even when you don't feel it. It's your nature. You have a good nature, Alessandro. Not everyone can see it, perhaps, but I can. Be proud of it.'

'You loved him?' But this wasn't the question Alex was asking and the Birdman appeared to have understood. He stroked the hair back off Alex's forehead and kissed him lightly. It was the first time he'd kissed Alex anywhere other than on the cheek. Alex would have let the man do anything with him, he knew that, but the Birdman, who also seemed to know it, stepped back in his odd light way and gathered his kaftan around him. 'I'm too old to have much faith in love,' he said. 'You're still young enough, and that worries me a little, but what can we do? We live and learn. If we're lucky.'

Which didn't satisfy Alex.

'But what *did* he do?' he insisted.

'Michel was a photographer,' said the Birdman. 'An authentic photographer. Not the kind who thinks every picture he takes is a work of art. He was genuinely talented, genuinely keen. His camera was the only thing he really loved, and even there he was promiscuous, unfaithful. He loved all cameras, I suppose. He'd pocket them as if he had a right to them. I saw him steal one from a bar table once, from a tourist, without even interrupting our conversation. He showed me how to make the work I did increase in value. He said that only a real artist could prostitute himself because only real artists knew the difference. Before him I was ashamed of what I produced; it was crude, vulgar stuff, fit only for cheap magazines. He showed me how to turn what I did into what he said the world would call art. He was amused at the idea that a little tricky lighting could make a naked arse worth so much more. He had plans for marketing our work in New York, in Paris, in galleries. Not under his name, of course – nor mine, come to that. He'd invented an alias.' The Birdman smiled. 'I don't remember it now. It sounded Japanese, but it wasn't. He made it up one night, jumbling cards with letters on them until something emerged from the chaos. It all came to nothing. We argued about money, or he did. He argued with himself in the end. I'd have given him anything to keep him. Not out of love, though, Alex, don't think that. Out of pride, a little, but also common sense. He was very talented,' the Birdman repeated. 'A genius, I thought, sometimes; I think he did too. For someone who sneered at art, he wanted to be an artist very badly, but in the wrong way, the self-despising Rimbaud way. You know who Rimbaud is? Of course you do. Forgive me, Alex, if I underestimate you. Michel wanted everything to be dirty because dirt ennobles. That was my charm, of course, in his eyes – the fact that he saw me as dirty. He'd found his Verlaine. A dirty old fat pornographer he could step on to get somewhere else. So I can't complain.' He took Alex's hand and squeezed it, a gentle, affectionate squeeze, as if to say everything was back to normal. 'That's what I mean about his being difficult. You wouldn't want to be like that.'

'That would have been why he wanted the photographs,' Alex said. 'There was something dirty about them as well. Not just that they were criminals and stuff. There was something wrong with them. None of us should have had them.'

'And now Michel is dead and the photographs have disappeared. Unless the bookseller has them after all.'

'That's true,' said Alex. 'I hadn't thought of that. Someone must have them.'

'I imagine the person who killed Michel will have had his reasons,' said the Birdman. 'He'd messed up once with your journalist friend. He wasn't going to mess up a second time. This time he made it look like suicide. He's no fool, but you'd expect that. Your Bruno died an appropriate death, one fewer nasty queer to interfere with little boys – who's going to investigate too deeply? And so did Michel, the suicide of a melancholic, a junkie, a poet *maudit*. What could be less surprising than that? Who'd question it?' He shuddered. 'I wonder what they'd have done to you if they'd found you.'

'But I still don't understand how they knew about Michel,' said Alex, afraid to ask himself how close he'd been to death.

The uneaten food is still on its tray – the woman never came back to take it. Looking at it now, the girl feels suddenly hungry, she can't understand why. White lumps of fat have congealed on the surface of the broth, the meat looks grey and damp. She wouldn't eat this if they paid her, but she'd give anything for something else, something her mother had made for her. We're having chicken this evening, she remembers wildly, chicken with small new potatoes and peas the way her mother does them, with bits of ham. She told me this morning and I didn't answer, I wasn't listening, I was too busy thinking about something Paola had said and now I can't remember what that was. All I remember is the way my mother looked at me as she put the biscuits back in the cupboard, not angry, reproachful. She wants to tell the big man to let her go, her dinner's waiting for her, but knows it will make no difference. Nothing she does will make a difference, she thinks, as the big man sits down opposite her. He nods to the other two men, who both step sideways, away from her. She can hear them breathe, but can't see them. It's as though she's there with him and no one else. You mustn't be scared of us, he says. What am I doing here? she asks him. I can't tell you that, he says, but you mustn't think we'll harm you. She knows she's supposed to feel reassured by this, but how can she believe him? She doesn't want to believe him, she realizes, because that would mean she trusts him. I do know you, she thinks, I know your face. I've seen you with my father, but that can't be true: how could her father have been near this man? I'm not going to talk any more, she decides, whatever they say or do to me. She presses her lips tight shut and she's happy to see that he notices this and puts both hands on the table, with their palms down first and then turned up, as if to show he's hiding nothing. We won't keep you long, he says, you don't need to worry about that. Everything will be all right. He looks down at the food. You can't eat this, he says, it's cold, and he clicks his fingers. His hands are very white as though he's used to wearing gloves. He has a ring with a big red stone on one of his fingers. Bring her something else to eat, he says.

ANDREW AND DANIELA **2008**

Andrew and Daniela are making their final choice of photographs for the exhibition. They are sitting together in the room above the shop with some *foie gras* and a bottle of extremely good prosecco Daniela produced from her bag as soon as she'd arrived. Daniela is in party mood. Following her up the stairs, Andrew was worried she might fall off her heels; he found himself lifting his hands towards her just in case. She's had her hair cut in Cleopatra style and dyed an orange red. From behind, from below, she might be seventeen and it's a shock, although he knows it shouldn't be, when she turns round at the top of the stairs and he sees her hard, tight face, her bright, over-made-up eyes surrounded by a filigree of lines. She leans towards him, almost into him, catching his arm with her hand as if she's about to stumble, and he thinks, Oh, my God, she's going to try it on – I thought we'd sorted that out years ago. But she lets him go immediately, reaches into her bag for the bottle and places it with studied care on the table, then pulls out a baguette and a small glass jar with a rubber seal.

'I can never get these damn things to open,' she says,

and he can hear from her voice she's already been drinking, although she isn't behaving the way she normally does when she's drunk. He's seen her drunk often enough: she's truculent, rude to waiters, even louder and shriller than usual. This evening, on the contrary, she's smiling, eager to touch him, worryingly affectionate. He takes the *foie gras* and pulls the rubber tag from the seal until it pops and the top lifts up. 'I knew you'd know how to do it,' she says, taking the jar from him, passing him the bottle. 'You have that air of masculine competence about you. You do have some glasses, I suppose.'

'Not for prosecco as such,' he says. 'I've got some wine glasses.'

'You're so formal, darling, so precise. How is it that I've never seen this side of you before tonight? Your Germanic side.'

He was right to be anxious: she is flirting. 'I don't have a Germanic side,' he says. 'I'm half Celt.' He opens a cupboard and takes out a plate and two glasses, the stubby hardwearing kind they use in wine bars, and an orange-handled steak knife he rapidly dusts against his leg as she breaks off the tip of the baguette and forces it into the jar.

'I was given this earlier today – this wonderful friend of mine brought it with him from Paris. He's just had a show there, he's massively talented, and he knows exactly where to shop for *foie gras*.' She giggles. 'Because I told him exactly where to shop for it.'

'And the prosecco?'

Daniela's dismissive. 'Darling, it was the only object worth salvaging from the sad little travesty of a show that old fraud Puglielli's managed to get financed by the region. Landscapes, darling, oil on canvas. Oil. On. Canvas. In this day and age. Without a saving trace of irony. I thought you'd be there.'

'Because of the lack of irony?' says Andrew. 'I told you I wouldn't be going when you told me about it. That's why we agreed to meet here.' He looks at his watch. 'Almost two hours ago.'

He's irritated with her for several reasons. The most confusing is her kittenish behaviour, which is not only inappropriate but, he feels, unexpectedly humiliating for both of them. 'It's warm,' he says, easing the cork from the bottle. 'You should have taken one of those freezer bags to the opening.' But what's thrown him most is that she's clearly in no mood, or state, to respond to his growing anxiety about the wisdom of putting on the exhibition. Martin has left him hesitant, wondering if the idea is even worth it; wondering what Michel would really want. He isn't sure any longer that he knows.

Daniela begins to laugh. 'What a clever idea! That would have been wonderful. Next time.' She slops some lukewarm prosecco into a glass. 'I'm so excited.' She pauses. 'About our lovely little show.'

'That's what I wanted to talk about.'

'I've pulled in a friend – well, a student – who'll do the catalogue for us. Put it together. You did get that piece from your English journalist?'

'There's a problem, Daniela.' He can't avoid it.

'Oh, well, never mind. We don't need it. I'll make my thing a bit longer. It wasn't such a good idea, in any case. What's wonderful about the work is that it has nothing to do with the world it pretends to represent. It's broken free.' She pats Andrew's hand. Her palm is moist and he has to stop himself pulling away. 'We've freed it, Andrew.'

'That's not the problem,' he says. 'Or, rather, Martin's not the problem. The problem is that the damn things *haven't* broken free of the world. They're all too firmly anchored to it.' He walks across to the box in which the photographs are still stored, then back to where Daniela is sitting, running her finger around the rim of her glass. 'Look at this,' he says, showing her the photograph with the girl. 'Martin knows who she is.'

'She's pixels on paper, darling,' says Daniela, barely looking as he lays it down in front of her on the table. He doesn't let it go: he's scared she might damage it in some way, deliberately, because it's getting in her way, or by accident, through simple clumsiness, tipping her half-glass of prosecco onto its glossy surface. 'Don't you get lonely, Andrew? Sometimes? I do.'

'Don't be infantile,' says Andrew, lifting the photo closer to her face, making it harder to avoid. 'Do you recognize her?'

'Should I?' Daniela wrinkles her nose.

'Martin did. When he told me who she was, so did I.'

Daniela glances at it a second time, looks away. Irritated or bored, it's hard to tell. 'I've never seen her in my life.'

'You're sure?'

'Who is she?'

Andrew holds the photo, image inward to his chest in an odd, protective gesture. 'Her name's Silvia Castellani. She was kidnapped in 1982. They never found her. There were posters all over Rome – you must have seen them. They were everywhere. I don't know why I didn't realize at once.' He looks at the photo again, as if checking. 'This must be the last photograph ever taken of her. That we know about at least.'

'But this isn't the sort of thing we want at all.' Daniela sounds deeply affronted. 'Some missing girl ruining everything.'

'I'm sorry?'

'But, *caro*, the last thing we want is some sort of sub-Weegee business,' she says, 'especially after that so-so Paris show of his a couple of years ago. All very well in its way, but who needs more unmediated scene-of-crime material, Andrew? In 2008. Please. So someone was there and had a camera. So when isn't that true, these days? The *verité* isn't in the being there, the reportage, it's in what happens *after* it, *around* it, the social construct of the crime. The *spectacle* of it. Just think of that English woman – what's-her-name – Myra Hindley, darling. That wonderful portrait done with those innocent children's hands by whatever-his-name-was. Genius. Sheer genius. That's what I want us to do here, the mug shot, the context. The anthropology of it. Even better, the *event* of it. I don't want to bother with all that other business.' Airily, she waves her hand towards the box. 'I thought you understood that, Andrew.' She smiles, a simpering, ingratiating smile. 'I thought you understood *me*.' When he doesn't answer at once, she adds, her tone slightly sulky: 'Besides, I wasn't even *in* Rome in 1982. I was in New York. I thought you'd have remembered that.'

Good God, Andrew thinks, but doesn't say. What a cunt you are. What a brutal, smug, insufferable cunt. But, of course, you're also right. There's no need to use this picture or any other picture that might upset someone. The show can go on. He tries to smile back, but can't quite manage it. He pours himself a glass of prosecco and drinks it in one go, then breaks off a piece of baguette, spreads it with *foie gras*, eats it hungrily.

'Now show me the ones we really can use,' says Daniela, raising her hands in front of her, almost to the level of her mouth, and clapping like a gratified child. 'All those lovely human faces.'

'So what happened to her?'

'Your guess is as good as mine,' says Andrew. 'Or anyone else's.' They have finished the *foie gras* and baguette and are reaching the end of a one-and-a-half-litre bottle of white wine Andrew keeps in a small fridge for emergencies. When this is gone, assuming they both want to continue drinking, they'll have to go somewhere else, which is Andrew's intention: he wants Daniela on neutral ground as soon as she can be moved without her noticing; before she can ask him again about loneliness. The photographs have now been chosen: fifty photographs, twenty-five faces seen from the front and side, some sad, some insolent, the majority vacant, as if they are thinking about somewhere else, some other place in which they are safe. Andrew tried to skew the choice towards people who might already be dead, for safety's sake, but Daniela seemed to realize this and became insistent, picking out shots of a boy with long hair tucked behind his ears and a tattooed bird on his neck, a girl who surely can't be more than sixteen, wearing a miniskirt and bra, who stands with her shoulders back, defiant, on the brink of tears. They are piled in front of them on the table. Two piles, full face and profile, like two decks waiting to be shuffled into one.

'In other words?' Daniela is stroking the cat as it sniffs the last traces of *foie gras* from her fingers.

'In other words, just about everyone's been called into play, from Stasi to the Vatican. You name them, they had a hand in it. Turkish fascists, the Mafia, Freemasons. Walt Disney.'

'And why her?'

'Her father worked in the Vatican. In administration, nothing special, I don't think. I mean, he wasn't a priest or anything. Well, obviously, if he had a daughter.' He's trying to remember what Martin told him, but already Daniela isn't listening.

'No frames,' she says.

'What?'

'I want them bare. Unadorned.'

'We could use drawing pins. Or clip frames. I've got some of those left over somewhere.'

She's deaf to his teasing. 'Or – no, I've got it. Totally, utterly elaborate, ormolu, curlicues, as if they were heads of state.' She nods with great vigour, then freezes, groans and clutches her head in both hands, cupped palms to cheeks, as the cat leaps off her lap. Andrew isn't sure if her impression of Munch's *Scream* is intentional. But Daniela would never imitate such a commodified image. 'Call me a taxi,' she gasps. 'I think I'm going to die.' One hand moves cautiously across, to cover her mouth, but to no effect. Before Andrew can do anything, she is vomiting onto the floor, white wine with lumps of phlegmy bread in it. She's making a spectacle of herself, he thinks, amused despite himself, how situationist.

He helps her stand, then walk, one step, another, finally lowering her onto the broken-down sofa-bed he's spent the past three hours keeping her away from, towards which she has glanced coquettishly a thousand times, between one full face, one profile and the next.

There are times this evening he's felt less the observer than the observed, as though these people, photographed almost thirty years before, criminals, outcasts, delinquents, responsible for who knows what illegal acts, whether petty or consequential he'll never know, were staring up at him; were judging him. He can't feel comfortable about this. With Daniela, though, he feels it's out of his hands. That's what makes her so valuable. The fact that she has no conscience, no sense of guilt. As though she really did believe there was nothing but context, nothing but spectacle, and no one was ever to blame.

She's slumped across the thin cotton bedspread he's used to cover the cushions, her mouth open, lightly snoring, her legs ungainly. She's got some sick on her cheek. If he had a camera he'd take a picture of her like this to show her, to see what she'd say. He supposes he'd better shift her onto her side in case she throws up again. He'd hate her to die like this, here, and at this time.

He kneels down to move her over but she's a dead weight. He can't get a purchase on her without standing up again. His own head has started to ache, a banging in the temple and the start of a throbbing stiffness at the back of his neck, on the left side, that has recently accompanied, even preceded, his hangovers. I must drink better wine, he tells himself, at least that. If I can't do anything about the quantity, I can at least do something about the quality of it. At once this feels like a good resolution, a gesture towards a healthier life. A new start. Here.

Trying to get back to his feet, he stumbles and finds himself on the floor beside the sofa-bed, giggling. 'I can't stand up,' he says, out loud, not once, but three times, enjoying the sound of his voice as though it belonged to another person, a wiser, more thoughtful person who might tell him something he doesn't already know. The last thing he feels before he goes to sleep, sprawled across the bare tiles, his aching neck slumped against the edge of the sofa, is Daniela's hand as it flops onto his shoulder and the cat settling tightly onto his lap.

The following morning, both of them ashamed in their own way, they fix the date of the show over coffee and cream-filled doughnuts brought from the bar. Andrew, it's decided, will clear out the room and arrange for the photographs they chose last night to be framed. They settle on simple wooden frames, flat, narrow, painted black, with plain grey mounts, no wider than a finger. The eyes will be covered by strips of crêpe ribbon, the kind once used for funeral armbands, cut down to size, identifiable as crêpe.

They are shy with each other, formal. Daniela doesn't seem to remember much of what was said and done the night before, which is fortunate for her self-esteem but also fortunate for Andrew, because her forgetfulness has awarded him an unexpected power. To his surprise, and relief, she says that she will pay for the catalogue. And posters. He agrees at once. He hasn't thought of posters. As she leaves the shop, she promises she'll send a journalist round a couple of days before the show begins. 'And we must have our photograph taken together,' she says, with a cautious smile.

ALEX **1985–2008**

Alex took to hanging around outside the bookshop. Sometimes he'd pick through the books on the table, his head down, never buying anything because that would have taken him into the shop and he didn't want to do that. Maybe later. He'd glance up occasionally, trying to see through the window, see what the man inside was doing. Most of the time he seemed to be reading, or staring at the wall. More than anything, thought Alex, he looked sad. When the man's head turned towards the street outside, Alex would look down immediately, take out whichever book was nearest to hand, thumb through it. He didn't want the man to see him; he was careful about that. He didn't want to be known, or recognized. He wondered if the photographs Michel had taken of him as he walked into the church that time had survived his death, and if they had, who owned them now. It was most likely to be the bookseller, he thought. From what the Birdman had said, Michel didn't seem the type who'd have had friends or tolerated much contact with his family either. He'd have one man at a time, assumed Alex, picturing himself as Michel despite what the Birdman had said. He *was* different, he knew that, but maybe not as different as the Birdman supposed. Alex had his dark side too. When he thought about the photographs Michel had taken, he saw his own darkness portrayed in them. That was what Michel had said, or something like it. Something about what he could see in the photographs being what counted. Alex envisaged himself as a dark angel, surrounded by light. Was that what Michel had seen in him? Was that what Bruno had seen?

One day, though, he became absorbed in a book about Caravaggio and didn't notice the bookseller walk out of the shop until it was too late.

'Caravaggio was a wonderful artist,' the man said, as Alex pushed the book back down into its slot. He nodded. He felt his cheeks flush hot. 'And quite a character as well. That's not the best book on him, though. If you're interested there's a better one inside.'

Alex shook his head. 'I've got to go,' he said. 'I'm meeting someone.' Why do I need to tell him what I'm doing? he thought. It isn't even true. He turned away, but the bookseller caught his arm.

'Take it.' He lifted the book from the rack and offered it to Alex.

Alex pulled back. 'I haven't got any money on me.'

The man smiled. 'I didn't think you had. Don't worry, no strings attached. Most of the books out here get stolen sooner or later, so I might as well intervene every now and again. It's good to see a book go to the right home.'

*

Alex stopped going to the shop after that, unnerved by what had happened without quite understanding why. Perhaps not unnerved so much as made uncomfortable, even guilty in a sense, as though he really had been about to steal the book. As though the man had understood he was being dishonest, as of course he was, but not in that way. He wasn't even sure the man had been trying to pick him up, although it had certainly felt like it. Maybe that was what had scared Alex, that he might have been available, even keen, if it hadn't been for Michel, for the photographs, for the whole fucking business, which Alex continued not to understand, and by which he continued to be enthralled. Because the bookseller wasn't bad. If they'd met some other way, he thought, who knows what he might have done?

Alex stayed with the Birdman until he finished his degree, switching to English and French for his final three years, then moved into a spare room of a flat belonging to a man he'd met at university, from Calabria, whose parents had bought him his own place, in San Lorenzo. They'd helped each other prepare for exams, but had never become close, which suited Alex. Everything he owned fitted into a rucksack and a couple of cardboard boxes. The Birdman called a taxi for him, helped him carry his stuff to the lift and from it. Alex had expected the Birdman to resent his leaving after so long, almost five years, but that wasn't the case. He seemed to be happy that Alex was settled somewhere else, proud of his initiative.

The Birdman helped him find his first job, through a friend who'd worked in a news agency supplying paparazzi photographs to foreign magazines. Alex stayed there for a while, filing photographs, dealing with foreign calls, writing articles based on stories he heard at the agency and, occasionally, selling them to teen magazines, until indiscretion lost him his job. He spent the next nine months providing commentaries to the photo sequences in porn magazines, stories about randy plumbers and housewives and *ménages à trois*, but rowed with the publisher over money, and stopped. He moved to London and worked in Iceland for a few months, stacking cardboard boxes in sub-zero temperatures, before meeting Roger, the editorial assistant of a building-materials trade magazine, in a pub in Camden. Roger slept with him, fell in love with him, invited him to share a one-bedroomed flat in Stoke Newington, and found him, through contacts, enough translation work to survive. He wasn't much older than Alex, which was a new experience for Alex, and almost as poor, but he treated Alex with awed, anxious fascination, as though he couldn't believe his luck. They worked out together in the local sports centre, walked from one end of East London to the other. Roger was an amateur psychogeographer, a connoisseur of hidden corners and mysterious fluxes, although he preferred to define himself as a topophile. 'It's all held together by love,' he liked to say. He taught Alex everything he thought and knew, standing on canal banks on windswept marshes and in the smoky saloons of pubs, his hands shaping places

out of air. He was bullet-headed, with an over-sensitive mouth, and a tendency to put on weight. Alex had never met anyone like him. He had ambitions to become a writer and the two of them would share his Amstrad, Alex by day, Roger by night. Alex found himself smiling for nothing, alone in the flat, his eyes on a pullover Roger had thrown on the sofa, a mug with an inch of cold coffee inside it that he hadn't had time to finish that morning before going to work. He wondered if he might also be in love.

When Roger started to lose weight, they both knew what it meant. Each time they went to a disco or gay pub, people were handing out condoms, collecting money in buckets for research, for hospices. People were dying around them, yet they'd felt safe, they'd been faithful to each other. They were tested: Roger was positive, Alex negative. It took Roger six months to die, of pneumonia finally after the last few weeks in which he had seemed to be running with a strange eagerness towards death, more exhausted by anger than by the illness, days spent in hospital and out of it, Alex not understanding, lost, in corridors, learning awful new words he would later do his best to forget, and would never forget.

And then, as if a wet cloth had wiped them from a board, four years of health and half a year of illness were cancelled out. Roger's belongings were borne away by a furious man who, horribly, resembled Roger and was his older brother. Their world was stripped bare, the bedding, the Amstrad, books, CDs they had bought together, Alex unresisting, without the strength left to fight. And Alex – negative despite himself – was homeless, single. He had never known what loss meant before that. To have everything taken from him, Roger's effortless, illuminating smile, their tramping together in mud-heavy boots across acres of damp ground until they were both too tired to talk, the laughter when Alex didn't understand a word and Roger would mime it, each charade an ulterior truth, a tighter bond. All of that gone, and with it, as a consequence of it, the will to search out work, which Roger had done for him, to find somewhere new to live, where he would be alone, and the friends he had made with Roger who no longer seemed to be friends in quite the same way, on whose floors he slept, or didn't sleep, until, with embarrassed determination, he was asked to leave. One night, hungry and drunk, with all he had left in an army rucksack he'd bought from Lawrence Corner one rainy afternoon with Roger, for a holiday they had never had the time or the money to take, he went to Victoria station and spent his last money on a train ticket to Rome.

The Birdman took him in a second time, helped him get back on his feet, listened to tales of Roger, rolled joints. He called him Alessandro, then Sandro, and this was no longer a source of irritation but of comfort; it made him feel more at home. After a month or so of being cosseted, sleeping in his own small room, which seemed to have been kept for him, although surely that couldn't have been the case, Sandro was ready to move on, and the Birdman was ready to point him to people who might give him a chance. Through one of the Birdman's contacts at Cinecittà, a midget who stood in for children in adult comedies, Sandro found himself working in the offices of a film distribution company near the station, using his French and English, the computer skills he'd acquired in London. He found a room in a flat with two language teachers from the university, both women, one Scottish, one German. He began to learn German, to distract himself. He dabbled in the film world, in distribution, in editing; he appeared in a couple of films, a walk-on and then a speaking part. Sometimes he would wake up with a sense of defeat so strong, so all-encompassing, he would lie there, winded, trying to remember what he had dreamed. Roger, sometimes Bruno, sometimes the two of them bloodily merged into one.

He slept around a lot, half wanting to die as either of them had done, undone by the arbitrary violence of disease or of others, of men like him, with faces transformed into weapons; bearers, in one way or another, of his death. Then these feelings passed, but he didn't fall in love. He didn't feel it was possible. He stayed in touch with the Birdman, helping him out when his midget friend, the Cinecittà contact, was murdered by a much younger man, not much more than a boy, his protégé. Around then he started to write, with the Birdman's encouragement, not just articles and pieces for porn magazines as he'd done before, but stories. A long story, based on the midget's death but with Bruno constantly in his mind as he wrote, was published by a smallish press in Rome and had a brief *succès de scandale*, but nothing much came of it, a handful of contacts, some sexual, some not.

Throughout these years, when he found himself in the centre, he would take a detour and stand for a moment, or longer, outside Andrew's shop. Andrew was growing older, as he was, but what struck Sandro was a weariness in the bookseller that didn't seem caused by age so much as trouble, the accumulation of trouble.

One night, Sandro had an upsetting dream, in which the figure of Andrew was folded into that of Roger, both of the men, enraged, accusing him of having failed them; a dream from which he woke crying out, crying out to be left alone. He splashed his face with water, shivering despite the warmth of the night air, went back to bed, but couldn't sleep. For some reason he didn't understand, because nothing he remembered of his dream had resembled it, he couldn't remove from his mind the image of Bruno strapped to his chair, legs spread, silenced by duct tape. He poured himself a glass of whisky and turned on the TV. Preachers, hot lines, a film with Bette Davis he'd never seen, which, despite himself, he watched to the end. Finally, as the room grew light, he sat down at his desk and started his article, but all he could think of was the solitary figure of Andrew, sitting behind his table in the empty bookshop. He didn't go back after that.

*

Ten years later he's sitting in a bar, thumbing through that day's *Repubblica*. He's finished his coffee and is about to leave, but his eye falls on a short piece on the Rome events page describing an exhibition. Beside a group of mug shots and the word, in block capitals, in English, EXPOSURE, there is a photograph of Andrew, older but instantly recognizable, and the art critic Daniela dell'Orto. They are standing outside the shop, side by side, their faces as frozen and formal as those in the mug shots beside them. The piece describes the exhibition as a 'phenomenological anthology', as much a work of art as the paintings of the German *Neue Sachlichkeit* movement. Dell'Orto is quoted as saying that 'These faces lose their primary value as the subject-object of the crime and assume a purely iconographic value, shaking off the dead weight of illegality and liberating themselves as pure aesthetic, codified within the contemporary art matrix defined by Warhol and Nam June Paik.' The article says that the exhibition opens in three days' time.

'Oh, Christ,' says Sandro.

The girl has been thinking about her best friend, Paola, how the last time they spoke, the day before it happened, she'd said that Paola was being stupid about some boy she'd met and Paola had said it was because she was jealous. She's been asking herself if this is true and now that she's come round to agreeing with Paola, because it is true, Paola was right, and, ashamed of herself for not having seen that at once, she can't stop feeling that the only way to put everything right is to speak to Paola again, and to apologize. The fact that she can't do this, can't just say she's sorry, is the worst thing of all, worse than not seeing her parents for however many days she's been here – five, is it now? six? – worse than not knowing how much longer she'll be kept here, worse even than not knowing what they'll do to her in the end. It strikes her that maybe if she can tell the big man this, that the worst thing is Paola's not knowing how sorry she is for being stupid, if she can make him realize how important it is to her to put things right with Paola, he might let her go. Paola has been her best friend for as long as she can remember, since the nuns' school, and they've never really argued. And now she'll be wondering where I am, she'll think I'm still angry with her and I'm not, I've forgiven her and I want to tell her that. If she could only talk to the big man, maybe he'd understand. But he hasn't come back, not since that time – she's seen no one but the woman, who still comes with the food, and takes the tray away after she's picked at whatever's on the plate. She's losing weight already. She's taken to sitting on the bed without moving for hours at a time, twisting a corner of her shirt in her hands until it won't straighten out again, however hard she irons it with her palm. She wonders if she's beginning to smell. She must be, she thinks, sniffing at her armpit. She hasn't had a proper wash since they brought her here. She's afraid to take her clothes off in case someone comes in and, anyway, she's got nothing clean to put on. And then, when she least expects it, the door opens and it isn't the big man coming back to talk to her, but the man who first pulled her into the car. And he grabs her again, by the arm, and drags her, kicking and screaming, out of the room.

2008

ANDREW AND SANDRO

Much later, when Andrew tries to make sense of it all, he will ask himself what happened first. He will try to reorder his scattered memories, assemble them as a whole. Because the qualities they share most are those of incompleteness, inauthenticity, as if they have been borrowed randomly from a film, or several films, whose styles jar. Sometimes it seems to him that he wasn't even there, that someone else stood in for him while he watched from behind a sheet of glass. And then he will find himself trembling and pushing away his memories with a sense of having been assaulted in some deep part of himself that nothing else has ever touched. 'They fucked me over' is how he puts it to himself. 'They fucked me over and left me for dead.'

It starts in the shop, two days before the exhibition is due to open. Andrew is waiting for the catalogues to be delivered from the printers. He has cut out the article from this morning's newspaper, photocopied it and Sellotaped it to the window beside a poster-sized version of the catalogue cover. Seeing the poster, with the photographs he and

Daniela have picked out now framed in black, the title – **EXPOSURE** – in white sans serif characters across the middle, the times and dates and address of the shop in smaller lettering across the bottom, his anxiety returns. The poster has made it all seem real, inescapable as it hasn't been up to this point. He has to go through with it now. And for what? He has worked out that, assuming he sells every single catalogue, which isn't likely, he will make enough money to forestall the closing of the shop for a matter of weeks, if that. He will struggle through the summer, a few extra sales of second-hand English paperbacks to passing tourists, and that will be it. He will sell the photographs, of course, if anyone wants to buy them, although Daniela has come up with some insane idea of establishing a sort of criminal archive, with these photographs at its heart, a Dadaist parallel to the database the police must have, except that these photographs will remain for ever unnamed, exemplary. He hopes she will already have forgotten this idea. In the meantime, he will have to fix prices for them all and produce a list, just in case. Everything has its buyer.

Right now, though, just after ten o'clock, he is worrying that his unease will only get worse when the catalogues eventually arrive. They're due this morning, two hundred copies to start with, fifty-six pages, glossy fold-out covers; he supposes that sooner or later he'll also have to pay the printers, whatever promises Daniela may have made that she'll handle it. Thank God it's in black and white. Colour would have trebled the cost. As agreed, there's nothing from Martin in it, which is probably for the best. Daniela's name-dropping, impenetrable text sits blissfully at the front, and will never, he imagines, be read by anyone other than her and a handful of her students, who rightly think it will serve their purpose to quote her own words to her in conversation. His own transliteration into English of the text, in the fond, vain hope that the catalogue will travel beyond national borders, has been printed in a smaller font and relegated to the last two pages. His name's tagged on at the end, in even tinier letters; he isn't proud of it.

Andrew is wondering what it will be like to hold a copy in his hand, whether it will make him feel better or feed his unrest, when the shop door opens and a man walks in. He's a few years younger than Andrew, good-looking in a tousled, slightly unshaven way, a type Andrew's always found attractive and, somehow, in this case, familiar. He feels as though he might have been introduced to the man at a party and then been separated from him, against his will, by circumstance. All thoughts of the catalogue disappear. Andrew smiles and steps forward. He's about to say something, ask if he can help in some way, when the door swings open again behind the man and a teenager pushing a trolley with two brown boxes on it comes in. The man steps aside to make room. Andrew signs for the boxes and waits until the boy has gone before sliding a knife beneath the tape and turning back the flaps of the one on top.

'You're the first person to see this,' he says, holding out

a copy of the catalogue. The man shakes his head – oddly, thinks Andrew – then, as if he's reconsidered, takes the catalogue from him and weighs it in his hands. He thumbs through the first few pages before giving it back.

'You don't know me,' he replies, to Andrew's surprise, in English. His accent is London, tinged with Italian, or vice versa.

'Are you sure of that? I was thinking perhaps I do,' says Andrew, standing with the catalogue, now closed, in his hand. This isn't just flirtation, however it might feel. He's seen this man before.

'I know where these photographs came from,' the man says, brushing Andrew's words aside.

'What?'

'I think you should call this show off,' the man says, impatient, although Andrew isn't sure who with. He's conscious of standing there, still holding the catalogue, not knowing what to say or think or do. Is this really how it happened, he will ask himself later, this suddenly? 'It might be dangerous for you to carry on with it.'

'Call it off? Dangerous?' Andrew is aware of slowing down, of behaving as if in shock. This awareness may be, he reasons, a sign of shock in itself. He is thinking about what the man is saying, but also about his English, how the man used the expression 'call it off' and the unlikelihood of that in someone who hasn't grown up in England. He is thinking that his face *is* familiar and that he's being wakened in some way he can't quite grasp by the presence of this man, whose name he doesn't know, but who must know him, and who seems, for reasons he doesn't understand, to care about what happens to him.

'I sold these photographs to someone called Michel.' The man's voice is low, his manner urgent. He is staring directly into Andrew's eyes, as if to convince him of the truth of what he's saying. Andrew wants to turn away. 'You know who I mean?'

Andrew nods. He can feel his heart beating in his chest.

'It was years ago,' says the man. 'I thought they'd disappeared for ever. I hoped they had.'

'I do know you,' says Andrew. 'I've seen you before.'

The man nods, more impatient than ever. 'That doesn't matter now. Is it too late to call it off?'

'Well, yes,' says Andrew. 'Absolutely.' But he doesn't mean it. He has never known more surely than now how much he would give to cancel the show. He hasn't slept properly for weeks, since the idea first came to him and he was foolhardy enough to speak about it with Daniela. Or was it the other way round? Had it been Daniela's idea, and he'd simply gone along with it? He can't remember. Since then, he's been in a sort of free fall and this is the first time he's felt able to act, to stop this madness. What he wants to say is, 'Yes, the game ends here, this minute. These meaningless, dangerous photographs will be taken from their frames and carried away from here, it doesn't matter how or where, and destroyed, wiped out, along with the catalogues and the posters and the whole bloody show.' But he can't find the words for this: it's all too new. 'Who are you?' he insists.

This is the way he remembers it. But at some point another man has come into the shop, an older, smartly dressed man in a grey suit, green and grey striped tie, an unnecessary raincoat draped over one arm. And this second man is holding out a copy of today's *Repubblica*, opened to the page, and asking him about the exhibition, if this is where it is going to be held, tapping the piece with his finger. But Andrew isn't listening. He's too taken up by Sandro, for this is the younger man's name, trying with all his mental strength to locate him. He *knows* he knows him, but from where? From when? He is barely aware of the smart man in the suit, who wanders round the shelves, taking out first one book and then another, glancing inside them, putting them back with care. Marking time. Normally Andrew would ask if he could help, direct the man to whatever he might be looking for, but Sandro is telling him, still in English, to close the shop so that they can talk, it's important that they talk, touching his arm as he does so, drawing him towards the door. In his memory, Andrew will see the three of them, as if from above, as they move around the shop, the way bees are portrayed as they dance, or the feet of waltzing couples, a choreography with a meaning that's beyond them all.

Eventually the man says he's from the Ministry of Fine Arts, from the government. He's courteous, congratulates Andrew on his range of books, some of them rare, highly collectable. He's holding a copy of Pellico's *Le Mie Prigioni*, not quite a first edition but in decent condition. Its value is minimal, but the man seems not to know this. Andrew expects him to ask how much he wants for it but, instead, the man opens it up and points to the bookplate inside. 'This comes from a public-library collection,' he says. He has a wart like a plump pink stud on the tip of his tongue, Andrew notices, and a smaller growth beside his nose, above the flare of his left nostril.

Andrew takes it from him. 'Many books of a certain age do, as you'll know yourself. Public libraries are being closed everywhere.'

The man from the ministry isn't interested in this. 'I can't see any sign of the exhibition. I thought this was the address.'

'It isn't in the shop.' Andrew gestures towards the staircase behind the man. 'The exhibition space is upstairs.'

The man takes a step towards the staircase. Sandro tugs at Andrew's sleeve, shaking his head.

'I'm afraid we're still putting it together,' says Andrew, blocking the man's way.

'We were notified of this event?' the man says.

'I'm sorry?'

'It's customary to notify the ministry of every public exhibition. If only to obtain the necessary permits. We have a specific office for that sort of thing.'

'That's been dealt with by the curator of the exhibition,' says Andrew. 'Daniela dell'Orto,' he adds, hoping her name will produce a more favourable reaction, knowing full well that Daniela has had no contact what-soever with the Ministry of Fine Arts or any other official body.

'I have no record of it,' the man says, in an odd, dis-tracted way, as if he's reading his lines from a card. He doesn't seem to have heard of Daniela.

'It's never been necessary in the past,' says Andrew, aware at once that he has contradicted himself. The man stands firm, waiting for Andrew to move, but Andrew doesn't budge; he's conscious his knees are trembling. He looks to Sandro for support, but Sandro is taking a half-dozen copies of the catalogue from the box and sliding them into a plastic bag. Before Andrew can stop him, he twirls his finger in the air to indicate they'll be in touch, gives him an unexpected grin and leaves the shop with the catalogues.

The man from the ministry spins on his heels and walks to the door, taking his mobile phone from his pocket, saying no more than a word or two before snapping it shut and sliding it back into his pocket. Andrew slumps into his usual chair, behind the counter, resisting the urge to hold his head in his hands. Moments later, three men enter the shop. The man from the ministry nods to them to stand in the corner, then walks across to where Andrew is sitting, positioning himself between the counter and the staircase.

'Perhaps we can take a look at the exhibition now,' he says. His tone has acquired a new authority, tinged with irritation. He's been messed about enough.

'I can't leave the shop unattended.' Even to Andrew, this sounds feeble. *He* sounds feeble.

'My colleagues will make sure your stock is safe.'

Andrew looks at the colleagues, three roughly shaven bruisers in jeans and black leather jackets, plainclothes policemen, he imagines. They are glancing around them, at the walls, the cluttered shelves of books, with expressions that mingle boredom and contempt. One is tapping a short stick in his free hand. Standing like this, shoulder to shoulder, they remind him of riot police.

'I'm sorry, but I really can't leave the shop unattended. I'd rather call someone to stand in for me for a moment.'

'I assure you that won't be necessary.' The man takes Andrew by the elbow and leads him, with gentle insistence, to the bottom of the staircase. 'I haven't got all day,' he adds, 'but this needn't take long.'

Andrew leads him up the stairs, turning at the last moment to see one of the policemen walk across to the counter. 'What does he want? What's he looking for?' he says to the man, twisting round, but by this time it's too late: they are almost in the room above the shop. The man's hand is on his back; he is close enough to Andrew for Andrew to feel the warmth of him through his shirt, the man's breath, pastry-scented, milk-scented, in his face as he turns to protest. The man is holding him firmly above the elbow now, as they stand together in the gallery, or what passes for a gallery, the room still untidy, the sofa-bed still open. Andrew slept here last night – he couldn't face going home alone. The cat wakes up, uncurls from the pillow, lets out a plaintive wail for food.

'So this is your exhibition,' the man says, his voice neutral. He lets go of Andrew and crosses the room to the furthest wall, pushing a tray with two empty coffee cups to one side with his foot, his folded raincoat still hanging over one arm. He's wearing what used to be called penny loafers, Andrew notices, oxblood leather, both still containing their original pennies; what a curious fashion that was – he hasn't seen a pair like this for years. The shoes are highly polished, the man's suit perfectly cut. Now that Andrew can see him properly, from a certain distance, he doesn't look the kind of petty bureaucrat the ministry would send for a job like this. Not to speak of the bully boys downstairs. Why didn't he listen to Martin? Maybe if Sandro had come round earlier, there would have been time to dismantle everything. And where is Sandro now? He realizes how scared he is, and how much he needs help.

Turning his back to the man, he takes his phone out of his pocket and opens the address book. He could call Daniela, but he senses she'd be useless. What is happening has nothing to do with her. He wants Martin here for this.

'Do you have permission to use these photographs?'

'Permission?' Andrew flips the phone shut.

The man who claims to be from the ministry swings around to face him, visibly annoyed. 'Permission,' he repeats. 'These photographs are state property. You do understand that, I hope? That these photographs do not belong to you?' He continues to glance at the exhibits in a hurried, yet concentrated way, moving from group to group around the room. He seems to be searching for something specific. Andrew flips open the phone a second time, but the man steps sharply across and takes his wrist. 'I'd prefer you not to make any calls just now,' he says.

'I don't understand.'

'Is everything here?'

'What do you mean?'

'The photographs,' the man snaps. 'Are all the photographs here?'

'All which photographs?'

The man leans over until his face is inches from Andrew's. Andrew, filled with disgust and – yes, he'll admit this – fear, wants to back away, but doesn't dare, doesn't know what the man might do.

'I don't think you realize the gravity of what you've done here.' The man speaks slowly, each word enunciated clearly, with increasingly evident annoyance. To avoid his eyes, Andrew focuses on the small growth on his cheek. It has a dark point at its tip, like a pupil; it's as if it were watching him. 'You have no right to possess or use these photographs,' the man continues. 'No right at all. And now you will answer my question. Are there any more photographs like this somewhere else or is everything here?'

Andrew nods. This isn't a lie, he thinks wildly, everything *like this* is here; the other photographs aren't *like this* at all. That's why Daniela didn't want them. These are the ones she wanted, these staring, truculent, exhausted faces, no longer in control of their destinies. The other photographs, the ones of the crime scenes, of shoot-outs and TVs stacked like boxes, of armed, masked men rushing from banks, the one of the girl in the car, are stashed away in a cardboard box he's taken back to his flat. He wishes to God he'd thrown them away as soon as he'd found them. He wishes he'd never seen the photographs. For a second, he curses Michel, who has thrust these dark, accusing faces into his life and left them here for him to deal with. From downstairs, he can hear scraping, the sound of objects being moved. 'What's going on?'

Ignoring him, the man calls for one of his bully boys, who runs up into the room, slapping dust from his sleeves. 'Take these photographs down,' the man says, waving his hand around the walls. The cat stands up and stretches, then walks into the corner of the room, turning to sit and watch whatever else will happen, as if it might later be called to account.

'You can't do that,' protests Andrew, but the man no longer seems to be aware of him. He is standing in the centre of the room, examining his cuticles, impassive, with an air of getting on with a job that needs to be done but offers no pleasure, no satisfaction. 'You don't understand. We're supposed to be opening on Friday.' Andrew's voice trails away, ignored. He watches the policeman lift the first few frames from their hooks and stack them against the skirting, holding them upright with his booted foot as he stretches for more. 'We've had all the catalogues printed.'

'Catalogues?' The man is suddenly alert. 'What catalogues? Where are they?'

'Downstairs.' Andrew's said too much already. He must learn to keep his mouth shut. He must learn to think twice before speaking. Once more, before he can decide what to do, the man takes his arm.

'Show me,' he says.

ANDREW

In the shop Andrew sees, to his dismay, that most of the books have been removed from an entire wall of shelves and piled haphazardly on the floor. Another police-man – if that's what he is, what any of them is – has arrived with boxes, into which he is stuffing the unshelved stock. They've already started on a second wall, lifting the volumes out in bundles, in horizontal stacks, as if they were glued together or nothing but spines attached to hardboard, those fake panels bought by people who don't read books but want the look of culture books lend to a room.

'You'll damage them like that,' he says. 'They're fragile.' But no one is listening.

This new man is younger than the others, stocky but slim-waisted and, unlike the others, blond; Andrew won-ders if he's from the north or if he's one of those fair-haired blue-eyed Sicilians, the distant product of Norman genes. He's startled to find himself distracted by this, distracted by desire at such a moment. The man from the ministry – although Andrew no longer believes this to be true and is thinking, Secret police, Special Branch, whatever they're called – looks round the room as if searching for a place to put down his raincoat.

'Those are the catalogues?' he says, pointing to the two boxes by the door. Not waiting for Andrew to answer, he tells one of the men to check. The blond one leaves what he's doing and walks across, while his boss picks up the copy of *Le Mie Prigioni* that he left on the counter before they went upstairs, opening it at the bookplate. And it is only now that Andrew sees his laptop has been taken from the counter, and everything else along with it, his note-book, his Rolodex, his copy of today's *Repubblica*, open at the page about the exhibition. And that's not all. The wooden drawer he uses to store his address book, his accounts book, his contacts list, invoices, scraps of paper, orders he hasn't dealt with, bills, has been pulled out of its place and is lying on its side beneath the table, emp-tied. There's violence in the way it's been tugged from its runners and hurled to the floor, an unnecessary violence that appals him. 'This is complete madness,' he says.

'Where did you get this book?'

'What?' He's suddenly incensed to see his stock man-handled like this. For the first time since this petty bureaucrat, who is anything but a petty bureaucrat, began to speak to him, as though he has finally grasped that he is being violated, Andrew feels entirely in the right. 'I don't know. How should I know? Good God, I've had some of this stock for decades.'

'This material is stolen,' the man says. The young policeman brings him a copy of the catalogue, returns to his work. The man flicks through it, first one way, then the other. He's after something, that's obvious, but doesn't find it.

'Don't talk nonsense.' It isn't *material*, Andrew wants to say, fixated by now on the man's use of this word, as though the violation he's being forced to undergo were no more than a matter of language. It's a book, and not worth stealing either. If it's worth twenty euros he'd be surprised. The man is ignorant, when it comes to books at least.

'We shall need to examine everything here.'

'Look, just what the hell is going on?' Andrew's voice is raised. 'You have absolutely no right to do this.' Abruptly, he pushes his way to the front of the shop, tripping over piles of books, stumbling against the boxes that contain the catalogues, banging his shoulder against an empty shelf. Before he can reach the door, one of the policemen bars his way.

'You're making this very difficult for yourself,' the man tells him, in an unexpectedly reasonable way, as if to say enough is enough, despite all this being Andrew's fault. Outside the shop a group of German tourists, sensible flat shoes and backpacks, has halted and a grey-haired woman in a voluminous skirt is peering short-sightedly in. When she sees the men, she pulls back hurriedly, muttering words of warning, and the group moves on. Andrew, who is close enough to reach out and touch the woman, this stranger who unexpectedly seems to be offering him a means of escape, finds himself being restrained. He struggles to free his arms, twisting in the policeman's grip, but to no effect, as though he isn't really trying at all. As though he's complicit in what's happening, this assault on his business, his freedom. 'You can't just come in here and strip my shop,' he cries, directing his voice as much towards the square outside as to the men who have entered his personal space, his privacy, to trample all over it. But no one, inside or out, appears to be listening. He is talking to no one. Even the policeman holding his arms has let him go and is back to his task of requisition. Andrew stands by and watches him take a large brown volume, a bound collection of newspapers from between the wars, forcing it into a box too small for it. 'You need a warrant to do this. Show me your warrant.' He can hear the hysteria in his voice, hear its weakness. He's enraged with himself for being weak.

'Where did the material for the exhibition come from?' the man asks, in a quiet, cajoling voice. 'We need to know.' He nods and the nearest policeman stands up and holds his arms from behind in a loose grip that, none the less, immobilizes Andrew. Once more, the man pushes his face into Andrew's, too close for Andrew to focus properly. *Material*, he's thinking. One more time and he'll scream. Everything is material. The policeman holding his arms is lifting them in such as a way as to tilt his upper body towards the man. They might be about to kiss. 'We need to know where they are,' the man insists, in a voice so low even Andrew hardly catches the words. For a second, the wart on his tongue can be seen. 'All of them. Every single one of them.'

The young policeman comes over with some magazines

he has found. They're old gay porn magazines, *Doppio-senso* mostly, though some are German, or from the States; the kind people used to buy before the Internet destroyed the market. Andrew recognizes them at once. He has a stock for the dozen or so customers who still prefer their pornography printed, older men, priests, who slide these magazines into their briefcases and, as a rule, buy something else before leaving, some large, obtrusive volume that provides an alibi or appeases the conscience. The magazines are wrapped in cellophane; this isn't to stop potential customers thumbing through them, Andrew's not mean like that, but because they're acquiring value as the years pass, and he needs to protect them. They're becoming kitsch, these improbable sequences of young men meeting in bars and going back to barely furnished rooms – time and time again, the same barely furnished rooms, the same geometric wallpapers and posters of bullfights and cushions the photographer's aunt had crocheted decades before – going back to these rooms to fuck each other, one on one, until they're surprised by bell-hops or window cleaners only too keen to join in. There's something retro about their pallid, undeveloped bodies and hungry eyes as they stare at the wall, bent over each other like coupling dogs. The magazines weren't hidden. There isn't any need to conceal them, other than taste perhaps, although Andrew isn't concerned about that. He keeps them on a low shelf near the counter, not out of shame or fear, not even to protect the innocent, but because they're the stock most likely to be stolen.

'What are these?' the man says.

Andrew laughs. 'I don't believe this.'

'This looks like paedophile pornography to me.' He flicks through the pile of magazines and pulls one out, shows Andrew the cover. A young man, stark naked apart from a jauntily angled sailor's cap and the tattooed head of a wolf on his forearm, his left hand, nails bitten, cupping his dick and balls.

'Don't be ridiculous. He's in his twenties.'

'You seem to be something of an expert.'

'I assure you there's nothing illegal about this *material*.' Andrew chooses the word with care, but also with irony, so that he'll be understood and, at the same time, show his contempt for the man. But, of course, the man won't understand. And Andrew's scared, more scared by the minute. He's being stitched up. 'It used to be on sale on every bloody newsstand in Italy.'

There is a scraping noise as two of the plainclothes policemen try to shift one of the now empty bookcases away from the wall. As if for the first time, as if he has been waiting for his attention to be drawn to the full horror of what has been done, Andrew looks around his shop. The floor is covered with books in untidy stacks. Boxes, half filled, stand open. Others are closed and sealed with tape, piled up beside the door. The air is choked with dust. Behind the bookcase, which is hanging half broken from the wall, its shelves cock-eyed, old newspapers appear to have been glued to the wall. Andrew has no idea why. It has never occurred to him to look behind the shelves; they remain as he found them, almost thirty years ago, when he first began to work for Joost. Some of the books on them were here when he arrived; he's never actually taken stock, never found the time to do more than make a rough count and promise himself, next year; he'll make a complete list next year. He hasn't even had the shelves painted, except once, along the outer edge. Anything more would have meant removing the books, a task he'd always imagined would take days. Yet now, in less than an hour, his entire shop has been dismantled, packed up and made ready to be carted off.

'We'll be able to talk more comfortably in my office,' the man says, his tone less authoritative than coaxing, as if Andrew had the option to refuse.

But Andrew knows this can't be true. 'You're taking me away with you?'

The man nods, brushes some cobwebs from his raincoat. 'Naturally, until we've had a chance to examine what we've found here.'

'I don't understand,' Andrew says, again.

'I'm sorry? What exactly is it that you don't understand, Caruso?' The man's tone is derisive. It is the first time he has addressed Andrew by name, and he has used his surname alone, without so much as a *Signore*, or the *Dottore* to which Andrew, though he would die sooner than use it, is entitled as a university graduate; without the slightest gesture of courtesy. That distance, finally, has been established. They are no longer equal. Andrew would retaliate, but he still has no idea what the man is called. That's odd, he thinks. He didn't introduce himself. He is about to ask his name when the man continues: 'We have found ample evidence of stolen goods, pornography, state material obtained through illegitimate procedures. Furthermore, you have refused to cooperate with our enquiries.'

'Through what?' And now Andrew, despite himself, wants to laugh. 'Obtained through what?'

The man raises his chin and glances towards the stairs. 'You don't expect to get away with this, surely. Those photographs upstairs belong to the police.'

As if on cue, the policeman responsible for dismantling the exhibition comes down with a box in his arms. Andrew can hear the sound of glass against glass as he stumbles on the final step, which is deeper than the rest; some of the frames are broken. Perhaps he can sue. 'But what have the police got to do with it?' he says. 'You're from the ministry. You said you were from the Ministry of Fine Arts. What does all this have to do with you? I thought you were here because I didn't have a permit.'

Another small crowd has gathered outside the shop; not tourists this time, but two of the waiters from the bar, the owner of the *baccalà* place across the square, a couple of older women who live nearby and call on Andrew to carry their bottled water upstairs for them. Hovering at the back of the group is Sandro. Andrew casts him a startled, desperate glance. Immediately, Sandro shakes his head, to warn him, and looks away.

'I need to make a phone call,' says Andrew.

'There will be time for that later.'

'Am I being arrested?'

The man pulls a face, as if offended by the vulgarity of the word. He shakes out his raincoat and slips it, finally, over his shoulders, then adjusts his shirt cuffs so that they are equally visible at each sleeve. He is wearing cuff-links, Andrew notices, gold and jet, with the Freemasons' square and compasses on them. 'Of course not,' the man says, adding, after a moment's pause: 'I hope that won't be necessary.'

'You mean I needn't come with you?'

'That, alas, would make it necessary.'

'But what about the shop?'

'I promise you everything will be locked up when my colleagues leave. Locked up and sealed.'

'You mean I have to leave my shop open like this for them to finish what they're doing?' Sealed. Like a crime scene. They'll be taking my photograph next, Andrew thinks. I've become an exhibit in my own show. Except that there won't be any show. He wonders what Daniela will do when she finds out. She has friends in high places, or says she has. He hopes she'll make it hot for this smug bastard. For a moment, at the thought of Daniela's wrath, and revenge, he feels protected.

'Don't make this difficult for yourself, Caruso.' The man holds out his hand. 'I need the keys.'

For a second, Andrew can't remember where he left them. Normally he just throws them onto the counter beside the laptop, but everything has been swept into one of the boxes being stacked in the middle of the floor, ready to be taken off and sifted through, he imagines, in search of God knows what. As he gazes round the chaos of his now unrecognizable shop, trying to concentrate on where the keys might be, he sees the youngest policeman tease away from the recently exposed wall a corner of the old brown newspaper that covers it and, with one swift gesture, tear it down. It peels off with surprising ease, in an almost rigid sheet that reaches to the floor. Beneath the paper, the wall has been printed with a stencilled flower design, faded in some parts, unexpectedly bright in others. All these years he's been surrounded by flowers, Andrew thinks, and never known. Against his will, he's delighted; he'd like to stay and help, to see what else has been hidden from him.

'I need your keys,' the man repeats.

Of course, he remembers, they're in the pocket of his leather jacket. It's where he left it this morning, not much more than an hour ago, though it's hard to credit all this has happened in so little time, time he would normally have spent selling the occasional book, doing the two Sudoku in his paper, wondering how long he should wait before lunch and what he'd have when he did, and whether he'd have a glass of wine to wash it down. It's hanging on a nail by the foot of the stairs; for some reason, it hasn't been touched. He points to the jacket. Then, when the man, caped in his raincoat like some bureaucratic superhero, has nodded permission, he walks over to fumble in the pockets. The first thing he finds is the business card with Martin's new mobile-phone number, the one he was given the night he learned about the girl. He holds it between his fingers, like a cardsharp, while he roots through the other pockets for the keys, then slips the jacket on, zipping it up to the neck. He doesn't know how long he'll be away. As they leave the shop, the man from the ministry leading the way through the bunched group of onlookers towards a dark grey car parked directly outside the bar, where no parking of any kind is permitted, Andrew manages to slip the card into Sandro's cupped and waiting hand. 'Call him,' he mouths.

ANDREW

Andrew expects the car to take him to the local police station, just round the corner, and wonders why a car is even necessary, unless it's to safeguard his reputation. For a second, as they hurry towards the vehicle, its smoke-dark windows catching the sun, he thinks the man might whip the raincoat from his shoulders with a bullfighter's flourish and fling it over Andrew's head to protect him from the curiosity of onlookers. But this doesn't happen.

Nobody talks as the car turns right onto Via Arenula and heads towards the river, then right again along the Lungotevere, taking the bus lane whenever it's free of cars. He's sitting in the back with the man from the ministry, with a driver and a second man beside him in the front. Riding shotgun, thinks Andrew. Watching out for Injuns. As the car speeds up, slows down, negotiates the lunch-time traffic, Andrew tries to breathe regularly, to calm down, to concentrate on his situation. He realizes that he is gripping his knees so hard his knuckles are white, and hopes the man hasn't noticed. He has always been prone to guilt, regardless of what he has done or failed to do; innocence has never offered him protection.

The car turns left, heading deep into a part of Rome he doesn't know that well, a district of lawyers' offices and expense-account restaurants for people who work in television, then suddenly swings right, left, right, until he's utterly lost, before gunning down a short slope as though the driver is afraid he's being followed, pulling up in an underground garage that must be as large as the building above it, already half filled with similarly official-looking cars of various dark hues. At a pinch, Andrew knows where he is, to the quarter at least, and where he isn't. He isn't, for example, in the Ministry of Fine Arts, or anywhere near it. Neither is he in a police station of any kind he's ever had the misfortune to see before today. Because he's been in police stations before this, once or twice. He knows what they feel like. And these cars aren't police cars.

'Here we are,' says the man, with an air of satisfaction as they come to a halt. He waits for the driver to open his door, indicating that Andrew should remain where he is until his own door is opened for him. Then the four cross the brightly lit garage together to a lift with stainless-steel doors, flanked by a small black panel with a single silver button bearing an upward arrow. The driver calls the lift and they stand in a loosely formed semi-circle, not talking, staring at the doors, waiting. They might be going to work, four colleagues who happen to drive up together and share the lift without speaking, exchanging no more than the nod of courtesy required.

For a handful of seconds, as the noise of the lift arriving

becomes perceptible, Andrew imagines himself turning round and walking off, as if he has left something in the car and needs to fetch it. He imagines himself striding up the ramp and out onto the street, where he will stop for a moment to get his bearings and then head left, then right, then left, towards the river, weaving between the cars double-parked at every crossroads until he is back where he belongs, in his bookshop, miraculously restored to order, the bookcases whole and standing against the walls, the volumes dusted and reorganized on their shelves. He has almost convinced himself this is possible when the lift doors open and the shotgun-rider, with a gloved hand in the middle of the back, nudges him gently inside.

Andrew doesn't see which button is pushed but judges, when the lift comes to a halt, that they're on the third or fourth floor. They have shuffled round, as people do in lifts, painstakingly avoiding one another's eyes, and now face the metal doors as they open onto a long window-less corridor. Andrew is lightly pushed out of the lift and taken into the first room on the left. It is empty apart from a wooden table, two chairs and a hat-stand. The man shrugs off his raincoat and hangs it on one of the pegs, then points to a small tray on the table. 'Put your personal belongings there,' he says, and watches as Andrew places his wallet, a handkerchief, some visiting cards and a used bus ticket on it. The man picks it up and leaves the room without speaking. Andrew waits to hear a key turn, but there is silence. He unzips his leather jacket and hangs it beside the raincoat.

It's a traditional hat-stand, beige wood bent into S-shaped curves, the kind you used to find in every office and even some homes. They had one in the hall of the flat he grew up in. His mother used to call it *the dead man*. 'Leave your things on the dead man,' she'd say, and it wasn't until Andrew was seven or eight that he learned she was simply translating from the Italian name for it. *L'uomo morto*. Sometimes, as a child, he'd rather wet the bed than cross the hall to the bathroom because that would mean passing within reach of the shadow of the dead man's arms as they stretched along the floor towards his feet.

The room has a small, letterbox-style window placed high on one of the walls, giving onto the type of internal roofless shaft buildings this size often have, intended to provide air, not light. The only light in the room comes from two fluorescent tubes set parallel at the centre of the ceiling, one or both of them faintly humming; the only decoration, apart from a large unframed mirror attached to the opposite wall, is a small wooden crucifix hanging above the door. It reminds Andrew of every institutional room he has ever known, as though they have all been condensed into this. School rooms, the room he waited in to be taught his catechism, the room in which he was told his father had died unexpectedly of heart failure, not by his mother, who was in the Dolomites at the time with a woman friend, but by a doctor, not much older than Andrew had been, embarrassed, inarticulate, inappropriately cute.

Most of all, it reminds him of the interview rooms in the labour exchange where he found himself working one summer during his time at St Andrews. He'd gone to stay with Sarah, his cousin in London. She shared a run-down flat over a chemist's in West End Road with Madeleine, the daughter of a famous model from the fifties, an aspiring model herself. Andrew slept on a child's mattress on Sarah's floor, surrounded by her T-shirts, tights, magazines, his feet hanging over the edge, his face against a slightly dirty, patchouli-scented pillowcase filled with his few spare clothes. Madeleine would come in most nights, weak with hunger after a day of eating salad leaves and drinking lemon juice, her mother's regime. She would sit cross-legged on the floor between Sarah's bed and the mattress in her underwear, bone-thin, bone-white, and talk about the food she'd resisted that day.

Andrew had signed on, unemployed, as soon as he'd arrived in London, and couldn't believe his hard luck when, three days later, he was offered a job at his own dole office, preparing other, more fortunate, people's claims. Each week he had to get ready long metal boxes of files, each file a dozen or more buff sheets of paper that represented an unemployed person, held together and attached to a cardboard rectangle by elastic and one of those metal tags threaded through a hole. It was hard to remember, sometimes, that they were people. This room is like the room they'd be taken to and questioned over their failure to find work, thinks Andrew now. Except for the crucifix and the mirror.

Andrew's seen enough TV series – he's hooked on *CSI*, *NCIS* – to know that mirrors on the walls of rooms like this are two-way; that, whichever side of them you're on, what you see is the same, reflected or directly, the same unwilling suspect. You see him as he sees himself, if he chooses to look, if he chooses not to twist away, to pretend. Otherwise it's like watching someone on *Big Brother*, knowing the person knows you're watching, knowing this must have its influence on what that person does, working this into your calculations exactly as the suspect does. Because whatever the mirror might be called the effect is not one way at all, but reciprocal. Already Andrew is behaving in a certain way, his face abruptly rigid, expressionless; he's tempted to turn his back to the wall in question, but resists the temptation because to turn one's back, surely, is to exhibit guilt. Ay, there's the rub, he thinks, the double rub. He doesn't know how to behave. He knows he's innocent, but he also knows, or thinks he knows, why he's here, which makes him an accomplice and gives him something to conceal. What would he do if he was really innocent, he wonders, because, whatever it is, that's exactly what he should be doing now. Would he be angrier than he is, more insistent on his rights, or would he be patient, assuming that everything would soon be sorted out?

He doesn't know. He's scared he might find himself swinging from one mood to the other, without any sense of what's most likely to convince them of his good character. In the dole office he was told to ask questions at random, to see if the claimants were lying, watch out for signs that might give them away as benefit cheats. He'd been sent on a half-day course on what to look for, averted eyes, the beads of sweat on the forehead, pens shaking in the hand, an inexplicable hesitation when asked, in the way he'd been trained to ask, if they'd exchanged their labour for money in the previous seven days. But how could he behave like that when he was one of them, despite being forced into a jacket and tie, dragged screaming – metaphorically at least – across the counter? How could he be obliged to betray his own kind, the lazy, the skiving, the unfortunate? He's always felt that way about authority, that to participate in it is to collaborate, to invite the contempt of those who refuse. He won't play along, he decides, whatever they do to him.

There's no ashtray on the table. It's part of the new international Puritanism, which sits so uneasily on Italian shoulders, however quickly they knuckle under for appearance's sake. That's probably where the man with the raincoat is right this minute, skulking on a fire escape with a Camel Light. Andrew hasn't smoked a cigarette for years, but he'd willingly smoke one now, one of the Nazionali he used to prefer. In recognition of the mirror, and to see what reaction it might produce, he reaches into his front jeans pocket as if to pull out a packet and is startled when his fingers encounter his mobile. He should have handed it over with the rest of his personal belongings. Cautiously, he extracts it, expecting the door to fly open at any moment. But no one appears, and a rapid glance at the screen tells him there's no signal. There wouldn't be, would there? he thinks. Perhaps the room, this floor, the entire building, is isolated somehow: there must be some stuff in the walls, some sort of insulation; he hasn't heard a sound not made by him, apart from the faint but constant buzz of the light, since he was brought here. It's odd how silence interferes with one's sense of time, he thinks, if that's what it is. Already he can't say how long he's been here. Ten minutes, half an hour – no, surely not that long. At least with his mobile he'll be able to keep track of time. Looking down, protecting it with his hand, he sees that it's just after two o'clock and that the battery is almost flat. He turns it off, slides it back into his pocket. For a moment he feels like a Boy Scout lost in the woods with only one match, two if he's lucky, although he never was a Boy Scout. His mother had wanted him to join, but he had dug his heels in, defended by his father, as anti-clerical as his mother was devout. Two o'clock means that he must have been here more than forty minutes, assuming the journey took fifteen, twenty minutes. But there's no way of knowing that either. However he looks at his situation he's faced by imponderables. He shifts in his chair, shrinking from the noise its feet make against the tiles, a noise that reminds him of the noise the cat makes when he opens her daily can of food.

He doesn't like animals. He always says animals are child-substitutes and a tie, as though his invariable life would lose some essential freedom if he were forced to think about feeding a cat or walking a dog or changing the shredded newspaper in a hamster's cage. No, he's joking when he says this; he's never considered a hamster. His mother was allergic to animals in a generic way and, for years, he supposed that he was too. When he realized he wasn't, by living with Sarah's Persian-tortoiseshell cross for six weeks, it gave him another opportunity to resent his mother. Now, moving the chair more carefully to stretch his legs, he's suddenly worried about the cat, which he has begun to consider *his* cat. Cats hate closed doors. He's had her around long enough to know that.

And thinking about her now – the last time he saw her was upstairs in the room, emptied of photographs, the walls stripped bare – he can't not wonder about the shop, the state it must be in. He's itching to take his mobile out of his pocket, to turn it on again and see how much time has passed since he last looked. But that's absurd. It can't be more than five minutes, ten at the most. He's worried they'll have locked the cat in, although he can't decide if that's better or worse than locking it out, returning it to its previous life on the street. He's not sure which he'd prefer, to be a prisoner or to be excluded. He'll demand to know what's happened to her when they come in. He glares at the mirror, as if to say, I'm ready for you now. And he's surprised to see himself.

He's become so used to the idea he's being watched he's forgotten that, whatever the mirror might conceal, it is still a mirror, will still reveal him. And here he is, his shoulders hunched, his legs sprawled out. He straightens up a little, shocked by how old he seems. Inside he's tight with anger and fear, however much he tries to control it, but what he sees in the mirror isn't so much an angry man as someone forlorn, abandoned, as though he's waiting for a bus that almost certainly will never come. Someone who's been trained to behave and has learned his lesson so well he thinks, when he thinks, that he's thinking for himself. But what happens if the bus does arrive? Because there is always that faint spark of hope. He smiles, then sneers, then smiles again, a cheeky, challenging smile, but he's too far away from the mirror – or his eyes aren't good enough – to see how much his face is changed by this. And what sort of changes would there be if he could see them? Because there is no one he can ask. He slumps forward, his head in his hands, as if to protect it from the eyes of the others.

ANDREW

The door opens and the man comes in, alone. Andrew starts at the sound of the latch drawing back, but otherwise makes an effort to show no sign of surprise. The last time he turned on his mobile phone it was half-past three, which means he's been sitting in the room for just over two hours, although he's had his eyes closed against the light and may even, despite himself, have slept for a moment or two. The phone beeped its little anguished beep, the battery almost exhausted, and he turned it off at once. I might not get another chance to see what time it is, he thought. Perhaps not even one more match.

The man pulls out the other chair and sits down, placing a clipboard in front of him, positioning it so that the edges are parallel with those of the table. He has taken off his jacket, but remains impeccable; he could even have changed his shirt. This one still has the creases from when it was ironed and folded, the way shirts are when they're new and wrapped in cellophane, when only the front and collar can be seen. Andrew glances down to check the cuff-links; they're the same as before, their square and compasses gleaming gold on the square of polished jet.

215

The breast pocket of the shirt has been monogrammed with the letters WA. W's unusual for an Italian. Walter? Wladimir, perhaps, though isn't it more usual to write it with a V? He can't remember. The A could be anything. He's on the point of asking the man to clear the mystery up, but the man speaks first.

'To begin with,' he says, 'I need your name and details.'

Andrew laughs, incredulous. 'I'm sorry,' he says. 'I'm not following this. You don't know who I am?'

The man uncaps a pen. 'It's purely a formality.'

Andrew puts his hands on the table, as if he's about to get to his feet, but thinks better of it. 'You trash my shop and drive me here with your goon squad, you leave me in a room alone for hours, then come in and ask me who I am? I'm sorry, I seem to be missing something.'

The man recaps his pen, takes the clipboard in his hand and stands up. 'We can do this whenever you're ready to cooperate. I'm in no hurry.'

He's out of the room before Andrew can call him back.

Andrew is thinking about the man who came into the shop this morning, who said his name was Sandro; about who he is, and what he might mean, and whether whatever he means will be good for him or not. He is thinking about the way he walked in, with that urgency. He didn't need to come round this morning, but he'd seen the paper; he had something that needed to be said. He had talked about danger, about the exhibition putting Andrew in danger, and these words are so reminiscent of comments

Martin has been making since he saw the photographs
that Andrew has an odd sense of being left out, as if he's
the last person to know something. This isn't remotely
true: Martin has been more than clear about what the
photographs might reveal. But this other man, this man
Andrew is still convinced he has met at some point in his
past, this Sandro who suddenly arrived from nowhere and
issued the same sort of warning, is something else. He'd
said he knew Michel, he'd sold the photographs to Michel,
which also produces a sense of exclusion. Andrew's always
been prone to this, this feeling that he's missing the main
event, whatever that might be. He's conscious of himself
as an outsider, and tries to take pride in it, but can't, not
always anyway. And there's the fact that he's attracted to
Sandro.

He closes his eyes and sees him again, through the lens
of desire, an inch or two shorter than Andrew, loosely
built, neither thin nor fat, his hair cut roughly, short round
the ears and neck, longer at the fringe, a cut that is slightly
too young for a man whose age Andrew would place at
ten years less than his own, the kind of hair that can be
chopped at in front of the bathroom mirror and pushed
into place, unlike Andrew's, which simply hangs; the kind
of hair Andrew has always wanted, still dark, just pep-
pered with grey. The face with one day's beard, the clothes
smart-casual, English-looking, shoes, not sneakers, he'd
noticed that at once, the desert boots Italian intellectuals
of the left used to wear and maybe still do away from the
capital; the kind Michel used to wear. The accent, that

charming, erotic mixture of Roman and Bethnal Green. The good, strong hands. The grey-green eyes, staring into Andrew's to persuade him of the truth of what he was saying. Gay? He hopes so. He hopes so with all his heart, because there was an air of possibility he hasn't felt for months – no, more than that. For years.

And now Andrew knows where he's seen him before. Not in the flesh, but in a photograph: walking into a church with the light of the street behind him, twenty-five years younger than he is now, but with the same fierce eyes, rough hair. Selling the pictures to Michel a week before he died.

The next time the man comes in Andrew's ready for him. Before he can even cross the room to the table, sit down, prepare his pen and clipboard, Andrew starts, his voice the sing-song voice of a child reciting his lesson.

'Andrew Caruso, born Rome, Italy, the twenty-fifth of September 1954, which makes me Libra. Father, Roman, of Sicilian origins. Mother, Scottish, of aristocratic origins. Only child. Educated in a variety of public and private institutions in Rome and Scotland. University graduate, for what it's worth, which is nothing. Practising atheist. Currently resident in Rome, Via Bartolomeo Bossi thirty-six, flat seven, rented. Proprietor of La Piccola Libreria in Piazza, a shop-cum-gallery selling first editions, antique and second-hand books, and putting on small exhibitions, bought from a Dutchman who now lives in Thailand, assuming he's living anywhere, and about to go bankrupt as a result of chronic lack of trade. Single, one recently acquired cat. Which reminds me, what have your colleagues done with her?'

He knows he's being cheeky, the way he used to be at school, and how foolish this sort of behaviour is, how little good it does him. Now, as then, it's unappreciated; all it does is slow the procedure down. But he can't prevent himself: it's his way of showing he's both innocent and knowing, both guileless and up to their every trick.

The man sits opposite Andrew again. 'You first came to our attention some years ago, Signor Caruso. We have a substantial file on your activities.'

'We?' Andrew notes the 'Signor' this time. That's better, he thinks, though he'd still have preferred 'Dottore'.

The man uncaps his pen a second time. 'Perhaps you could give me the more pertinent of those details again.'

'Me? We? Who are *you*, actually?'

The man ignores this. The pen is poised above some sort of form. 'You say your mother was Scottish. You have Italian citizenship?'

'You know I do.'

'You did your national service?'

'I didn't need to. I was my mother's only support. As you well know. If you've been keeping an eye on me, that is.'

The man detaches a folder from the clipboard and pulls out a photograph, which he pushes across the table to Andrew. Andrew picks it up, turns it the right way round. The image isn't that clear, but it's clear enough for Andrew to see himself, his red hair long and loose, waving what looks like an iron bar over his head. His face is distorted by shouting, his shirt torn off his shoulder where someone must have pulled it, trying to hold him back. He can't be more than twenty-three, twenty-four, which would make it 1977, the season of his public rage. He doesn't know where he is, but he must be on a demonstration of some kind. Andrew Caruso versus the World and its Masters. From the quality of the image, the photograph must have been taken with a zoom lens, and blown up, so that only this detail is visible. He's not alone, but he's at the centre of the scene, as though it was all about him. There must be thousands of photographs like this, taken from rooftops and police vans, from the hot years, '68 and '77, and more recently, of students waving flags and heavier things than flags, *weapons*, as he's doing here. He looks at himself again, his eyes and mouth black pits in the pallid face, the hair aflame as if with its owner's passion, so young, so furious, so *right*. It reminds him of recent photographs of the Genoa G8, photographs of overturned bins on fire and bloodied faces, of balaclavas and banners, of a dead boy lying on the road, and of how ineffectual, how vainglorious this sort of protest is. He puts the photograph down.

'What do you want from me?'

The man looks up. He licks his lips. The wart, or whatever it is, on the tip of his tongue appears briefly, round and glistening as a rosy pearl. 'Your personal details, Caruso.'

'You have photographs of me taken more than thirty years ago. What other personal details do you need?'

'What do you think we need?'

'I don't know what you need.' Andrew's tone is exasperated. 'Perhaps if you could tell me, I'd be able to help.'

'We've been looking through your list of contacts. Quite a few of them are familiar to us.'

'I don't know which contacts you mean.'

'You make your living, such as it is, by dealing in stolen goods, Caruso. Books, prints. Essentially you're a fence.'

'This is ridiculous.'

'What other name would you give to someone who buys valuable objects from thieves and sells them on?'

'I buy *objects* from whoever comes into the shop to sell them. I assume they've been acquired legally. In any case, I can't remember the last time I bought anything valuable.'

'I don't think we understand each other.'

'I understand you perfectly.' Andrew's voice is louder then he intends. He's shaking his head. 'You're trying to frighten me, to threaten me. You show me a photograph that's thirty years old, in which I appear to be committing a crime for which I wasn't charged then and won't be now. You tell me I deal with thieves and you have proof of it. You're trying to scare me, that's obvious.' He spreads his hands; he wants to appear reasonable. He *is* reasonable. 'What I don't understand is why.'

The man stands up again, for the first time showing impatience. He has been sweating; his shirt is wet beneath the arms. 'There are also serious irregularities in your tax returns.'

'Now I'm Al Capone.' Andrew snorts with laughter. 'I want my lawyer.'

The man leaves the room.

What Andrew doesn't understand is why they don't ask him what they want to know, and why, if they do, he doesn't think he'll tell them. The man made it plain in the shop that, whatever reason he may have given for closing the show and carting off Andrew's entire stock in cardboard boxes, what he was really doing was looking for a photograph that wasn't there. Which he no longer seems to want to talk about. Andrew assumes the photograph he wants is the one of the girl Martin spoke about, Silvia Castellani, the girl who went missing. He doesn't just want the photograph, though. He also wants to know where Andrew got it from. So why doesn't he ask straight out, instead of playing this absurd game of intimidation? And if that isn't what he wants? If there is something else in the show that no one has noticed? It must be something deeply incriminating to justify this farce into which Andrew has been drawn: the ministry, if the man really is from the ministry, the police, if they really are police and not hired thugs, this two-way-mirrored room, which is obviously designed for interrogation, but by whom, for whom? He doesn't know. Whatever it is, it's bigger than Andrew, and maybe Martin, imagined. He's being held here against his will and he doesn't know who's responsible. All he knows is that it involves more people, it's dirtier and less careful of human needs, than either of them had thought. It is, as Sandro insisted this morning, dangerous. Is this why Andrew doesn't want to involve Michel?

Because it isn't enough to think that Michel is dead and beyond harm. Not for Andrew. And not only for Michel's sake. Michel might lead them to Sandro. For the first time, Andrew wonders if he will leave this room alive.

SANDRO AND MARTIN

'Is that Martin Frame?'

'Who is this?'

'I was given this number by Caruso.'

'Caruso? The singer?'

'Andrew Caruso. The bookshop owner.'

'And who are you?'

'My name's Sandro Cano. You don't know me. Caruso told me to call you. He gave me your card.'

'How can I help you?'

'I'm calling for Caruso. He's just been arrested.'

'He's been what?'

'Arrested. I'm standing outside his shop now. It's been sealed off by the police. They've taken everything they can away with them.'

'I think we'd better meet.'

'I think you're right.'

'There's a bar near the shop. On the right as you walk out into the square.'

'I see it.'

'I'll be there in half an hour. Thirty-five minutes at the outside.'

'I'll be waiting. How will I know you?'

'I'll be looking very worried, Mr Cano. And I'll have a walking stick.'

Martin's there in twenty-eight minutes. Alina has driven him, dropping him off on the corner of Via Arenula, and he's walked faster than he should to get to the bar, cursing his stick as it skids off the curved backs of the cobblestones. This is no fucking city for old men, he says to himself. Or anyone else, these days. Jeans shops everywhere you look. Andrew arrested. I knew this would happen, or something like it. And I shall have the pleasure of telling that painted windbag, Daniela dell'Orto, what a fine mess she's got them both into. Because this must be about the show. He'd seen the piece in the paper this morning and thought, Good God, what is the world coming to? What is *language* coming to? He'd said as much to Alina, who smoothed his feathers before settling to her studies.

He reaches the bar, walks in. A second later, a man strides over.

'We'll be more comfortable sitting down,' he says, pointing to the tables arranged outside the bar. 'And more private.'

Martin nods, follows him onto the street. He's never seen him before, he's sure of that, and can't quite place him. His name's Italian, his accent that of someone who's lived in London. He's not a young man, although he's younger than either Martin or Andrew. He looks as though he's lived, but has found his feet. He's wearing the sort of corduroy jacket professors wear, but he doesn't have the air of a professor. There's a shabbiness about him that looks slightly contrived, an attention to detail that belies it. He's carrying a plastic bag with what appear to be books inside it. He might be a writer, thinks Martin, or someone who'd like to think he is. The name, Sandro Cano, rings a tiny distant bell. Well, I'll know soon enough, he decides. Before they reach the table, he glances across to the shop, makes a low whistle. The shutters have been pulled down and red and white tape fixed firmly across them, as Sandro had said. 'It looks as though Andrew won't be selling any books today,' he says.

'Or tomorrow, I don't think.'

'Indeed.'

As soon as they're both seated, their backs to the shop, Sandro puts the plastic bag on the table between them and, after glancing round, pulls out a copy of something Martin recognizes instantly as the catalogue.

'They arrived while I was there this morning. Two boxes. I grabbed these copies before the police took them away with everything else.'

'I think you'd better tell me exactly what happened.'

'How much do you know about this exhibition? These photographs?'

Martin's surprised. He didn't expect to be questioned. 'Are you someone I should know?' he says. 'Some friend of Andrew's I've never met?'

'Andrew Caruso and I met this morning. Officially for the first time.'

'He gave you my number, you say?'

'Yes, but I don't know why. Why you, I mean, and not someone else.'

Martin is finding it hard to conceal his exasperation. 'I'm sorry, Signor Cano,' he says, 'but I think we're getting off to a rather bad start here.' The waiter is standing beside the table, but neither of them pays any attention. After a moment he walks off and leans against the glass of the bar, his tray dangling from his hands.

'You're quite right. I'm sorry too.' Sandro smiles abruptly, briefly, as if he has just thought of something that amuses him. 'He gave me your card as he was being led away. Let me try to explain what I saw. Then we can talk about what we know.'

'That sounds reasonable.' Martin calls the waiter across. 'But first I think I should offer you something to drink.'

'Beer.'

Martin orders two beers. 'And nuts,' he adds. 'Can't drink on an empty stomach, these days,' he explains to Sandro.

'The catalogues arrived and then a man came who said he was from the Ministry of Fine Arts. I don't think this was true. He was very well dressed, expensive clothes, handmade shoes. English style, the kind you never see in England. He pretended to know something about books, but Caruso wasn't convinced, I could see that, and I think the man could see it as well. He started to nose around, to ask Caruso questions about the exhibition. He wanted to go upstairs. I tried to stop this happening, but it was impossible to talk without saying too much. I didn't want the man to notice me. Then he made a phone call and some other men came. I left the shop a little before that – I took some of the catalogues and watched from out-side. Caruso and the man went upstairs – that's where the exhibition is, right? – and the other men started to take all the books from the shelves. They were looking for something, I think, but maybe not. I think they may have been doing it to scare Caruso. When he came down again and saw what they were doing, his face went white. They put the books into boxes. They pulled the shelves from the walls and ripped off the paper behind them. Again, I think this was to scare Caruso. The paper was old, news-paper from the forties, the fifties maybe, a long time before Caruso came. Then they took him off in a car. I stayed here and saw them carry away the boxes and also boxes from upstairs. I think the pictures from the exhibition were in those boxes, right? The photographs?'

'When did this happen?'

'I got to the shop around half-past eleven, maybe a little before that. Caruso was taken away at ten to one.'

'Why didn't you call me straight away?'

'I wanted to see what else the men would do. I waited until they'd finished clearing away the shop and sealed the shutters. Then I called. There was no answer. It said you were unavailable. I waited a little more and called again.'

'I didn't turn it on till after lunch,' says Martin. 'Hate the damn things.' The waiter arrives with their order. They wait for him to leave before continuing.

'You saw the exhibition?'

Martin nods. 'Well, not exactly. I saw the photographs.'

'In the catalogue, there are only photographs of faces. In the exhibition?'

'As far as I know, the same.' Martin looks at Sandro more closely. 'What other photographs might there have been?'

'Of crime scenes, people who haven't been arrested.' Sandro sips his beer.

'What do you know about these photographs?'

'That was my question to you,' says Sandro, with the same unexpected smile as before.

'Well,' says Martin, who is also, to his slight surprise, amused, 'I think that one of us is going to have to spill a bean or two. Nothing ventured, nothing gained.'

Sandro nods, then spreads his hands, palms up, as if to indicate he has nothing to conceal. 'I know where the photographs came from. I mean to say, I know how they came to be in Caruso's possession. I sold them many years ago to a friend of his, a Belgian photographer called Michel. I don't know his last name.'

'And how did they come to be in your possession?'

'They were given to me to look after. By a friend of mine who wanted me to be discreet.'

'But, rather than look after them, you sold them to someone else?'

'Well, yes, that's true. You see, the friend they belonged to died unexpectedly.' Sandro raises an eyebrow.

'Who was this friend?'

'He was a journalist.'

'As I am,' says Martin. 'Was.'

Sandro acknowledges this information with a nod. 'Maybe you've heard of him. Bruno Conte. He worked for *Il Messaggero*. He was murdered.'

'Rings a bell. It wasn't a gay murder, was it? Donkey's years ago now.'

'It was made to look like that. But, no, I don't think it was. I think his death had something to do with these photographs.'

'I think you may be right.' Martin reaches into his jacket pocket, extracts a folded, crumpled sheet of paper. 'Do you recognize this?' he says, opening it out, smoothing away the creases.

Sandro looks down, then picks it up. 'This is one of the photographs?'

'Yes.'

'Do you know who she is?'

'Yes, I believe I do.'

'Does Caruso?'

'I told him who she was. You recognize her too?'

'When Bruno died I went to live with someone who looked after me. That was how I came into contact with Michel. There was another friend of Andrew's there who told me about this shop. You know Andrew is gay?'

Martin smiles. 'Yes.'

'This other friend was called James Bond – that's how I remember his name. But he called himself—'

'Jamie. Jamie Bond. He worked for me briefly. I'm beginning to think we have a lot in common, Mr Cano.'

'Please. Call me Sandro.'

Martin holds out his hand. 'Martin,' he says, as Sandro shakes it, wondering why they hadn't shaken hands at once. How strange trust is, he thinks. 'Call me Martin.'

'It makes sense to me now, you see. I haven't thought about all this for years. I haven't wanted to. Bruno's death made it painful for me, so I pushed it to one side. We do that, don't we? Pretend things haven't happened. But the friend I went to live with, the one who looked after me, he tried to find out a little more about Bruno, and why he was murdered. He did it for me, I think, to help me achieve closure. That's what we say now, isn't it?' Once again, the abrupt, unexpected smile. 'Closure. And then you show me this girl's face and I see how it all fits in. I didn't remember this photograph. I had no memory of it at all until now.'

'What did your friend find out?'

'That Bruno was investigating a ring of men – powerful men, my friend said – who used girls for their pleasure, who kidnapped girls. This is the Castellani girl, isn't it? The one who disappeared, whose father worked at the Vatican? I don't know why I didn't realize it then. Her face was all over Rome for months. This is why they killed Bruno, because somehow he'd found this photograph.' Sandro folds the sheet of paper and lifts it to his mouth, as if he's about to kiss it or blow it away. 'And then he gave it to me.'

'And you sold it to Michel, along with all the others.' Gently, Martin takes the photocopy away from Sandro. 'How much did he give you for them?'

'Half what I'd asked for. He died as well, you see, before he had the chance to pay me the second part. He died as well.'

'Yes,' says Martin. 'He died as well.'

'The car they took Caruso off in,' says Sandro, briskly, changing the subject, 'I don't know what kind of car it was, but it wasn't right. None of what happened here feels right. You have his number?'

'I do. At least I think I do.' Martin pulls his mobile phone from a pocket and stares at it. 'These things do have memories, don't they?'

Sandro laughs. 'Try and call him now.'

ANDREW

Andrew has been alone in the room now for what feels like hours. He has passed the time, or part of it, by thinking about the girl who disappeared, wondering what kind of room she was kept in, assuming she wasn't killed immediately – wondering whether it was like this room. He'd forgotten her name until Martin reminded him and it all flooded back. Silvia Castellani. It's extraordinary what you can forget. Everywhere you went, for what felt like months and may have been more than that, her smiling, slightly out-of-focus face was plastered on walls and lampposts, hoardings and rubbish bins and bus shelters throughout the city. Always the same blurred face, the same photograph, taken on holiday, perhaps, or at a party, which would surely have reduced the chances of her being recognized. Andrew remembers he read once about Marilyn Monroe walking with some friend, maybe Lee Strasberg, and Marilyn remarking she could be anybody, she was completely unrecognizable unless she turned *it* on, then throwing the Marilyn Monroe switch that transformed her into the icon. Perhaps this is what Daniela means. That's the beauty of icons, he thinks. They're not what you are at all – except when, as in the girl's case, you want to be recognized, because your life depends on it. You sit in a room and wait to be rescued and all people have to go on is that single face, which was you for no more than a moment, and then you were gone.

Fiddling with a button on his shirt cuff, he thinks about what Martin told him, about the speculations surrounding Castellani's disappearance. Kurdish separatists whisking her off to blackmail the Pope, international finance, Stasi attempts at destabilization, Bulgarian gypsy gangs, the trade in human organs or white prostitution for the Arab market, the Vatican Bank, Andreotti – because there is always Andreotti, Blackfriars Bridge, the death of Calvi. Everything from the Third Secret of Fatima to the Band of the Magliana. The only thing that's missing, he thinks, smiling against his will, is alien abduction. It's Marilyn all over again, a bubbling stew of conspiracy theories, the high and the mighty and the low, organized crime and irreproachable public figures hurriedly rubbing shoulders in corridors, exchanging glances, as each goes about his business.

But even to think about it is to waste my time. There's no natural bottom to this sort of thing, he decides, and he dismisses the thoughts of the girl as swiftly as he allowed them entry, casting his eyes about the walls of the room he's been held in now for God only knows how long. He'd look at his mobile phone to see, but he's nurtured this healing vision of himself on the pavement outside, flipping it open and calling someone – Martin?

Daniela? – to say he's free; he wants to have some battery left for that. Is this the kind of place they kept her in, though? he wonders, because he can't, after all, not think of her. Some shabby anonymous office like this, with a buzzing light and a crucifix? Or somewhere cold and dark, somewhere underground, the way they used to hide those held for ransom during the kidnapping days when no one with money was safe. Maybe she never left Rome at all. Maybe she's still here, within a mile of where he's sitting, watching television, a cat on her knee. Some people believe she's still alive, not only her family – you'd expect that – but experts on the case. He's surprised how much he knows. He hadn't realized he was listening while Martin told him everything, and all he'd done was nod and go ahead with the exhibition, like the stubborn, incautious, optimistic idiot he is.

He closes his eyes against the fluorescent light and sees her staring out through the window of the moving car, scared witless, as far removed from the smiling girl as could be imagined. Is this why he hadn't realized who she was at once, when he'd looked at the photographs that first time, two months ago now, although it seems a lifetime? Is this why it had taken Martin's trained, journalistic eye to spot her? But even Martin hadn't been sure, at first. It might not be her at all. He might have misunderstood everything. If only they would tell him what they want. If only he could talk to Martin. Yes, he decides, the minute he gets out of here, he'll call Martin.

Because there is no one else. There is no one but Martin.

Certainly not Daniela, he doesn't include her, but everyone else? His friends, his lovers, such as they were? How did this happen? Where did they go? 'Into that good night,' he says to himself, the first time under his breath, the second time out loud – whether they can hear what he says or not is immaterial to him. And gently, too, without the slightest hint of distress. Every bloody one of them, in one way or another, not calling, not answering calls, their letters and, more recently, emails unread, because it's as much his fault as theirs; he takes the blame for it.

'It's my own fucking fault,' he says, out loud again, his head thrown back. He doesn't care what they hear or see, not now; all at once they've stopped scaring him, who-ever they are, although he doesn't know why. Nothing material has changed. If he had to define what he feels at this moment he'd say it came closer to tedium than any-thing else, as though he were waiting for papers to be authenticated or a dentist to carry out an annual check-up. He's bored.

He glares at the mirror, then stands up and walks across, pressing his face to the glass to see if anything can be glimpsed of them, the ghost-like presence of his observers. But when he pulls away and refocuses his eyes there's nothing to see except the pattern left by his breath, and a neat round patch of grease from the tip of his nose. Per-haps he's mistaken and it really is nothing more than a mirror with a solid wall behind it. He taps, tentatively at first, then with genuine force, an unanticipated flurry of anger, wanting to break through it, frighten someone, attract attention. For a moment, as if caught in an inexplicable draught, he feels hysterical, unstable, but that's only natural. Who wouldn't feel unstable, locked in a room for hours on end, with, he has just realized, a growing need to pee? This time he bangs on the mirror with the open palm of his hand. 'I have to piss,' he says. He repeats this, each word underlined by a slap against the glass. I. Thud. Have. Thud. To. Thud. Piss. Thud. Adds, for good measure, remembering where he is: *Devo*. Thud. *Pisciare*.

Some moments later the door opens. The mirror reveals to Andrew, who doesn't immediately turn, the youngest of the four men who wrecked his shop. The blond one. Andrew turns and repeats, this time with an air of apology, '*Devo pisciare*.' The man has taken off his jacket and rolled up his sleeves, revealing a tattoo down the length of one muscled forearm, its blue-black ink in contrast with the coarse blond hair. He must have been sitting in some other overheated room like this one, possibly the one behind the mirror. The tattoo is a row of letters in some sort of Gothic script, so ornate the word can't be read, which might be to the good: it's the kind of lettering amateur Fascists prefer for their graffiti. If he *has* been behind the mirror, thinks Andrew, he's been watching me. He wishes it could have been the other way round. He's fantasized about mirrors like this, assuming it is two-way, mirrors behind which he could sit and watch men going about their daily business. They wouldn't have to be young, or available, or even sexy. It isn't about sex, or not overtly. He'd be perfectly happy to see them eat and read the paper, do a crossword, scratch their knee, pick their teeth. It's about their intimacy, to which he's normally denied access. He has never achieved that level of intimacy with anyone, if intimacy is what it is, the right to observe, unobserved. He subscribed once to one of those secret webcam sites, but it's not the same. Whatever the webmaster claims, they know they're being watched, they're playing to the camera. They titillate. If that's what they're doing, Andrew would prefer it done honestly, face-on to the lens.

The man nods and holds the door open, waiting for Andrew to cross the room. 'I have to accompany you,' he says, his accent the kind Swiss Italians have, the odd and, to Andrew's ears, slightly comical lilt that renders its speakers innocuous, whatever they might be saying. He uses the familiar form – *Ti devo accompagnare* – unlike Andrew's interrogator, who has never wavered in his use of the formal *lei*, however much contempt he might express with it.

They leave the room together, the young man at Andrew's side, one hand above Andrew's elbow to guide him. The corridor is empty. No people, no chairs, not even a calendar or framed print of the president to relieve the institutional gloom of the place. After ten, fifteen yards, the man steps forward and opens a door. Andrew expects to be ushered in, locked in, perhaps, but the man comes with him. It looks like he's going to be accompanied all the way.

They're in a communal toilet, urinals down one wall,

cubicles along the other. Hesitant, Andrew waits to be told what to do, glancing at the man as if he needs permission to piss. But the man, arms crossed now, avoids his eyes. He knows I'm gay, thinks Andrew; he's embarrassed, ashamed for me, contemptuous, perhaps. Escorting a gay man old enough to be his father to the lavatory: it's hardly what he joined the force for, Andrew thinks, assuming he really is a policeman. He's imagined this scenario so many times; indeed, he's seen it acted out in a hundred adult films, in magazines like the ones he continues to sell in the shop – or did until this morning. This is the point at which the man in uniform makes some crude advance, affectionate or violent depending on genre, and the prisoner, or captive, or unwary traveller, is expected to succumb. Andrew's imagined this happening in airports, police stations, prison cells, the back of armoured vans; imagined the body search, the fingers in the mouth and anus, the summoning perhaps of a colleague for some three-way sex in which all the roles are blurred. It's the very stuff of porn. But it isn't going to happen. Not here, not now. Andrew walks over to the urinal, extracts his slightly tumescent cock, aims and waits, suddenly pee-shy, for the flow to start.

Back in the room, just as the young man is about to close the door, Andrew asks what they intend to do with him. He's been wondering how to word this all the way along the corridor. He doesn't want to sound intimidated or defiant. He wants it to seem the most natural question in the world, as if he were asking a flight attendant what time the pilot expected to land. He's pleased, in the end, with his delivery: calm, indifferent-sounding, the merest request for information. He's less pleased with the response.

'I can't answer that.'

'What have you done with my property?'

The man shakes his head. 'I told you. I can't answer your questions.'

But Andrew isn't to be put off now. 'Tell your boss I'd like to talk to him,' he says, sitting down at the table in the chair he has come to regard as his. How quickly routines are forged, he'll think later, when this occurs to him, when the other man still hasn't shown and he is sick with fright and hopelessness once again, his imagination running riot, and he can't remember what deal he'd thought, in a flash of unwarranted buoyancy, he might broker for his release. 'And you can tell him I'm hungry as well.' This isn't true, but it strikes him that eating is a basic right he's being denied: he wants to see what will happen. He wants to be given the chance to refuse to eat, to go on hunger strike. He wonders how long they will have to keep him here before he smears the walls with his own shit. Isn't that what people do in these cases? he thinks, abruptly amused, despite himself.

The young man leaves the room. The minute he's gone, Andrew wishes he had stayed; it would have been company at least. An official shoulder to cry on. Suddenly he's reminded of an incident he's not thought about for years.

He'd been to see a film with a friend. Afterwards they'd arranged to meet up in a *birreria* near Piazza Navona with someone else, someone Andrew didn't know, but after they'd finished their second beer and he hadn't turned up, they'd decided to move on. Those were the days before mobiles, when people used brass *gettoni* and public phone boxes to communicate, and Andrew's friend, whose name was Luca, stopped in a bar in Campo de' Fiori to call *his* friend, whose name Andrew can't recall, and see why he hadn't shown. He called his home number, but there was no answer. 'I'll just try his boyfriend,' Luca said, *gettone* paused above the slot. 'The unreliable bastard might be there.' Andrew remembers standing beside the phone, kicking his heels, watching Luca's face change as he made the call, the irritation, the shock, the horror, the concern passing like coloured slides before a light. Finally, Luca put the phone down and turned, pale beneath his tan, to Andrew. 'His boyfriend's killed himself,' he said. 'The police are there. We have to go.'

The man had locked himself in. Luca's friend had banged on the door, shouting, imploring him to open it, eventually calling the police when he smelt gas. If he hadn't, the entire block might have been blown sky-high. There was some awful tale about the man having planned his suicide years ago, an extended death wish that had finally borne fruit. But what Andrew remembers most distinctly about the night, as they crowded together on the landing – he and Luca, and Luca's friend, with curious neighbours and firemen and paramedics – was the way one of the policemen there had put his arm round the shoulder of Luca's friend as he sobbed and shook and blamed himself, had embraced and comforted him, drawing him in, his voice too low for Andrew to hear what was said. What Andrew remembers feeling, more than sympathy or pity or fellow-feeling, was a deep and shaming envy, in spite of everything. This was soon after Michel's death, when no one had offered him such comfort, but it wasn't so much that lack which shocked him, when he thought about it later, as the knowledge that, in order to be held like that, to be whispered to like that, he would live with his lover's loss. He would cope with it. It would be worth it.

Soon after it occurs to him that the young man may have been sent to set him up, to see if he'd make a pass or compromise himself in some way, the way police entrap men in public lavatories. And, of course, they could easily say he had – it would be his word against theirs. Which means he might as well have done. Appalled by himself, by his shallowness, he wants to cry. If it wasn't for the possibility they might be watching, and the fact that he no longer has his handkerchief, he would.

When he can't take it any more and has lost all realistic sense of time, he turns on his mobile phone and sees that it's just after half-past six. By his calculations he's been here five hours. He hasn't spoken to anyone since the young man left him alone some three hours ago, he'd say, although surely it's more than that. It feels more like days than hours. He turns the phone off immediately, terrified that this, his only remaining contact with the world outside, will fail him, but not before the warning beep that tells him the battery is almost exhausted. He stares at the door, and then at the standard-issue crucifix above it. He sits in the almost-silence, twiddling the button on his cuff.

MARTIN AND SANDRO

The flat's empty when Martin arrives with Sandro. In one sense this is a pity, thinks Martin. Alina would have offered them coffee or one of her choice of teas – Earl Grey, orange pekoe, gunpowder green – and biscuits, perhaps a slice of the pecan tart he found her baking yesterday from a book of American recipes; her sardonic parody of afternoon tea. Still, needs must, thinks Martin, extracting a bottle of red wine from a rack on the floor beside the fridge and proffering it, label up, to Sandro, who smiles his approval. 'It's nothing special,' says Martin, reaching into a drawer for one of those fold-out metal corkscrews waiters use, levering out the cork in one easy professional sweep, 'but it's perfectly decent. At my age I've learned to respect my liver. The way one respects a wily old enemy one knows will win.' He gestures towards a wall cupboard with his head. 'You'll find a couple of glasses in there. Not those ghastly buckets, we aren't trying to impress anyone. Yes, yes. They'll do perfectly well.' As soon as the wine is poured out, he glances at his watch and pulls a face. 'Dear me, still so early. My wife will not be happy about this. She doesn't appreciate the potential of a merry widow-

hood. I suggest you deflect the flak when she gets here.'
Sandro looks puzzled. 'Sorry, old boy, natural mistake to
make. I forgot you aren't a native. What I meant was I suggest you take the blame,' explains Martin. Sandro touches
his glass to Martin's. 'So you're in the information business as well,' Martin says.

'I'm in all sorts of business, necessarily. I have no steady
job,' says Sandro. He tastes the wine, considers it, nods
his appreciation. 'I cover the waterfront.'

Martin's amused. 'Quite. Though I can't help wondering
where you learned that expression.'

'Tennessee Williams used it once, on television, but I
think his meaning was a little different. I learned it from
a man called Roger in London. It's what he liked to say
when people asked him what he did for a living. He
worked for a magazine, you see, about bricks and tiles. It
wasn't very romantic. He liked to pretend he was a volatile,
impulsive type. In a sense, he was.'

'So you worked as a journalist in London?' Martin has
been put in his place, and is both delighted and intrigued.
He's decided he likes this young man.

'No, that was later. I'm not really a journalist, not like
you, Martin. Not a proper journalist, though I suppose I
am in the information business, as you say, because everything is information, isn't it, in some way? I'm a jobbing
writer – I mean I go from job to job. I do some teaching
sometimes, English to Italians, Italian to everyone else. I
help out a friend of mine who's been good to me, who
needs my assistance. I don't have a career. You live in Italy.

You know what it means here to have a career, the compromises you make with yourself, and others. Careers are dead-ends, in any case. To tell the truth, I think I was scared by Bruno's murder, more scared than I knew then, and for a long time. I've always tried to keep my head below the parapet.'

'I've come across your name, nevertheless,' says Martin. 'Despite your efforts. I can't think where, but Sandro Cano rings a definite bell.'

'I wrote a book some years ago. It wasn't a bestseller, but maybe you saw it in bookshops before it was remaindered? It was about the friend of mine I mentioned, something that happened to a friend of his. A murder.'

'Another murder? Your friends don't seem to have much luck,' says Martin.

Sandro shrugs. 'I didn't know him well. He helped me once when I needed a job, so I knew him a little, to say hello and have a coffee. But my friend, the one I look after sometimes, is a man called Morelli. They'd known each other for years, even worked together. I wrote about it because I didn't know what to think. It reminded me of what happened to Bruno at first, the violence of it, and then, when I looked again, everything seemed different. I think that's what writing does to you.' He grins, a sudden scornful grin, as though he resents the truth of what he's saying. 'It makes everything look different so that you don't know where you stand.'

'Good writing does,' says Martin. 'I'd like to read it.'

'Even so, it isn't a very good book,' says Sandro, visibly

pleased. 'But I think I can find you a copy somewhere. Perhaps in a box beneath my bed.'

'And you know Jamie Bond?'

'I knew him. Through Morelli. Sometimes I think everything that happens to me in Rome has happened through Morelli in one way or another. I didn't know him long. He'd already finished with Caruso. He used to pass his time in Morelli's flat like a lot of other people, from everywhere. Morelli called the place his *caput mundi*. Only in Rome, he said. Jamie told me about Caruso when he heard I had something to sell.'

'But you didn't sell the photographs to Andrew?'

'No. I would have done, that was my plan, but he wasn't there. Michel was in the shop. I thought I was lucky because he said he was interested in photography. Caruso wasn't, he said, I should deal with him. And so I did. He didn't want to meet me in the shop, we met in that little church just near. If Caruso had been there he might not have bought them. They weren't his kind of thing, although maybe I'm wrong. I think that would have been better, though, if I had tried to sell them to him and he'd said, no, he didn't want them. I wish now I had thrown them into the river and walked away. They carry death with them.'

'That's a bit melodramatic, old boy,' says Martin. 'Photographs don't kill. Not by themselves, at least.'

Sandro shrugs, not convinced. 'Can I see that photocopy again?' he says.

Martin unfolds the sheet of paper and hands it to him.

'I haven't seen this for many years,' he says.

Martin reaches to refill their glasses but the bottle is empty. He gets up to open another.

'This man behind her,' says Sandro. 'It's hard to see his face. Is it this blurred on the original?'

'No,' says Martin. 'But hang on a minute.' He opens the new bottle, then leaves the room. While Sandro waits for him to come back, he hears a key turn in the lock. A woman walks in, with shopping. She's younger than Sandro, considerably younger than Martin; his daughter, perhaps. Not Italian, not English either. But Martin had spoken about a wife, about having to – how did he say it? – deflect the flak. Immediately Sandro pours himself some wine from the just opened bottle, so that she won't assume only Martin is drinking. He's about to stand up and introduce himself when the woman asks him, in Italian, if she knows him, and he can hear at once that he's right, she isn't Italian, and that she comes from the east somewhere, Eastern Europe. Poland, Russia, the Ukraine, he isn't sure. He stands up, offers his hand.

'*Mi chiamo Sandro Cano.*'

For a second it looks as though she's about to giggle.

'I'm sorry?' he says, slipping back into English. Perhaps she doesn't understand Italian after all. He nods towards the other room, to reassure her. 'Martin's through there.'

'No, no, you must pardon me. I thought you said you were Sandokan. You know, that pirate type they made those films about all those years ago. For children. Do you remember?' She shakes his hand firmly. 'I'm Alina.

Martin's wife. Now, please, tell me your name again. I promise not to laugh.'

'I see you two have met.' Martin's standing at the door with a magazine in his hand.

'Well, yes. I have met your famous pirate friend.'

'He's actually Andrew Caruso's friend,' says Martin, with a grin, 'and whether he's a pirate or not is still uncon-firmed. I suspect he is.'

'Andrew's friend?' Alina glances round for Andrew.

'We don't know where Andrew is,' says Martin. 'That's why Sandro's here. Andrew appears to have been arrested.'

Once again, Sandro tells his tale, or the part of it that concerns the events of the morning. When he's finished he shows them both a copy of the catalogue. Alina thumbs through it with growing irritation. 'You stupid, foolish men,' she says.

Martin snorts with laughter. 'That's hardly fair, my dear.'

'Playing your stupid, foolish games with authority. You don't know what authority can do to small people. You have no experience of it.'

'You're right,' says Sandro. 'I don't think Andrew under-stood the risk.'

Alina looks sharply at Martin. 'I thought you spoke to him.'

Martin nods. 'I did, I honestly did, Alina – there's no need to glare at me like that. But there was just no stop-ping him. He was adamant that the show go on. To be frank, I've never seen Andrew so determined about anything. I'm very fond of the man, you know that, but he isn't the sort who normally sees things through, particularly if they're difficult or – God forbid – dangerous. I think this show meant more to him than he quite understood. It certainly meant more than I understood. The girl in the photograph struck me as a bit of a risk, and that's why I told him to think twice before going ahead. But I didn't imagine for a second that anything like this might happen. Assuming, of course, that the two things really are connected.'

'You think they might not be?' says Sandro. 'There could be other photographs? Other stories?'

Well,' says Martin, 'every picture tells its tale. Let's face it, putting a complete rogues' gallery on the walls of a public space could easily open more than one can of worms. What strikes me as odd, though, is the speed of it. Good God, the piece in the paper came out this morning and – what? three hours later? – these people are tearing the shop apart and dragging Andrew off for questioning. It's more than some old lag with a grudge and a couple of friends in the force.' He picks up the catalogue, thumbs through it as Alina has done, puts it down with an exasperated sigh. 'She isn't in here, of course, but they weren't to know that.'

Sandro still has the photocopy in his hand. He opens it out and lays it on the table where all three can see it.

'You have made a photocopy of that photograph?' Alina is visibly displeased. 'I didn't know.'

Martin grimaces at Sandro, then pats Alina's hand; she

makes a clicking noise with her tongue and moves her
arm away.

'This man,' says Sandro.

Martin opens the copy of *Espresso* he has brought from
another room, pointing with an air of triumph at a photograph. 'I'm pretty sure this is our man.'

The article is part of a series on the mysteries of Italy,
stories of terrorist bombs for which no one has claimed
responsibility or been convicted after thirty years, the death
by poisoned coffee of a disgraced financier in a Roman
jail, a porn star's fatal illness, the disappearance of government trillions earmarked for villages destroyed by
earthquake. The usual stuff. This article talks about a
scandal that briefly rocked the Vatican some years ago,
when a Swiss Guard was shot by his commanding officer,
who then committed suicide. The photograph shows the
murderer and his victim with a group of other men. Martin
prods excitedly at one of these men with a chewed-down
fingernail. 'Pure chance. I was thumbing through the thing
in the loo and there the fellow was, staring up at me. It
is him, isn't it?'

'I'm not sure. It certainly looks like him. Who are all
these people?'

'It doesn't say. Vatican apparatchiks, I imagine. I suppose I could find out. A couple of phone calls.'

Sandro empties his glass, studies the photocopy again.
'Where is the original? It must be clearer than this.'

'I don't know.'

'Maybe this woman' – Alina opens the catalogue at the first page – 'this Daniela dell'Orto has it.'

The two men look at each other.

'She still doesn't know about this?' says Martin.

Sandro shakes his head. 'Not if she hasn't passed by the shop and seen that it's sequestered. Is that the word? Is that what the police do in England? I don't have her number. Do you?'

Martin shakes his head. 'It shouldn't be that difficult to find.'

ANDREW

Andrew has been thinking about Daniela dell'Orto for the past half-hour or so, as a mental exercise more than anything, to keep his mind away from where else it might lead him, down into deeper, irreversible panic. He's wondering what she meant about loneliness that evening when they were crouched together in the room above the shop, choosing the photographs. She'd asked him if he ever felt lonely. She did, she said. Was it part of some drunken seduction routine she'd decided to play or something else? Did she mean it, in other words? Not about him. About herself. He doesn't see Daniela as lonely, but that's because he doesn't see her as a person with *interiority*, as they say in avant-garde circles like hers. She has no *interiority* to *elaborate*, that's how she'd phrase it, though not about herself, he's sure. About someone she can't stand and wants to put down. She was right, though, to ask him. Because of course he's felt lonely. He's never not felt lonely, if being lonely means being aware without respite of being alone.

Perhaps, paradoxically, he's *less* lonely now than ever before, locked in this room with the dead man in the corner holding his leather jacket, and the mirrored wall, from which he might never escape – *will* never escape, mentally at least. He's convinced of this now, the light almost entirely faded from the window high above his head. He's never felt less alone than he does at this minute, in this room. He feels observed: he's the centre of their attention. It's heart-warming, almost: to be anything but alone in this room, which is gradually filling up with the weight and clamour of himself, the stink of himself, and the whole self-wrought disaster of his life. To be lonely, surely, is to be empty, hollow, but right now Andrew's filled with self-loathing, which leaves no room for loneliness. He has no money, no friends, no lover, no future; his filthy, ill-equipped, untidy flat is rented and might be repossessed, his shop – by which he means his livelihood – has been ripped apart by the police. There is no way out to be seen, and no one to care much about it. He doesn't care, certainly. Neither wanting nor expecting to, he's none the less learned the meaning of the phrase *I'm past caring*, as though this was a stage, perhaps the ultimate stage, on a downhill journey he's been making for the past fifty-five years. He's been making assumptions about Daniela, but who knows? It may be that I'm the one without *interiority*, he thinks, with a sort of acid satisfaction.

One Friday at the labour exchange he'd prepared his box of claimants, and was signing them on, and the time had come for a certain Ignatio, *Mister* Ignatio, a shaven-headed hatchet-faced Maltese, his neck tattooed with a dotted line, to present himself. Andrew can still remember the time, between two fifteen and two thirty, and Mister Ignatio failing to show, and Andrew conscious of being watched by the people who worked there, his colleagues but not, for the most part, his friends. Two forty-five and Ignatio still hadn't shown. By four o'clock Andrew knew that what he had to do was deny Ignatio his right to sign on. The rules were clear: he'd missed his chance. But still Ignatio wasn't there. The claimants came, and signed, and went. Eventually, with no more than twenty minutes left, Andrew had to pee. He asked Mr Scriven, the manager, to stand in for him, hoping that, while he was skulking in the bathroom, Ignatio would walk up to the counter and slap it with his customary violence, with his hard-edged karate-trained hand, then sign with his usual X, not because he was illiterate – Andrew had seen him read and write – but because to sign his name would be to demonstrate respect. When Andrew came back, with only five minutes left and the doors to the public about to be closed, he was struck by the silence in the overheated barn-like room, its reek of unwashed clothes and sweat. He looked along the working side of the counter and saw his colleagues, one behind the other, like birds on a wire; to the left, beyond the counter, the straggle of late-arriving claimants, each with his or her excuse. At his box, where Mr Scriven should have been, there was no one. And then a door banged and Ignatio strode in, bow-legged, chin thrust out, his short arms swinging. And Andrew reached for the claim, knowing he would sign the man on however late he was, whatever punishment might ensue. Only to find, to his horror, that the claim wasn't there. He looked round for help, but his colleagues were gathered together, out of sight of the claimants, weak with laughter as Andrew – the new boy, the half-Italian, the student who would soon be gone – checked, and double-checked, and Ignatio clenched and unclenched his tattooed fists. Andrew was quite alone; he had no allies. No one will help me, he thought, as he turned his eyes towards the ceiling and waited for Ignatio to reach across the counter and slice a new mouth into his throat.

If he had to choose the moments, though, in which he has felt most alone, they wouldn't be times at home, in the flat, in front of the TV or watching webcams of foreign exploited youths he'll never meet, and knows that, and wouldn't want to meet – they'd have nothing in common. If he had to, he'd choose those occasions he's been to an exhibition and had ideas he'd have liked to share, or to a restaurant and found himself with the bill after only twenty minutes, or in the cinema alone, those dreadful moments when the film is interrupted by an interval, ostensibly for the changing of reels, though that can't have been true for decades, and everyone except Andrew engages in fervent discussion about the film they're halfway through. Those are the moments. Sometimes he'd take a book or pretend to be writing notes, as though otherwise he'd become the subject of their mocking attention.

The sickness he suffers from, he thinks now, isn't

existential, isn't interior at all: it's a functional loneliness, and it has to do with being *seen* to be lonely. He's ashamed of his loneliness. He's ashamed, and his shame is all he has.

The man comes in, throwing some photographs onto the table. They fan out like large, brightly coloured playing cards. Andrew recognizes images he's downloaded from porn sites.

'What do you have to say about these?'

Andrew doesn't even need to look. Unless they've slipped something in among them, which can't, of course, be ruled out, there's nothing illegal. It isn't a question of his being careful, as some people are: he's simply not interested in boys, and never has been, even as a boy himself. Then he had wanted young men who knew what the world was about. He'd hang around with them, hoping he'd be noticed; in order to be noticed, he'd behave badly, then take the blame while they laughed and moved on, recognizing him as different and maybe dangerous, someone who attracted attention, but the wrong kind. Then, as he grew up and calmed down, and the world became ever more incomprehensible, these were the men he got stuck with, cynics, deadbeats, romantics. What was that Joni Mitchell line about romantics boring people in dark cafes?

'I don't have anything to say.' He's had enough, he's exhausted. 'How long do you intend to keep me here?'

The man picks up one of the photographs, throws it

back down with a gesture of disgust. It skims across the table and lands on Andrew's lap. 'We haven't finished with you yet,' he says, his hands on the table, his face thrust towards Andrew. 'This filth is yours. You know that, don't you?'

'Each to his own,' says Andrew, in a tone he intends to be insolent, but which comes out as merely weary. He turns the picture around so that he can see what's there. He barely remembers downloading it, and has no recollection at all of what he'd noticed that made it stand out from the rest, other than a certain cheekiness in the eyes of the man who is staring between his raised feet at his partner; a cheekiness tinged with awareness of the absurdity of his situation as he lies on a table with his arms round his thighs, his feet still wearing a pair of short white socks, soiled from the floor of the studio, or motel room, or wherever this particular sequence was filmed. Perhaps that's what the man is referring to, he thinks. White shows the dirt.

'We need to know where the other material is.'

Finally, thinks Andrew.

'I don't know what other material you mean.'

'Where did you find the photographs?'

'Which photographs? These ones? This filth?' Andrew's irony isn't noticed. 'It's readily available on the Internet. I can show you where to find it if you like.'

The man sweeps the photographs to the floor with the edge of his left hand; he has to repeat the gesture, more clumsily, with a rage and violence that shocks Andrew to the core. One of the photographs refuses to be swept away, is stuck to the table. Andrew watches as the man peels it from the surface and tears it into two, into four, into eight. He'd do it again, and again if he could, transform this image of two men fucking into sixteen and more, increasingly tiny, innocuous arrangements of form and colour, but he doesn't have the strength. He flings them down with the rest, then puts both hands on the table once again and pushes his hot red face into Andrew's, his hot red breath on Andrew's skin. How odd that Andrew should have thought about Ignatio earlier. Why hasn't he expected this? I must have been mad, he thinks, to suppose they won't use force.

'Did you buy them? Who sold you them?'

'I found them,' Andrew says.

'Where?'

'Outside my door,' he says. He has a picture in his head of a basket, woven from rushes, with the photographs tucked beneath a blanket, being left on a step. They could do him some serious damage, he realizes, just as he realizes that no one in the world knows where he is. He's like the girl: even though they've never met, their paths have somehow converged. Is this what they did to her? He flinches at the thought – more than a thought, at the almost perceived sensation – of his fingernails being drawn from their beds.

The man grunts with exasperation, stands up and leaves the room. No, no, wait, Andrew tries to say, or thinks he has said, but all at once it's too late. He is left alone once more with the humming fluorescent light and the dead man draped with his jacket and his tormentor's raincoat, a scattering of pornographic images on the floor, images that he has chosen from that infinite Internet wealth of images, and a small wooden crucifix above the door. He can't stop seeing the girl. He starts to cry.

It's more stifling by the minute. They're turning the heating higher, Andrew decides, unbuttoning his shirt a little lower, rolling up his sleeves. He looks at the pale skin on his arms, the way it looks slightly dead, except one can't say that: something is dead or it isn't dead. Death doesn't admit degrees. His skin, though, dry and hatched with hair-fine lines, the freckles faded and blurring into un-defined stains, *is* slightly dead; it's in some hinterland he doesn't want to admit the existence of. 'I'm falling apart,' he says to himself. He thinks of the Abu Ghraib photos, the nakedness, the dogs, the smirking woman. Please, God, not that. Is that how the girl was treated? Did they feed her? Did she starve to death, the way Madeleine did, in London? Or did they kill her straight off because her only use to them was dead?

The young blond man with the tattoo comes in. Not looking at Andrew, as though there were no one in the room, he stoops to collect the photographs and fragments of photographs from the floor, sliding them into a large yellow envelope, the kind lawyers use. Andrew barely glances at him. He sniffs back his tears. 'What are you going to do with me?' he asks, his voice unexpectedly thick, clogged with crying. The man walks out. It's hotter than ever. Outside the window, the light has gone completely. It must be nine, ten o'clock by now.

'Why am I here?' says Andrew, to the closed door.

Andrew has forgotten what he originally wanted, before he stumbled on the mug shots and the crime scenes and the photographs of piles of stolen goods that have brought him to this room. What he wanted, months ago now, was to find some work Michel had left and to sell it, to use what small worth he could salvage from Michel's posthumous state of almost-fame to pay his debts, to exploit his death, to move on. Anything saleable would have done.

Now, his cheeks dry, playing with the dangling button of his cuff and waiting to be released, or charged, or disappeared, because he knows that any of these things could happen, he rewrites his past few months. He imagines that what he planned had nothing to do with profit, with poor old lonely Andrew and his mundane financial difficulties, but was solely a tribute to his dead lover, Michel, an uncontaminated gesture of love and redemption. He's whitewashed everything else out. He imagines that the work he might have found in one of those boxes in his corridor, which contain all that has value in his life, which contain nothing of any lasting worth, would have come to be the focus of everything he has lost, not only Michel but Jamie and all the others – stands, as they say, of a night or a week or a month or so – and finally of himself: the focus not just of what survives but of what his carelessness and stupidity have taken from him, the focus of his capacity for love and of the depth of his loss. He imagines that what he found would have freed him, because that's what he wants, finally: he wants to be free of Michel, and of everyone else, himself included.

In his mind's eye, unbound, he sees a different catalogue from the one Daniela has had made for him, an elegant laminated cover with the final self-portrait of Michel, pixie-like, naked, perched on his pile of newspapers, which his loathing of the ordinary interests of the world would have stopped him reading – cross-legged Michel, with his Tintin tuft, desirable, malevolent, ungraspable, just days from his self-willed death, his eyes only seeming to be directed towards the others and Andrew, but actually turned in on himself, hoping perhaps to see what it is he wants before he goes, or to wonder about it, to ask the camera why.

Because now, with no idea of what the next hour may bring, what Andrew thinks he wanted the show to do was to commemorate and to celebrate that loss. He knows he has stumbled into something over which he has no control. But, other than that, he is ignorant, which is to say – he genuinely believes – that he is innocent. His initial desire, to make money from Michel's work, and the subsequent forgetting of it, like a board defaced and then wiped clean to make room for something more worthy, is all he has to hold on to. He is sitting in this room, with the dead man and the mirror, sweating into his shirt, wishing they'd finish the job.

And then the button comes off in his hand. And there is a sound in the corridor.

MARTIN AND DANIELA

Daniela's out of Rome, in the house of an artist she knows near Perugia, although it takes some time for them to discover this. She's never heard of Martin Frame, she says, she doesn't talk to journalists she doesn't know, how did he get hold of her mobile-phone number in any case, it's strictly personal, she demands to know who gave it to him, she's working and won't be interrupted. Martin presses the speakerphone button, lifting a warning finger to his mouth, then names the contact who provided her number, an American expatriate artist who paints dead flies in minute detail, arranged in convoys, or singly, the size of crows. She calms down. 'Well,' she says, 'if you're a friend of Jonathan.' Martin tells her he was supposed to have contributed to the catalogue of Andrew Caruso's exhibition, the exhibition she has curated. He knows Andrew well, he says. He has something important to tell her, something that concerns the show. 'Speak now,' she says, imperious. Martin pulls a mocking face at Sandro and Alina, who are listening to every word.

*

It takes her three hours to drive back to Rome. She comes directly to Martin's flat. She is breathless, hysterical, as though she has run all the way from Perugia, her sharp heels clicking against the asphalt of the *autostrada*. She has a plaited handbag the size of a suitcase, which she throws to the ground and then stares at, as if expecting it to move. Martin and Alina's flat is on the fourth floor, overlooking a corner of the Forum, the jagged remains of a colonnade. She runs across to the window, borne forward still by the momentum of her journey. It's dark outside but the columns are lit from below and have a ghostly splendour. This view is one of the world's things Martin most loves.

'How trivial that lighting is,' she says, turning back to the room. 'You'd expect something more from the Fascist heirs of the empire, but there you are. Class isn't water. Speer would have done no better, I suppose.'

'Can I get you something to drink?' says Alina. Daniela looks at her for the first time. It's obvious she can't quite place her, can't decide if Alina is a maid or not.

'Wine,' she says. 'White, if you have it.'

'You understand what's happened?' Martin is irritated. He is also, like Sandro, rather drunk. He sits down, indicating that Sandro should do the same, but Sandro prefers to stand. He is leaning against the wall, by the door, his arms crossed, his expression hostile.

'I know what you've already told me and nothing more. Andrew isn't answering his mobile. He infuriates me – this habit of his of making himself unavailable. Sometimes I call him for days, day after day. He never thinks to call me back. And yet his life is quite empty. He should be grateful.'

'I told you that he's been arrested. He probably doesn't have his phone with him.'

Daniela raises her shoulders, shakes them, an artful little mambo of self-righteous vexation. 'Even so.'

'We really have no idea where he is. I called a friend of mine in the police,' says Martin, noting the way Daniela raises an eyebrow at this information. 'As far as they know, he doesn't seem to be anywhere at all, certainly in none of the places one would expect him to be if he'd been arrested in that area. Sandro here says the man who took him away claimed to be from the Ministry of Fine Arts. I imagine you have some friends there.'

'As you do in the police? We all have our appropriate circle of friends,' Daniela says, her head turned away from Martin, as if speaking to someone else, who isn't there. Alina offers her a glass of wine on a small silver tray. Daniela takes the glass but doesn't thank Alina, apparently thinking her status too equivocal to require acknowledgement. 'I can't believe you're aware of what you're saying.'

'It isn't that difficult to believe, surely,' says Martin, exasperated. 'You and he have organized an exhibition of what are essentially stolen goods. It's hardly surprising the authorities should show some interest.'

'What nonsense!'

'And you've done it without permission from anyone,

as far as I know. I warned Andrew of the risks he was running. I don't know if he spoke to you about this.'

She shakes her head. 'Of course not. If I'd imagined there was any risk of interference, uncalled-for interference, from the authorities' – her lip curls – 'I'd have called off the show immediately. That's a Ricci, isn't it?' she says, pointing to a charcoal drawing on the wall of a gaping mouth, a boat. She seems surprised to find it here. What did she expect? wonders Martin. Posters of bullfighters? *Ceci n'est pas un pipe?*

'Well, they've taken the lot.'

'They've what?'

'I told you on the phone,' says Martin, with satisfaction.

'The line was dreadful,' she snaps. 'I couldn't hear what you were saying.'

'They've taken the entire exhibition and every book in the place as well. They've carted off every movable object from the shop, including Andrew's computer, his account books, his personal records. Sandro saw it all happening from outside.' Once again, he indicates Sandro, who nods but doesn't speak. His eyes are fixed on Daniela, watching her every movement as though he's convinced she'll make off with something of value. 'They took all the catalogues too.'

'Oh, no,' she says, finally shocked. 'But they're already paid for. In cash. I don't know what I was thinking of.'

'Sandro salvaged these,' says Martin, showing her two copies. The other four are locked away in his study.

She takes the top copy and glances through it in a rapid, professional way, looks unhappy about something, closes it. 'This is the last thing I need at the moment,' she says. 'There's talk that I might be given the Maxxi.'

'The Maxxi?'

She glares at Alina. 'The new modern art museum. I don't expect you've heard of it.'

'Oh, yes.' Alina smiles. 'The Zaha Hadid design.'

'Precisely,' says Daniela.

Sandro walks across the room and snatches the catalogue from Daniela's hand. Startled, she recoils. 'You do have contacts at the ministry, then?' he says.

'Of course.'

'Andrew was taken away by armed men, six, seven hours ago now. And what we're doing is standing around, discussing how wonderful you are and how important your career is.' He strides into the hall and picks up her bag, flings it on the floor beside her. There is the sound of something breaking. 'Is that where your fucking phone is?' he says, pointing to it, as Daniela, with a stifled cry, bends down to open the bag and pulls out half a plate.

'You fool,' she says. 'You've ruined it.'

'For God's sake,' Sandro cries.

For a moment, Martin thinks he's about to strike her and is ready to step forward, but Alina's there first. She takes Sandro's arm, holds him back. What an odd scene we must make, thinks Martin, ready to shake Daniela himself.

'I don't think she understood,' Alina says, with barely

veiled contempt, nodding at Daniela, who is ferreting in the bag for the rest of the broken plate.

Martin crouches beside her. 'Please help us,' he says. 'It's in your interest as well – surely you see that.'

'I will *not* be told what to do. How dare he?' She glares at Sandro.

Martin glimpses something small and shiny. 'Is that your mobile?' he says.

With an irritated sigh she pulls the phone from her bag. 'Is there somewhere I can be alone?' she says.

Alina nods. 'Come with me.'

When the women have left the room, Sandro collapses onto the sofa. 'I'm sorry,' he says, and Martin hears the slight slur in his voice and wonders if the same slur is audible in his. This might explain dell'Orto's appalling behaviour, although maybe such behaviour needs no explanation. Maybe this is just the way she is, and is allowed to be. He's seen her on various occasions in the past, surrounded by a gaggle of yea-sayers out for some kind of advancement, skinny, her voice over-loud. He's come across her work in journals and newspapers and given it the moment's attention required to ensure that it's not worth reading, that it's an offence to both language and thought. Close up, she's older than he imagined, nearer his age than Andrew's. He guesses she's had surgery: her cheekbones are slightly more prominent than they ought to be. 'There's no need to apologize,' he says. 'I think we've treated her remarkably well.'

'Even if I did smash her plate.'

'I wouldn't worry about that. She has appalling taste. I'm not surprised she's an art critic.'

Sandro grins. 'Let's hope this damages her career at least.'

'She won't let that happen. She'll ditch Andrew well before anything mud-like attaches itself to her.'

'I don't suppose there's any more wine to be found?' says Sandro.

'My dear boy, what do you take me for?'

Thirty minutes later, Daniela comes out of the bedroom, Alina's arm round her shoulders. 'I must say at once how sorry I am,' she says, and it is evident from her voice that she is close to tears. 'I didn't take you seriously. Your story. It was so absurd. Like some bad film. But you're right to be worried. Nobody knows anything. Nobody. I've called a dozen people and nobody has even heard of the show. I don't know if they're lying or not. They might be. I can't believe a show of mine would mean so little. But they all agree that no one from the ministry would close down a show as you tell me this man has done. It's simply not standard operating procedure, as people say now.' She sits down, next to Sandro, who moves to make room. She squeezes his knee with her small, thin hand. 'You say you saw him handcuffed?'

'No,' he says, 'not handcuffed.'

'But they were police?'

'I don't know who they were.'

ANDREW

The man from the ministry comes into the room, closing the door behind him. He has put his jacket back on, which gives Andrew hope that something might be about to happen. He crosses to the table with an air of great purpose, four small neat steps in his oxblood penny loafers, halts for a moment, with a glance towards the mirror, then places Andrew's wallet and keys before him, where the photographs had been until he swept them to the floor. It's hard to believe he's the same person: his rage has been transformed into mild, bureaucratic benevolence. 'It's time for us to go,' he says. Before Andrew can react, the man's walked over to the corner to take his raincoat from the dead man. He shakes it out and slips it on, buttoning it up to the neck, adjusting the collar in his prim, fastidious way, then lifts Andrew's leather jacket from one of the other pegs and lays it on the table, beside the keys. Andrew's instinct is to ask why, why now, but the door opens again and they're joined by the two men from the car that brought him here, and he decides it's wiser not to talk. This, after all, is what he wants, to leave the room, even if he doesn't know where they might be taking him.

Silent, obedient, he does what he's told. He stands up, puts on his jacket and slides his wallet and keys into his pocket. He wonders what they've done with his handkerchief, but knows better than to ask.

'I'm ready.'

He's led back out to the corridor, then to the lift, but no one holds him this time. Other than that, they've pressed reverse, he thinks. We should be walking backwards in that odd way film has when its steps are retraced, as though catching up on itself in tiny jerks. He stumbles; his right leg had gone dead while he was sitting at the table and is now returning, agonizingly, to life. The driver catches his arm, supports him for a moment. It's a pity it's not the blond, Andrew thinks. At least they've given him back his keys. That's a good sign, surely. A sign they don't intend to kill him or keep him for ever. Already he's calmer. He must have been mad to think they meant him harm. In the lift they stare at the door, the men behind and to the sides of him and, once again, Andrew tries to work out how many floors they're passing, which floor he's been held on these past ten hours. He's about to ask what time it is, but he's worried, irrationally, that any comment he makes, any request, might reverse the direction once more, fast forward him straight back into the room. He's not safe yet.

For a moment he considers the possibility that this whole day might not have happened at all, that he might be the victim of a hallucination brought on by stress and fear, and weariness. Only the pain in his leg, more acute as the seconds pass, convinces him of the truth of the lift, as it halts and the stainless-steel doors slide open to reveal the underground car park, or what must surely be the car park, because there is nothing but darkness, pitch-black darkness. They could be anywhere, thinks Andrew. They could be in the bowels of the earth.

The man to his left steps out and flicks a switch and Andrew, in the blaze of light, sees the dark grey car he was brought here in earlier. It's been driven closer to the lift and is no more than a dozen yards away. The rest of the garage appears to be empty apart from the regular pattern of concrete pillars; the other cars must have been driven away. But he doesn't have time to look round because the near back door is opened and a firm gloved hand on the top of his head protects him as he's eased down onto the seat, the way he's seen people – criminals, suspects – pushed into cars a thousand times on the news, as though they've been rendered incapable of getting inside without banging their heads on the roof. Is this what they did outside the shop? He can't remember. It feels like a lifetime ago.

This time, the man from the ministry sits in front, beside the driver, while the second man sits beside Andrew in the back. The car revs up the ramp into the street, gates swinging closed behind it. It's dark outside and the road into which the car emerges is poorly lit after the bright-ness of the garage. Andrew tries to see the name of the street, any sign that will tell him where he is, but the glass in the windows becomes gradually darker towards the top, making it hard to see above the sides of the parked cars lining both sides of the road. He cranes his neck for something he recognizes but each road seems the same, a string of cars parked bumper to bumper, the driver almost scraping them as he speeds through this part of Rome, both familiar and mysterious to Andrew, without a single landmark he can identify. Finally, after minutes have passed, he gives up and slumps back into the seat. He realizes he's been holding his breath and sucks the stale, overheated air of the car into his lungs.

When the driver comes to an unexpected halt ten minutes later, Andrew looks out of the window and sees a high stone wall, a gate, darkness beyond. The man sitting next to him leans over, his body heavy on Andrew's, and opens the door. Then, as if Andrew were a sack of rubbish or an unwanted dog, he's pushed from the car onto the verge. He finds himself sprawled there, his hand immediately smarting as it scrapes on gravel, his feet being kicked away from the door as it swings shut behind him and the car accelerates away, too fast for him to see its number.

He's been walking for fifteen, twenty minutes before he realizes where he is. He was dumped from the car on the Via Aurelia Antica, outside one of the back gates to the Doria Pamphili park, and now he's walking through a residential area that may be, though he isn't sure, Monteverde Nuovo. The first thing he did after struggling to his feet and nursing his grazed hand for a moment was turn on his mobile, but without result. The battery's flat. He's holding it in his hand now, its smooth black plastic comforting against the broken skin of his palm, as he walks in what he hopes is the direction of the city centre. The charger's in the shop. He has the keys at least, he thinks. His next act was to look inside his wallet. He remembers he changed a fifty-euro note that morning because the woman at the bar till made a fuss. But the money's no longer here. His cards are gone too, his bank card, his Amex card, the only one he had left. Oh, shit, he thinks.

When he hears the gurgle of a drinking fountain, he stops to wash the grit from the graze, and drink, gulping the water down in a sort of frenzy until he chokes and starts to cough. He's hungry, desperate suddenly for food. All around him, the streets are empty of everything but cars, the occasional shop front closed behind shutters, the foyers of the blocks of flats lit up from within, the noise of televisions coming from half-open windows above his head. It strikes him how impossible, even shameful, it is to be lost in a city, without resources. Finally, turning a corner, he sees the dome of St Peter's in front of him, gleaming against the night sky, almost tangible. 'So that's where I am,' he says to himself, almost breaking into a run. He hears his breath, his heart. I'm free, he thinks, and a whimper escapes him, an odd, strangled sound of relief and no longer suppressed fear. Calm down, he tells himself, and anyone who might be listening. 'Calm down,' he says, repeating it out loud, like a mantra, until his voice sounds normal.

He sees a movement in the distance, two people walking together slowly, in conversation, leading a large dog. He tries to catch up with them without hurrying too much. He doesn't want to scare them. He's worried they might run off and leave him, or set the dog on him. He feels exposed, delinquent.

They slow down as he approaches; presumably they've heard his footsteps, or the dog has. He greets them, '*Buona sera,*' he says, his voice sounding strange to him all over again. He's like someone come back to life, like Lazarus. He asks them what time it is.

'It's half-past eleven,' the woman says.

Their dog, a Labrador, is sniffing at his leg. 'Thank you,' he says, and walks off.

It's a good half-hour before he gets to the bookshop. Which means it must be midnight. The *baccalà* place is closing for the evening; the bar still has customers sitting outside at the tables, tourists by the look of them. His shop has its shutters down. He's bending over to slip the key into the lock when one of the waiters from opposite comes over. He's out of his apron, on his way home. Behind him, the owner is closing chairs and carrying them inside to be stacked against the wall.

'They brought everything back,' the waiter says.

Andrew straightens up, lifting the shutter with him. 'They what?'

'They finished a couple of hours ago. They kept the place closed up so I couldn't see what they were doing, but they took in all the boxes. They must have been in there for an hour or so. They took the tape away when they left. What the hell was that all about?'

'What tape?'

'That tape they use to stop people going in. Police tape.'

'Who were they? Who brought the stuff back?'

The waiter shrugs. 'Don't ask me, my friend. I've never seen them before. The boss says they're the ones who were here this morning.' He turns and calls out to the owner to come and talk, but there's no sign of him.

Andrew unlocks the door, walks in, flicks on the light. He can't believe what he finds. The bookcases have been placed once more against the walls, the books unpacked and shelved. His computer is sitting on his counter, his Rolodex and accounts books beside it. There are some banknotes, folded neatly into two, and his plastic sitting on top of them. Apart from the general air of order, the shop might never have been touched. He walks across to one of the shelves. If the books had been the right books he would have wondered if he'd imagined the whole thing. But no: the section in front of his eyes has a worn-out paper label taped to the front of the shelf marked *biografie*, yet the books are a hodgepodge of titles, novels, travel books, old chemistry textbooks, theology, picked from the box and stacked at random. The order is only apparent. He glances down to where the gay porn magazines are usually kept, but they haven't been returned, and he can't see them anywhere else. The copy of *Le Mie Prigioni* that had so interested the man is no longer on the table. It might be anywhere, Andrew thinks. He hopes he never sees it again. There is no sign of the catalogues, but he doesn't care about that. He runs upstairs.

The cat is fast asleep on the sofa, curled into a tight black ball. The walls are bare, apart from the regular grid of small brass-headed nails on which the photographs were hung. It's over, he says to himself. He sits down on the sofa, beside the cat, and holds his head in his hands, which are shaking slightly. What does he do now?

He wakes up with the cat on his lap, the light still on. He has no idea what time it is. He reaches for his mobile, remembers it needs charging. He remembers the man, the car, the room. He looks at the walls, as if to check. 'Everything gone,' he says, 'every fucking picture gone.' He doesn't know whether to laugh with relief or cry. He goes to look for his phone charger, finds it in the carefully replaced drawer of his desk, the flex wound neatly round the plug. He connects the phone and turns it on, waits for his SIM card to click in.

It's half-past one. He has a series of missed calls, most of them from Martin and Daniela, and a text from Martin, which tells him to call as soon as he receives it, at whatever time that might be.

'Martin?'

'Andrew. Thank God for that. We've been worried sick. Are you all right?'

'I think so. I've only just woken up.'

'Where are you?'
'In the shop. Above the shop.'
'We'll be right there. Don't move.'
'I want to go home,' says Andrew.

ANDREW AND MARTIN

Alina drives Martin and Andrew to Andrew's flat. Sitting in the back, craning forward until his face is almost beside Andrew's, Martin has been asking Andrew for details of the previous day, but Andrew seems distracted, whether by tiredness or by something that's penetrated more deeply than tiredness it's hard to tell. Because there is also what Martin recognizes as the after-scent of fear about him. Rather than continue to question him, he explains that Daniela is trying to find out more about the role of the ministry in the whole business, but Andrew looks scornful and shakes his head. 'He wasn't from the ministry. The ministry had nothing to do with it.' He shows interest only in Sandro. 'He called you? He told you what happened?'

'Yes, he's been with us all afternoon and evening.'

'Where is he now?'

'He's at home.'

'Your home?'

'His own home.'

Andrew isn't satisfied. 'Where is that? Where does he live?'

'I'm not sure,' says Martin. 'I didn't think to ask.'

Andrew slumps back into his seat and closes his eyes until the car pulls up beneath his building. Standing at the door, he fumbles with, then drops, his keys. 'I'm sorry,' he says, stepping back as Alina picks them up and tries them all until one fits. Neither of them has been to Andrew's flat, though he's been dropped off in the street below before now, with Alina opening the door for him on occasions in the past as well. He doesn't entertain, he always says, he's not equipped for it, and Martin's occasionally wondered if this is the case, or if he's merely not invited them. It's true that he can't imagine Andrew cooking, not even for himself. Andrew's not the domestic type.

The flat's on the third floor. There's no lift, and they climb the stairs slowly, Andrew rocking a little, leaning against the wall every now and again as if to get his breath. He's taken the elastic band off his ponytail and his hair is hanging loose to his shoulders; this is the first time Martin has seen him like this. From behind, he could be a boy, his slim hips, the leather jacket, a boy coming home from a party.

Alina still has the keys. When Andrew stops in front of a door, she comes forward to open it, the double-headed security key ready in her hand. Andrew walks into the flat and turns on a light.

'I should have guessed they'd come here as well.'

He walks along a corridor lined with boxes tipped on their sides, their contents emptied out onto the floor. Martin has seen the shop, how it's been left, and found it hard to believe that what Sandro had told him was true.

He's never seen it look so neat. This isn't true of the flat. He doesn't know what kind of state Andrew normally keeps it in; he imagines it isn't the cleanest flat in Rome. But he's never expected anything like this. He wonders how much of it predates their visit. Andrew is trying to make his way along the corridor without walking on top of books, magazines, newspapers, files of photocopies. After the first few hopeless steps, he gives up and pushes the mess to one side with his foot, not caring what damage he does. He disappears into a door at the end of the corridor, comes out a moment later.

'They've found them,' he says. 'I'd left them by the bed. They were mixed in with a bundle of other stuff. I was going to sort them out today. It is Friday, isn't it? They held me there until they'd found them and then they let me go. I suppose I should be grateful. If I'd thrown them away or given them to Daniela or you, I'd still be in that room. I'm surprised it took them so long.'

Martin and Alina are standing just within the flat, in a sort of hall. Alina pushes the door closed behind them. Andrew bends down, hands on his knees, and starts to stack books into a pile, then knocks it over with the back of his hand.

'I'll make some coffee.' Alina goes into one room, comes out. 'I'm sorry,' she says, as though she's intruded, or been shocked. Martin wonders what she's seen.

'The kitchen's through here.' Andrew stands up and moves aside to let her into the room behind him. 'It's a bit untidy, I'm afraid.'

Martin puts his arm round Alina's shoulder. 'You sit down for a moment. I'll make the coffee.'

Andrew is standing in the corridor as if he's forgotten where he is. Then, with a start, he hurries back along the corridor, trampling over everything, and disappears once again into the room at the end, which must be his bedroom.

'I'm all right,' says Alina, briskly. 'You should go and see what he's doing in there alone. I'm worried he might do something stupid.' When they hear a window being opened, she covers her mouth with her hand. 'Go now.' She pushes Martin away from her. More cautious than Andrew, he picks his way over the debris.

Andrew is standing by the window. The air's cold at this time of night, but Andrew doesn't seem to have noticed. He's taken off his leather jacket and thrown it on the bed, on a tangle of greying sheets, three corners of the bottom sheet detached from the mattress, the pillows thrown to the floor. Clothes have been taken from drawers and hangers and hurled about the room. Framed pictures lie face-down on the bare tiled floor, fragments of broken glass around them. It looks as though a bunch of wires has been ripped from halfway up the wall, but that might have happened ages ago, might have belonged to anything. A stereo, a computer – who knows what Andrew does in this room apart from sleep? I had no idea, thinks Martin, washed by guilt. This poor sad man.

'They didn't take this,' says Andrew. Martin walks across.

'What? What didn't they take?'

Andrew is holding a photograph. He shows it to Martin. Martin sees a naked man, cross-legged on a pile of newspapers.

'It's Michel. You never met him, I know that. This is all his fault.'

Martin picks up Andrew's leather jacket and puts it round his shoulders. 'We aren't leaving you here with all this. You're coming home with us.'

Andrew nods. He puts the photograph of Michel and an old green pullover into a plastic bag. 'Thank you. There's nothing of any value here.'

Andrew is sleeping in the living room, on the sofa. Alina tried to persuade him to go to bed in the spare room but he fell asleep as soon as he sat down. Martin eased off his boots while Alina fetched a blanket. 'It's been a long day,' she whispers to Martin, as they turn off the light and go to their room. Alina reads for five minutes but is sleeping before she has time to close the book, her mouth slightly open, her chin slumped onto her chest. Cautiously, so as not to wake her, Martin slides off her glasses and puts her book on the bedside table. She's reading a Kathy Reichs novel, as though her daily studies of the intricacies of the human body weren't enough to slake her thirst for it, alive or dead. He wonders for a moment what she saw in the other room of Andrew's flat. I'll ask her tomorrow, he thinks, if I remember. He turns off the light, lies down, eyes closed, but he can't sleep. He doesn't expect to. He's trying to make sense of the day that's just come to an end, and the kind of sense it makes is both familiar and disquieting to him. There's a mixture of subterfuge and brutality, the kind of subterfuge designed to unsettle, the kind of futile brutality whose only purpose is to frighten that he can't reconcile with the police. The order of the shop, insolent in its perfection, the wanton disorder of the apartment. Perhaps they'd simply lost patience by then. And Andrew himself, unhurt apart from a slight graze on his hand, too tired and shaken to talk but not ill-treated, not harmed in any visible way. Not that the eye sees everything – Martin knows that well enough.

As they drove back to the flat, Martin tried to get a name out of Andrew. Surely someone must have given him a name.

But Andrew shook his head. 'I asked,' he said, in a pleading way, as though afraid he'd be told off for having failed, 'but he wouldn't tell me. None of them would.' When Martin, ignoring Alina's warning glance, asked if he had any idea where he'd been taken, Andrew shook his head again.

'Somewhere behind the Vatican. Round by the courts. Where the lawyers have their offices.'

'Prati?' said Martin. 'Somewhere in Prati?'

Andrew turned then and looked at him, but Martin couldn't see the expression on his face in the darkness of the car. Whatever the expression might have been, it was all the answer Andrew gave.

'Did they threaten you?' Martin said. 'Mistreat you in

any way?' At that point, Alina lost her temper with him. 'For God's sake, Martin, leave him alone. There'll be time enough for that tomorrow.'

First thing in the morning, Martin remembers what he wanted to ask Alina.

'What exactly did you see last night, in the room next to the kitchen?'

Alina laughs. 'You miss nothing, do you?' she says. 'You only pretend to be a frail old man.' She's getting dressed. He watches her step into her skirt and pull it up to her waist.

'I remember when women used to put their skirts on over their heads and wriggle them down in a very sexy manner. That's how old I am.'

'Women wore underskirts, my darling. And corsets. A woman's life was far more complicated when you were a young man.' She zips up, twists the skirt round so that the zip is at the side, takes a blouse from a hanger. 'I saw a plate with some food on it, and there were beetles, no, not beetles, cockroaches. I haven't seen cockroaches for quite some time. I have no idea what the food was. It had been there a long time.' She shudders. 'We can't let him live like that, Martin.'

In the kitchen, when Martin is making coffee for them both, Alina says she wants to call the police, but Martin dissuades her. 'That's up to Andrew. I don't see what good it would do. I don't think the police would even believe us. They'd think it was some sort of publicity stunt.'

'Is he still asleep?'

'Dead to the world.'

Alina sucks in her breath. 'Don't say that.'

'It's only an expression, my dear,' says Martin. 'An idiom.'

'Words are never only.'

Martin's mobile rings from the living room. It's been set to the traditional English ring tone by Alina, whether through affection or misplaced humour, he isn't sure. *Brrr-brrr*, it goes. *Brrr-brrr.* 'Oh, shit. That'll wake him if nothing else does. It's like a voice from the past. Why can't I have some meaningless pop jingle like everyone else?' He hurries from the kitchen.

At first he can't find the phone. By the time he does, flinging cushions round the place, Andrew's awake. He doesn't seem to know where he is. He lies on the sofa unmoving, apart from his eyes, which scan the room. Finally he looks at Martin. 'Christ. I don't think I've slept like that for years. I can't believe it.'

'It's an ill wind,' says Martin, with a cheerfulness he immediately regrets. Alina has told him off a hundred times for being flippant, but flippancy, sometimes, is all he has. Andrew, though, doesn't seem to mind. He smiles and, raising his head a little from the cushion, nods agreement. Martin looks at the phone in his hand, which has stopped ringing now. 'I suppose there's some way of knowing who that was, but I can never seem to work out what it is.'

'Missed calls,' says Andrew, sitting up. He's taken his

shirt off during the night. His naked shoulders are stark white, with a sprinkling of freckles, more fragile than Martin would have imagined. His hair is tangled and pushed up to one side, his left cheek corrugated red where it's been pressed against the cushion.

'I expect you'd like a shower,' Martin says. 'I'll get you a towel.'

Andrew sits up, wrapping the blanket round him, bare white feet swinging down to the floor. 'I don't suppose I could have a coffee first, could I? Before I shower?'

'Absolutely,' says Martin. 'Priorities.' He leaves the room.

Alina is waiting to see who called. He gives her the phone, making a hopeless face.

'It's not in your memory,' she says. 'But, then, who is?'

'I'm suffering from amnesia?'

'Don't be silly. You had a call from the same number yesterday, just before two. I expect it's Sandro.'

'Can I call it back?'

'I think it suits you to be incompetent,' she says, with what he hopes is – at least in part – affection. 'It turns me into your secretary. Of course you can, darling. Later today, if we have time, I will give you a brief lesson on the use of the mobile phone in the twenty-first century. You'll be surprised.'

'Heaven forbid.'

'You have Sandro's number?' Andrew is standing at the door, with the blanket round his waist.

ANDREW AND SANDRO

Sandro's sitting by the door, reading a pile of newspapers, when Andrew gets to the bar. It's the *latteria* near Piazza Farnese above which Andrew once lived with Jamie in his cold-water flat. Sandro, who isn't aware of this, knows the place well. He's ordered a large bowl of cappuccino, and one of the flat pastries the bar sells, shaped like a heart or one of those leaf-shaped fans that remind him of Thailand, which he doesn't really like, biscuit-like slices that crumble as he tries to eat them. Searching in vain through the national and local pages of the daily papers for news of Andrew's detainment, the sequestering of the shop, the impounding of its contents, he doesn't see Andrew come in. He only becomes aware of him when Andrew pulls out the chair opposite, its feet scraping the tiles, and sits down, hands on the table. He raises his head and smiles.

Andrew looks exhausted. He has pulled his hair off his face and tied it back in some way, but strands have come loose. He hooks them behind his ear, a second and third time, continuing to do so even when there is no longer any need. He has a fine face, too thin and drawn but subtle, thinks Sandro, hard to read; worth reading. Green eyes, pale lashes, his hair no longer the red it was when Sandro first saw him, twenty-five years ago in the back of the bookshop and later, offering him a book about Caravaggio from the tray outside; it's a sort of tawny shade now, like an old fox Sandro once spotted by a railway line in Dalston. The colour's fine; it's the length that doesn't convince. You should cut it, Sandro would like to say. It would knock ten years off you. I'll tell you one of these days; I'll cut it myself if necessary. You aren't that much older than I am.

'I'll get you a cappuccino,' he says, standing up. Andrew smiles back, in a rueful way, as though throwing himself on Sandro's mercy, or good grace. He's wearing the same leather jacket he had on yesterday when they took him away, and an ironed T-shirt that looks too large for him and makes him seem frailer than he is.

'A bowl. I need it.'

'And one of these biscuit things?' Sandro points to what's left of his.

'I suppose there isn't anything else? Less friable?'

'It's a speciality.' They grimace simultaneously, then smile. 'I'll see.'

'I haven't been here for years,' says Andrew, when Sandro returns with the bowl, no biscuit. He raises his eyes to the ceiling. 'I used to live on the top floor. Freezing in the winter, unbearably hot in the summer. I used to think it was decadent. It appealed to the poet in me. Not that I've ever written anything worth reading.'

'Bruno brought me here the first time.'

'Bruno?' Andrew shows sudden interest.

'The man who gave me the photographs,' says Sandro, because they have to talk about them, however hard it may be. 'It was one of his favourite places. He said Rome was changing and the old places needed to be supported or they'd get knocked down and replaced and Rome would become like everywhere else. It's probably a good thing he died when he did.'

'He died? Why did he give you the photographs?'

'He was scared.' Sandro leans in, lowering his voice. 'I think you're lucky to be alive, you know that? I thought you'd finish like Bruno.'

'How did he die?'

'He was murdered. For a long time after, I expected to be arrested for his murder. Then I expected to be . . . not arrested – kidnapped, I suppose, as you were, because I had the photographs, because I knew there was something wrong with them. And so I freed myself by selling them to Michel. Or I thought I had.'

'You killed him? Bruno?'

Sandro laughs. 'I killed Bruno? Of course not.'

'But why did he give them to you in the first place?'

'I don't know. I think he panicked. I was nineteen. Perhaps he thought that made me safe.'

'You were friends?'

Sandro nods, smiles deprecatingly. 'Well, a bit more than friends.' He is pleased to see Andrew relax. You're slow on the uptake, he thinks. Then: That's nice. I'm glad you're slow. 'He was the first man to take me seriously. That mattered very much.'

'They've trashed my flat,' says Andrew. He doesn't seem to have heard. 'Totally. They haven't actually destroyed anything, but they've left their mark everywhere. The way people crap in places they've robbed. Though I've heard that's more of a release of tension than anything else. Can you believe that?' He stares into Sandro's eyes. 'Do you know who they are?'

Sandro shakes his head.

'Have you got a car?'

'Yes.'

'I don't suppose you'd like to drive me round a little?'

To start with, Andrew seems to know where he's going. They cross the river onto Via Giulio Cesare, heading towards the Vatican, barracks on one side of the road, offices, shops on the other. It's late Friday morning and even the bus lane is clogged with traffic. Sandro waits to be told where to go, moving with the flow, in second, in third, back in second. Andrew says turn here, then no, straight on, twice. 'Left,' he says suddenly, and Sandro swings the car into a narrower street. 'Right,' and they're two, three blocks at most from Piazza Risorgimento. Andrew is crouched forward, both hands on the dashboard like an excited child, except that his face is rigid with concentration; he's glancing around him, at doors and cars and corners, alert, breathing deeply, in and out like some sort of spiritual exercise, as though expecting to be attacked at any moment and wanting to be ready to ward it off. To Sandro, he's like someone performing martial arts, suspended at the point of flying across a room. As they pull into the square, Andrew shakes his head, furious, all poise abandoned. 'We've come too far this way,' he says, his left hand waving in Sandro's direction. 'Go down there,' he says, jabbing a finger to the right. And Sandro does. He's remembering the time he drove the Birdman to Rebibbia, how scared he was that the news would be bad, how disappointed when there seemed to be no news whatsoever. Morelli has always looked after me, he thinks, and now it's my turn to look after him. And now I'm looking after Andrew as well.

They carry on driving. They're near the main law courts. Andrew starts and tells Sandro to slow down, then shakes his head. Twice, Sandro pulls over and Andrew jumps out of the car and stands for a moment on the pavement, walks across to gates and the narrow drives between buildings, returns to the car. Once, he beckons to Sandro and Sandro double-parks, but he's barely left the wheel when Andrew turns round and waves his finger from side to side. 'False alarm.' They shuffle with the traffic from block to block. At one point, Sandro points out they've been along this road at least three times before and Andrew slumps back into the seat.

'Let's try down here.' He's pointing left.

'We've done that one too. I don't think there's anywhere

we haven't been. I don't mind carrying on, though. Don't think that.'

'I can't remember.' Andrew sounds irritated. Sandro's already turned left when Andrew touches his arm. 'I'm sorry. I'm angry with myself, not with you.'

'I understand that.'

'It's just that it must be somewhere.' But it's obvious from Andrew's tone that he's losing faith.

'Can I offer you lunch somewhere?' says Sandro.

'I'm really not hungry. I've wasted your time.'

'Come back to my place. I can make us a plate of pasta or something. I'm not a bad cook, you know.'

Andrew closes his eyes, then opens them and turns to Sandro with an anxious look, as though he has just thought of something. 'Yes. That would be nice.'

Sandro lives above a fish restaurant in San Lorenzo, in a flat shaped like a shoebox with a window at each end. There's a small terrace behind it, overlooked by the balconies of surrounding buildings, with a table and two chairs on it and a couple of plants in pots. Sandro moves one of the chairs so that Andrew can sit down and see into the kitchen, while he chops bacon and fills a pan with water. '*Alla gricia* OK?' he says.

'My favourite.' Andrew glances at the layers of balconies above him. 'It's slightly like being in a bear pit down here.' He smiles. 'I'm sorry, that wasn't very tactful of me, was it? It's actually very nice.'

'The worst thing is when they empty their ashtrays onto

my head.' Sandro slides the bacon into a pan. 'No, wait a minute, I'm wrong. The absolute worst thing is when they throw down their used condoms.'

Andrew laughs out loud. Sandro, startled, looks across and sees his head thrown back, his arms hanging loosely by his side, and is glad to have amused him, and a little aroused. Andrew's the kind of man he's recently become attracted to, a few years older than he is, with a sort of worn-in hippie air; someone who's never been inside a gym or tanning centre. He'll make this clear, he decides, and see what happens.

'I suppose it's a sign of civil responsibility they use condoms at all,' Andrew says.

Sandro emerges with a bottle of white wine and glasses. 'Martin showed me the photograph he thinks has caused all this trouble.' He opens the bottle and pours them each a glass. 'I didn't remember it, not really. I never looked at them properly when I had them – I was too scared of them after Bruno's death. But he says he knows who the man in the car is, or he thinks he does. The man behind the girl.' He goes back into the kitchen. 'Hungrier now?'

'Yes. Can I do anything?'

'Relax.' Sandro comes back with two plates of rigatoni.

Andrew jumps up. 'I'll get the forks,' he says, but Sandro glances at his breast pocket.

'Forks and napkins. I've thought of everything. I told you I was useful in the kitchen.'

They start to eat. 'This is excellent,' says Andrew. After a few mouthfuls, though, he puts down his fork. 'Martin talked about it this morning. He was going to see some friend of his who may know the man's name. I told him not to bother.'

'Not to bother?'

'I don't see what good it will do. Any more than our wild-goose chase did this morning.' Andrew covers his face with his hands; his fingers are thin but strong, like a guitarist's. Perhaps he is; music would go with the hair. Sandro reaches across and presses the back of his own hand momentarily against Andrew's, an impulsive gesture intended to remind Andrew he is not alone. Rubbing his eyes, his eyebrows, Andrew brings his hands down and round to the back of his neck. 'I slept on Martin's sofa. I've got a stiff neck.' He looks at Sandro. 'You made a very good impression on Martin, you know.'

'He made a good impression on me.' Sandro is pleased. He's wondered what the other man thought of him.

'But he won't let things go, that's his problem. He says he wants to get to the bottom of this. I told him, "You're behaving like the English journalist you say you are. You think things have bottoms, that all you have to do is dig, dig, dig and you'll get to the truth of the matter." He's lived here for thirty years, longer maybe, he's been involved in all sorts of shady business, not only journalism – did you know that? – but he still believes in solutions. I'm only half Italian, you see. I want to believe, but I can't, not entirely.' His eyes search Sandro's face. 'You're one hundred per cent?'

'Yes. One hundred per cent Roman. All I know is

intrigue. It was in my mother's milk.' He's relieved when Andrew smiles; he knows he's being laughed at and doesn't mind. 'Perhaps you're too shaken by what happened yesterday.'

But Sandro still doesn't know what *did* happen yesterday. He knows that Andrew was taken off because he saw it happen. Then, this morning, after speaking to Andrew and arranging to meet him, he'd spoken again to Martin, who told him about the flat. But that was all. 'He doesn't want to talk about it,' Martin said, and Sandro understood. Who would? He looks at Andrew's face for signs of bruises, cuts. Was he beaten up? Whoever these people were, they were surely professionals. They would leave no marks that weren't both invisible and to calculated effect. But his own question now is also probing, just as Martin's were. He should leave well alone. Andrew, though, doesn't seem to mind. On the contrary, he seems to have been waiting for the chance to talk.

'Shaken?' he says, with an angry laugh. 'I can't believe it happened. I woke up this morning and I thought, What? These people walk into my shop and take me away and hold me for ten hours and then just throw me into the fucking street. They destroy my flat, they steal my property. And they have no right. That's what I can't accept, not really. The fact that they did that to me even though they have no right.'

Sandro's about to say something to calm him down but Andrew continues: 'I've spent decades thinking no one has the right to do this kind of thing. No one. Not the police, not the army, not the CIA. I've marched against it, signed petitions. And then these goons walk into my life and they aren't the police, as far as anyone can tell, and they aren't the army, and they aren't the CIA, or the FBI, or MI bloody 5. And suddenly I'm making distinctions, because suddenly the police *do* have this right. The police *can* arrest people and seize goods and interrogate – not that they did, not really – and all the rest of it. Because I wouldn't mind that so much, I'd have some sort of redress, I'd know who to complain to, who to sue for loss of livelihood. I could go to my lawyer and the papers. But what in God's name am I supposed to do with what happened yesterday?'

He spreads his arms. 'I could tell you every single thing I went through, every single thing they did, and of course you'd *believe* me, you'd have to, but deep down, where it matters, none if it would make any sense. Deep down, what you'd be doing is humouring me. Because it can't have any consequences, you see, and without having consequences it has no meaning. It might as well never have happened, and so it didn't happen. That's what I tried to tell Martin. But he wouldn't listen. I tried to tell him that it didn't happen.'

Sandro has no notion what to say to this. It's just as well that Andrew appears to expect nothing from him. He seems suddenly deflated, slouched in his chair as though everything he has said has emptied him in a literal sense. 'I'm sorry,' he says, in the end. Your pasta's getting cold, Sandro thinks.

But Andrew hasn't finished. 'I understand what people mean when they say experiences are incommunicable,' he continues. 'We all assume that what happens to us is the same as what happens to everyone else; that's what empathy is, I suppose. It's not so much putting yourself into other people's shoes as putting their feet into yours. And then something comes along that doesn't resemble what other people go through. I'm not saying I've been tortured or stuck in a concentration camp or anything, but, in a way, this must be what it's like, this feeling that you might as well not talk about it because no one will ever understand. You know when someone tells you some terrible story, some story that goes beyond anything you've ever experienced yourself, and all you can think while you're listening is, Thank God, thank God that wasn't me?'

'Some stories you don't forget.' Sandro pushes his half-full plate away from him, his hunger gone. 'They don't need to happen to you. They stay with you anyway. They stay and they won't go, whatever you do. Sometimes it's worse than when you've lived through them yourself. When they happen to you, I don't know, you find the strength to cope with them.' He's thinking about Roger, about Roger's dying. 'When it's someone else, there's no escape.'

'I'm sorry.' Andrew reaches for the wine, filling both glasses. 'I'm being self-pitying. It isn't very attractive.' He moves Sandro's glass towards him a little, to encourage him to drink, perhaps to apologize. 'In the bar this morning you were talking about your friend. The one who died. Was it Bruno?' he says. 'You said he took you seriously.'

'Yes.' So you did hear, thinks Sandro. You were listening after all. He takes the glass and sips. At this moment, he's lost for words.

'It's good to be taken seriously. It doesn't happen that often.' Andrew shakes his head. 'I'm sorry you lost him.'

'Look,' says Sandro. 'Tonight.' He pauses, rubbing his neck as Andrew did a few moments ago. It must look like a gesture of solidarity, it occurs to him, unconscious at first and now, as he smiles a slow, hopeful smile, no longer unconscious: aware of itself and intended to seduce. But seduce is the wrong word. To offer something. 'If you don't want to spend another night on Martin's sofa.'

All at once, Andrew looks stricken. Sandro, who has expected any reaction but this, who – to be honest – expected Andrew to leap at the chance, is thrown off kilter.

'I also have a sofa,' he says.

And now Andrew looks disappointed, though he's obviously trying his best to conceal it. I'll have to tread carefully, thinks Sandro. I don't want to spoil everything. But what is there to spoil? He isn't even sure that Andrew wants him. All Sandro knows is that, in the past, he's slept with Jamie, Michel, young men. But that was a long time ago, when Andrew was also, if not young, considerably younger than he is now. Maybe his tastes have grown with him. Sandro is their age, or Jamie's; if Michel were still alive he'd be almost fifty. He'd look no better than Sandro does, and might look worse.

'I don't know what I'm going to do.' Andrew sounds utterly helpless. He stares at his plate of pasta, almost untouched, then finishes his wine.

'I have things to do,' says Sandro. 'You can help me, if you like.'

ANDREW AND SANDRO

They walk together through the tunnel beneath the railway lines towards the Esquilino, Sandro leading the way along the narrow pavement. Andrew watches his legs, his feet, the swing of his shoulders in his oddly professorial jacket, a style that's too old for him and, paradoxically, makes him look younger. He's about the same height as Andrew, perhaps a little shorter, but there's a weight to him that makes Andrew feel small. Not fat, maybe not even muscle: a presence. And there's a lightness about him too – a weight and a bounce, if that's possible. What did he mean about having a sofa I could sleep on? Andrew wonders. Was it just an act of generosity? Or did he mean what I thought he meant? When he touched my hand like that, with the back of his hand, I didn't know what to do, how to behave. I don't want pity, but what he was offering didn't feel like pity, or not only that. I know what pity feels like, Andrew thinks, self-pity anyway. So what was he offering? What is he offering? What kind of friend was Bruno? He's afraid to ask. As they come out of the tunnel, filthy, its air unbreathable, Sandro turns and smiles, but doesn't speak, as if to say, That's over. We're out of it now. We can breathe again.

They walk past where the porn cinema used to be, and a second-hand bookshop, also closed down, as Andrew's will be before the year's out. This is the first day he hasn't opened the shop since he was taken into hospital with appendicitis more than fifteen years ago. He's dragged himself in through illness, hangovers, strikes, because without the shop he's nothing, he has no purpose. Side by side now, they walk past closed and open doors, parked scooters, a shop that sells mattresses, which makes him think of beds, and sex. When a car slows down beside them, Andrew quails with fear and, to his horror and shame, finds himself trying to hide behind Sandro, like a child behind a sofa. But the car drives on, oblivious to him. 'I'm sorry,' he says.

But Sandro doesn't seem to mind. He gives Andrew's arm a reassuring squeeze. 'Relax. I'll look after you.'

Hearing this, Andrew's eyes well with tears. Whatever it means, whatever Sandro intends it to mean, it's good to hear it said. They walk together towards Piazza Vittorio.

Andrew recognizes the door immediately, without even needing to step back and look up at the windows on the second floor. While Sandro is fishing in his pocket for the key, he looks at the brass plate with the list of names beside the bells and there it is, just as he remembers. Morelli. It can't be more than a month or two since he was here last, when the fat man in the kaftan came out of this building and walked off in his slippers in the direction of the station. And now it occurs to Andrew that maybe he wasn't going to the station at all, but to Sandro's.

They walk together into the dark hall. Andrew expects Sandro to call the lift, but he heads over towards the staircase. 'It's only on the second floor,' he explains, 'and I hate these old lifts. I always think they're going to break down.' As they climb the first flight, Andrew following Sandro, two tall thin Somali boys brush against them, giggling as they head out of the building. They're wearing T-shirts and low-slung jeans, their pants showing above the waistband. One of them tells the other to get a move on or they'll be late, with a perfect Roman accent. They're no more foreign than I am, thinks Andrew, less probably: I've never quite belonged in this city. He's awash with a sense of loneliness, flailing in it. Then Sandro opens a door and they walk into the Birdman's flat.

'It belongs to a friend of mine,' says Sandro. 'He's in hospital, at Fatebenefratelli. I come round every day to make sure the place is all right.' He leads Andrew into a large room with a low stage against the wall on the left, a ring of ill-matched chairs facing it to make a sort of theatre. But what Andrew notices first is the row of windows opposite, the afternoon sunlight glinting off dangling wires covered with fat and peanuts in their shells, prismed in the swaying of cut-off plastic bottles. This is what I saw from below, he thinks, the fat man feeding his birds. 'I just have to fill the water bowls and check there's food.'

Sandro leaves the room, but continues to talk, raising his voice as he turns on a tap, opens cupboard doors. Andrew doesn't move. 'They don't really need it but it's his life. Feeding the birds is his life.'

'He must be lonely.'

Sandro comes back with a watering can, a bag of nuts. 'I don't know. He's had a full life, if that counts for anything. I see a lot of him. He's been good to me, more than once. Longer than anyone else. I don't think he's lonely. I think he's alone a lot, apart from the birds, but that isn't the same, is it? He's a generous man, which helps.'

Andrew nods. 'Can I take a look round?'

'Go ahead. I won't be long.'

Andrew wants to say that he's been here before, not inside the flat, but beneath it, like a stalker. But that would mean explaining how he'd come across the address, which would mean talking about the photographs, and he doesn't want to do that. Not now. He stands in the corridor of this other man's flat and breathes deeply, breathes in the fusty, bird-scented air, with an acute sense of how another's life has been lived, and of how his own life might measure up to it. It's hard not to see his home brutally, obliquely, mirrored in this one; its order and space compared with his turmoil and disorder, which was only made in part by the men who went there yesterday and pulled the books off the shelves and emptied the boxes onto the floor. He peers into the kitchen, its surfaces bare and clean, the sink empty, into the bathroom, with its plants along a narrow windowsill and paintings on the walls, into a small white bedroom, with a single bed pushed against the wall.

'That's where I used to sleep,' says Sandro, standing behind him, close enough for Andrew to feel the heat of him. 'When I didn't have anywhere else.' Andrew's afraid to move away, to lose this momentary almost-contact. Sandro grips his arms above the elbows, moves him slightly to one side in what may be a functional gesture, but doesn't let him go at once, so that they're standing side by side, with Sandro's arm still pressed against his back in a sort of embrace. And then, before Andrew can respond, he's gone, crossing the room to take something from a shelf above the bed, and Andrew is swaying in the sudden absence. 'Look.' Sandro's holding out a book. 'You don't remember, do you?'

It's a book of reproductions of paintings by Caravaggio. And Andrew, in one aching breath-stopping second, does remember. He remembers giving a young man this book and seeing the young man walk away with it and thinking, I've blown it. What an idiot I am.

'You used to be a lot more forward,' says Sandro, in a teasing, even taunting tone.

'You never came back. I thought I'd scared you off.'

'You did.' He's waiting for Andrew to take the book from his hand. 'But not in that way. I admired your nerve. I was scared on my own account, not yours.' Andrew reaches for the book, which Sandro has opened. He expects Sandro to let it go, but Sandro continues to hold his side of it, so that the book is shared by them, binds them, four bare hands framing the face of the young John the Baptist as he turns away from the light and glances to his left, his tousled hair in his eyes, still half asleep, beneath his neck a V-shaped flush of red, which might be shame or sun, a labourer's tan, standing out against the whiteness of his torso, one rough, work-coarsened hand on his bare knee and the other half resting on, half pressed against, a trestle of some sort, beside an empty bowl. A boy about to leave. There is a moment of something that might be embarrassment, or more than embarrassment, before Andrew gently lets go of the book.

'I think I've lost my nerve,' he says.

Sandro looks around the room, beaming with pleasure as he replaces the book on the shelf with the others. 'Well, it must be somewhere.' He takes Andrew's hand and pulls him into the hall. 'We'll have to look for it.'

'I'm not sure—' says Andrew, his voice so low he can barely hear himself speak.

Sandro lets him go. 'I still have things to do. I have to take some things to the hospital, to Morelli. Do you want to come with me? You can stay in my flat, if you'd prefer that. You can wait for me there. I won't be long. If you haven't got anything else to do, that is?'

Everything has been decided for me, thinks Andrew. How did this happen? Is this what I want? And if not this, what? 'No,' he says. 'I'll come with you. I'd rather do that than be alone.'

*

Morelli is in a ward on the second floor, with a window that overlooks the synagogue. There are two beds in the room, the one nearest the door, which is empty, and Morelli's. Andrew stands at the door to begin with, uncomfortable, aware he might not be wanted, unsure of the relationship between Sandro and this bald no-longer-fat man in flowered pyjamas, who is reaching an arm out, his hand extended as if he expects it to be kissed; unsure, too cautious to be sure, of the relationship between Sandro and himself. Sandro squeezes Morelli's hand, then takes the man's head between his own two hands and kisses his forehead. 'Come on,' he says, turning to beckon Andrew into the room. 'Come and meet my guardian angel.'

'The boy's too kind,' says Morelli. His voice is little more than a faint wheeze. If Andrew were further away from him he wouldn't have made out the words. This poor man's dying, he thinks, and he is filled with tenderness and a shame he can't understand, as though the wrong man has been chosen. 'Always too kind. He's my guardian angel now, and has been for years.' He observes Andrew, beckons him closer. 'I know who you are,' he says, with satisfaction, as though he's found the solution to a problem that's been bothering him. Andrew glances at Sandro, questioning. But Sandro shakes his head.

'I've brought you some salami. And a bottle of gin.' He lifts up a plastic bag, tilts it for Morelli to see inside. Morelli smiles and pats Sandro's hand with his own frail, hairless one. He's breathing hard, as if sucking the air through a layer of cotton wool. For a moment he closes his eyes, leaning back into the pillow. His eyebrows have been plucked, his skin is pale, unblemished, without a wrinkle. How smooth and perfect he is, thinks Andrew, how Buddha-like. 'I promise you there isn't a single thing in this bag that will do you good,' says Sandro.

'How well you understand my needs,' Morelli whispers, his voice a barely audible rasp. Turning his head with effort against the softness of the pillow, he looks at Andrew again, more sharply this time. 'It isn't always easy, you know, to understand a person's needs.'

'I know that,' says Andrew.

Morelli closes his eyes once more.

Sandro sits beside him on the bed. 'He'll go to sleep now.'

They stay for just over half an hour. Andrew leaves the two of them alone for a while. He goes downstairs and finds a place to wait in a courtyard filled with men and women in pyjamas, smoking cigarettes, talking or not talking, sitting in pairs or groups or alone. An old woman in a nightdress and knitted jacket asks him why he's here and he tells her he's visiting a friend. She wants to know if his friend is very ill, and Andrew nods. 'I'm here to die as well,' the woman says. 'I'm all alone in the world.' She says this in an odd, chirpy manner, as though discussing her holiday plans, that breaks Andrew's heart.

'I have to go,' he says.

'That's all right,' she says. 'I understand.' She takes his hands in hers, with surprising strength. 'Go to your friend.' She wishes him *tante buone cose.* Many good things.

Before they leave, Morelli wakes up and signals to Andrew that he wants him. Andrew walks across the room as Sandro stands, straightening the sheet beneath him, and moves away. Morelli says something, but he doesn't catch it. He leans closer, Morelli strains forward, which only makes it harder for him to speak. He sinks back. Andrew bends down until he can feel the man's breath against his skin. There's a warmth coming from him he doesn't expect. This time he can hear without any strain at all what the dying man has to say.

'Look after him. I'm everything he has.'

Later that evening, in Sandro's flat in San Lorenzo, Sandro tells Andrew about Roger, about one day in particular. 'We just set out,' he says, 'early that morning, without any real idea of where we might end up. Roger decided that what we had to do was to walk until we noticed some man we thought worth following, you know, someone sexy, and then we would just follow him until we saw someone else who appealed to us more, and then we'd follow *him*. And what we would do as we walked was make a note of where this took us so that we could mark it on a map later. He had a notebook in his pocket to write down the names of the streets. He had this theory that the shape it would make on the map would tell us something significant about desire, about us. He was mad, really, but he was also thoughtful and serious and I think it was play, really. He was playful. I called him *homosexual ludens* once; he loved that. We walked and walked

– it was summer and hot, for London anyway, we were starting to sweat. I wanted to stop and have a drink somewhere – and then we saw a postman Roger liked, a black man with dreadlocks. But he spotted us straight away and told us to fuck off. We couldn't stop laughing. Then we were walking past a building site and there was a man up on the scaffolding, in a pair of cut-off jeans and boots, very sexy, magazine-style sexy, and so we stopped and stared up at him for a while until Roger started to laugh again and said, "This is no fucking good, we can't just *stand still*. It won't show on the map." And then it started raining and we went into a pub, and that was it, really. The end of our lustful psychogeographical mapping of East London. That was three weeks before he told me he had Aids.' Sandro pauses. 'I loved him with all my heart and I'll never forgive him for dying.' He reaches across the table and, with his thumb, strokes what looks like a tear from Andrew's cheek, then pushes the empty wine glasses to one side in a reckless, drunken way, all of it pushed against the kitchen wall, the bread basket, the pepper-mill, the bowl with the cheese. He leans over, ungainly, his chair sliding back, his stomach pressed down against his empty plate – the oil will stain his shirt – one elbow on the table to maintain his balance; all this to kiss Andrew, finally, on the mouth.

'I think it's time I took you to bed,' he says.

ALINA

Six months later, Andrew and Sandro are invited round
to dinner by Alina and Martin. They're early: they hadn't
expected to find a parking space so easily. Alina lets them
in while Martin puts olives and nuts in bowls and opens
a bottle of prosecco, watching the regional news on a
small television in the corner. She takes their coats from
them, the weather's changed in the last two weeks, and
tells them to go into the living room and sit down, she
won't be long. She turns for a moment to watch them as
they dither beside the door, then laugh and push each
other through. She wasn't sure to start with, about Sandro
mainly: she was scared that Andrew would be hurt. But
she's changed her mind. She was the first to notice they
had the same initials: AC. She was the first to point out
the assonance of their names, Andrew and Sandro, when
they constantly misheard her and were answering for each
other without realizing. Martin finds this sort of thing
quaint, akin to tea-leaf reading, but Alina's convinced, in
some dark unexamined corner of her being, that there are
no coincidences. Six months ago, she doubted Sandro's
motives, but what she sees in him now is love and a

constant regard for Andrew's needs, a regard that has given Andrew a new self-regard she'd never have imagined he could achieve, a pride in himself that seemed unattainable a year ago. He's changed. But it's not a one-way process. When Morelli died, Sandro depended on Andrew, and Andrew knew, and did what was needed, and it was beautiful to watch.

It's lovely to see them together, thinks Alina, as she goes to join them in the living room, calling to Martin to bring everything through if he can manage. Martin calls back that he can, he's perfectly capable despite his dodgy leg. They're on the sofa, Andrew turned towards Sandro, still laughing about the chances of their finding a parking space like that, judging them close to zero. After years of looking like an ageing hippie, Andrew has finally had his hair cut short, with a crooked side parting and an unruly fringe, which makes him look younger than he is; he's also put on a little bulk around the chest and shoulders, which gives him substance. She imagines he's been working out, or eating better. Sandro, on the other hand, has softened, loosened up in some way, as though an outer shell has been removed and he can relax into himself. When the two men are sitting or standing side by side, as they generally are, there's a growing resemblance between them, to both their benefit. They wear each other's clothes, new clothes as far as she can tell, though maybe they already belonged to Sandro. Neutral clothes that suit them both. There is much about Sandro's past life that remains unclear to her, although he's happy to talk about it. There's no reticence about him; he's almost embarrassingly frank. He tells his stories, and Andrew listens and nods, and Martin raises an eyebrow now and then, and Alina thinks, How improbable it is that we should be here, the four of us, with our different lives converging on this one point, around this table. We understand so little of how the world works.

This evening they have something to celebrate. The new shop will be opening tomorrow afternoon, Saturday. Andrew and Sandro have spent the last two months disposing of unwanted stock, painting, repairing shelves. They have transformed the room upstairs into a reading space, with two small sofas and a coffee machine, and new shelves for the books they've decided to keep. It can't have been easy for Andrew. More than once, Martin has dropped in and seen him in a state of trance, a book in his hand, while Sandro works around him and the cat sleeps in her bed.

The new shop will concentrate on the performing arts: books, magazines, DVDs, a poster or two. Sandro has contacts; he's convinced they'll make a go of it. He hasn't just put his energies into it: he's inherited money from Morelli, and possibly the flat, although the lawyer of an ancient aunt in Calabria has laid a claim for the place. In the meantime, Sandro continues to feed the birds, provide clean water. Some of the pictures from the flat have been brought to decorate the walls of the reading room, as they call it. Among them, Andrew found a framed photograph he recognized immediately as Michel's work, although he'd never seen it before. An image, both cruel and tender, of a sleeping dog beside its sleeping, drunken owner on Ponte Sisto. He hung it next to the one that Michel had taken of Sandro, when Sandro was Alex and barely more than a silhouette surrounded by light. He showed them both to Alina, told her what he'd been told by Sandro, about Michel's time with Morelli. Another connection, she thought, but didn't say. She's helped with the shop too, in a break between exams. They all have.

They hear Martin laughing. A moment later, he comes into the living room with a tray. 'I should have opened this in front of you,' he says, pouring the prosecco. 'But I assure you it popped quite satisfactorily.' He hands the glasses round. 'You'll never guess who's just been on the news.'

'Someone we know?' says Andrew.

'Yes,' says Martin, 'although more by her recent absence than anything else.'

'Give up.' Andrew takes an olive, offers the bowl to Sandro.

Martin rubs his hands with merriment. 'Your erstwhile colleague and friend Daniela dell'Orto.'

Andrew flinches. Please don't start, thinks Alina, casting a warning glance at her husband. She's told him more than once, a dozen times, to let go of what happened to Andrew and he's finally understood that what he wants and what Andrew wants are not only different but incompatible. Daniela's a particularly sore point.

'Erstwhile doesn't begin to describe it. The woman

hasn't answered a single call of mine since the day it happened. I must have called a thousand times. I tried phoning her once from Sandro's mobile, minutes after she'd let my call ring, and she answered at once. Then, when she heard my voice, she turned the fucking thing off. She changed her number after that. She's dumped me. I'm toxic waste as far as she's concerned.'

'She did send you that email,' says Sandro.

'Right. Telling me to leave her alone and to move on and not to pester her with crazy accusations. And to get a life. I'm quoting here.'

'So why is she in the news?' says Sandro.

'She's been appointed director of the new modern-art place out by the Vatican.'

Andrew slaps his leg. 'I don't believe it. She didn't have a cat in hell's chance of getting that six months ago.'

Nobody speaks for a moment. Then Sandro starts to laugh. '*Il bel paese*,' he says.

Alina stands up. 'I'll just see how everything is in the kitchen.'

She's prepared ossobuco, one of her favourite recipes. She loves the glutinous quality of the veal, the unctuous sauce it produces, densely flecked with the green-white of celery and scraps of carrot. She's made a gremolata of lemon peel and garlic and parsley to stir in before serving. It ought to be eaten with risotto, and this is also a favourite of hers. Alina loves food, not just for its flavours, or nutrition, but for what she calls the alchemy of it.

Risotto's like bread, magical, the way the rice is transformed from hard, brittle, separate grains into a food fit for gods, creamy but still with bite, if it's done as it should be, with the care it deserves, with the care all food deserves.

She's already chopped the onion and softened it in butter, along with a spoonful of extra jelly from a marrowbone the butcher put aside for her, because this is how they do it in Milan, and Alina is nothing if not authentic. The cookery book's propped open behind an empty wine bottle, but she doesn't need the recipe. She can make risotto with her eyes closed, and would do if the sight of it slowly becoming itself weren't such a pleasure. She reheats the onion, measures out rice in a jug, turns up the heat beneath the broth.

She isn't even aware that Martin has left the television on behind her until she hears the name Silvia Castellani mentioned. Tipping the rice into the pan, turning it with a wooden spoon until it's coated with the butter, she turns to see who's speaking and sees the face of the girl, the photograph that covered the city, except that she wasn't here to see it: it was years before she came to Rome. She only knows about it because Martin has shown her. Martin has told her about the girl's disappearance these past few months. He's identified the face in the car behind the poor girl, only to find the man has been dead for more than five years and wasn't – in any case – of great importance, a go-between. He's told Alina because no one else will listen. Andrew doesn't want to know. Sandro might, but he's never alone. And so Alina listens because someone must listen to Martin, who has put so much effort into understanding the whole story, as though he were the one to have suffered; so much effort, so little result.

And now there's a woman saying she knows where the girl was taken, she was there when it took place. Alina doesn't know who the woman is – she missed her name. The woman's older than Alina and looks as though she's had a rough time. Her lips have been pumped with whatever the stuff is they use these days, her hair dyed jet black. She's what Alina's mother would have called a prostitute, but Alina knows that it isn't easy to judge any longer. She might be a lawyer, a politician. She's saying that not only Silvia Castellani but other girls, too, were taken to the same place, some cellar in Monteverde Vecchio. She's saying that her husband, or lover perhaps, was part of a criminal gang in the Magliana, and Alina has heard Martin talk about this gang, suggesting they were almost certainly involved. She's saying that this man kidnapped the girls on behalf of someone high up in the Vatican. She may have misunderstood this: she's checking the rice and almost burns her finger, which distracts her. Perhaps the Vatican is involved in some other way. She pours in a glass of white wine, stirring carefully until the liquid has evaporated. The woman says some of the girls were sold on to the gang, who did what they wanted with them, she doesn't know about that. She was never told. But Silvia Castellani was kidnapped for a purpose, and taken to this house. It wasn't for money. She was kidnapped on commission, the woman is saying, and Alina adds some broth and stirs very slowly, to release the starches from the rice, but not too fast: the last thing she wants is a pudding. She was kidnapped because a cardinal wanted to send a message to someone, someone who would understand. She had the impression, the woman says, that the person for whom the message was intended was more important than this cardinal, who's dead now, which is why she feels she can speak, finally, after so many years of silence. She can't forgive herself. But who on earth, Alina wonders, adding another ladle of broth, could be more important than a cardinal? In the end, she was killed, the woman says, and her body was taken and dumped in a cement mixer outside Rome, where all the new building was going on. How horrible, thinks Alina, with a shudder, watching the bubbles on the surface rise and break.

And now it's the turn of a man in a suit and tie who says the woman is unreliable and shouldn't be trusted. She has a history of drug abuse, alcoholism. She left her husband, a professional athlete, for a criminal. Her story doesn't add up, in any case: there are details that cancel each other out, dates that don't coincide with what actually happened. Alina sprinkles the saffron into the bottom of the ladle, scoops up a little broth and swills it round until the saffron has dissolved, then adds it to the risotto and watches it change colour, like something catching fire, a deep, resonant yellow, sun-like. Beautiful, she thinks.

A little more broth, but she's careful not to overdo it. And now for the rest of the butter, and the Parmesan she grated earlier. Stirring these in, she turns one last time and sees the face of the girl fade away, replaced by that of an actor whose name she can't remember. So that's that, she thinks.

She hears them laughing in the living room. She could have called them through to hear this news, but she's glad she hasn't. They'll know soon enough, she decides, sprinkling the gremolata over the ossobuco, stirring it in, then carrying it across to the table, returning to give the risotto a final stir. The story will be on the front pages of tomorrow's papers and the raking over of the dying embers will begin and the men, because they are always men, will gather round to warm themselves once again, as though any heat is likely to be given off. There will be programmes on late-night television, with starlets and opinion-makers and Vaticanologists, and articles in magazines, and the woman who has finally decided to speak will be eulogized and then crucified for what she has said as the country divides into those who think everyone in power is guilty and those who have vested interests in believing something else. Of course everyone in power is guilty, Alina thinks. You might as well deny that people will do anything to protect what they have. The powerless know this perfectly well and would say so, if only those in power thought to listen. And why on earth would they want to do that?

Besides, what would be the point of ruining a perfect ossobuco, an impeccable risotto? Tomorrow will be soon enough.

The girl is gone. Her body has been fractured, beaten, broken into a thousand pieces, scattered across fields and seas, entombed in the concrete pylons of bridges and the cloistered cells of convents, reduced to the mercy of silence. Her body has been fed to Turkish wolves and box-filed in cellars beneath the echoing streets of Potsdam and Sofia. Her body has been traded to nomads, has been bought and sold, plundered for its organs, been married off to a herder whose language she doesn't speak, been ripped and sewn and ripped again. Her body has been ground to dust and mixed with water to be modelled into effigies of the girl she was, who will soon be forgotten as her parents and those who imprisoned her also die, will soon be worn back down into dust and water. Her body has been captured by light and fused on paper coated with gelatine and silver, fused from alchemical salts in darkness and liquid baths to re-emerge as an image endlessly reproduced, a single girl with a smiling face printed a dozen thousand times, shown on TV and published in newspapers and magazines, attached to lampposts and shop windows, folded and slipped into wallets, gathering dust

THE GIRL

on the walls of police stations, the offices of bureaucrats, parishes and station waiting rooms, the resounding halls of airports, the desks of customs officers, wherever power has pitched its tent and been found wanting, because despite them all, despite their efforts, she is gone. Her smile, her hair, her eyebrows, the glimpse of her teeth behind her just-parted lips, the texture of her skin, the poise of her head on her bare, defenceless neck, her tenderness and nerve in the steady uncaring attention of the lens, all of this face, its every feature, as familiar and unknown to us as our own – all gone.

ACKNOWLEDGEMENTS

I'd like to thank David Isaak and Clarissa Botsford, without whom this novel might never have been written.